Had that ridiculous seance summ

Behind her stood a naked man, streaming blood from a hideous pattern of stab wounds in his chest. Though he was losing quantities of blood, he showed no inclination to collapse. His opalescent blue eyes were fierce with determination, the eyes of a man who refused to die no matter how ghastly his injuries. Before Janis had any opportunity to break her paralysis, the stab wounds—she was sure they were *fatal* stab wounds—faded before her eyes until there wasn't a mark on his body.

Those blue eyes gleamed in the intruder's lean, tanned face. His thatch of blond hair glittered in the light from the chandelier, but she particularly—and inanely—noted his eyebrows, sideburns and body hair, dark with golden highlights in a masculine pattern of triangles that could awaken the libido of a stone.

She had no control over filling her eyes with all of him, even with the sight of herself in the mirror, practically enveloped by him, her face unnaturally pale, her eyes darkened by shock.

His glowing blue eyes on hers in the mirror, he reached to grasp her left wrist. She knew that touch instantly from when she had been at the piano across the hall. This time, his grip was warm, but still demanding attention.

More adrenaline coursed through her, preparing her for flight or fight. She whirled and slammed her Italian leather briefcase...into thin air.

Her defense stopped her in mid-action, facing the dining room table. No one had stood behind her—she was quite alone in the room, lunging at nothing!

But the strong, warm fingers still gripped and twisted at her left wrist, and the coiling heat which had somehow overjoyed her was replaced by utter terror.

I don't believe this! I won't believe this!

If she wasn't hallucinating, she faced instant changes in the way she looked at life, heaven, hell, eternity— Halloween!

Although there are several reputedly haunted houses in San Diego with charming and chilling legends attached, I dedicate this book primarily to my inspiration—Old Town's Whaley House—one of the two officially haunted houses in California, the other being Winchester House in San Jose.

I thank my long time friend, Miriam Pace, for suggesting I send my story to ImaJinn Books.

And, finally, I thank my patient husband who keeps the computer upgraded, the atmosphere conducive to my best efforts, and reminds me to come out of the office often enough that I know other worlds do exist.

THE GHOST AND MS. DEMURE

***

Marian Jones

ImaJinn Books

THE GHOST AND MS. DEMURE
Published by ImaJinn Books, a division of ImaJinn

ISBN: 1-893896-29-3

10 9 8 7 6 5 4 3 2 1

PUBLISHER'S NOTE:
This book is a work of fiction. Names, characters, places and incidents are products of the author's imagination or are used fictitiously. Any resemblance to actual events or locales or persons, living or dead, is entirely coincidental.

Cover design byMarian Jones

ImaJinn Books, a division of ImaJinn
P.O. Box 162, Hickory Corners, MI 49060-0162
Toll Free: 1-877-625-3592
http://www.imajinnbooks.com

ONE

Janis Carter drew all the first floor drapes while her Heritage Homes Association Vice-President and Treasurer followed at her heels. "Can't I talk you women out of this? You have no idea the damage hysteria could do to our reputation, and who can tell what some female will do during one of these so-called `seances.'"

Her sympathies were with him. "I'm only the paid director, Mr. Thorpe. The Board, except for your vote, accepted Dr. Wythy's application to do the astral photography project—and *any other* research she wished to do at Wharton House after hours this week."

Tall and loose jointed, a lot more than twice Janis's age, Millard Thorpe usually bore a remarkable resemblance to an elderly horse. On this occasion, he more closely resembled a mule. He whispered, "She's a flake!"

"She's a noted psychology professor emeritus with a legitimate interest in parapsychology. She's absolutely ethical. And when she doesn't raise any ghosts, she will give us fair and helpful publicity in her reports, because she will still believe in the possibility of spirits wandering around even if she couldn't raise them. I don't believe any more than you do that she'll be successful. I've chosen the most level-headed, minimal number of people possible to be present. Everything will be all right. I promise."

Janis wished it were over. She was still shaken from the minor car accident that morning—due, she was sure, to a careless mechanic doing the routine earlier tuneup, no matter what the garage owner had said. She had no way of going home to soak out the stiff neck, for in a weak moment she had invited her one-time psychology professor from Claremont to be her house guest while in San Diego. Her long, difficult day would not end when the doors to Wharton House were locked for the night.

Mr. Thorpe raised both hands in a gesture that said, *Then it's all on your shoulders!* and went for four folding chairs. While he carried them from adjacent Badger House's kitchen to the Wharton House front parlor, the chief docent at Wharton House clumped about in her elephantine way, rearranging the authentic Victorian parlor clutter. Nancy Rogers also doubled as the Association's volunteer PR person and carried a flash camera around her neck like an albatross.

The over-the-shoulder camera bag bumped like a marching drum on her all-too-solid rear as she moved the antique oil lamp to safety atop the Queen Anne writing desk. Millard Thorpe arranged the folding chairs around the lamp table. Dr. Maggie Wythy adjusted the light from her seance lamp. Its eerie glow distorted shadows and colors. Dr. Wythy's layers of burgundy and ocher tie-dyed chiffon shifted to monochromatic grays.

"No pictures during the seance itself," Dr. Maggie ordered. "There's no telling how the flash might affect the spirits. Run the tape recorder if you like, but be absolutely silent except for the mantra chant. If anyone breaks the concentration, I'll not answer for the consequences."

Millard Thorpe winced. Her words set up those present for "consequences" of hysteria such as caused the mischief prompting the Historical Association Board of a generation earlier to refuse further requests for para-psychological research. The Board majority had not turned completely over, but neither had it learned permanently how hysteria and suggestibility could create rotten publicity.

Dr. Wythy told Nancy to give Janis her photographic equipment and sit at the table. Janis stored the camera bag behind the stove.

"Just stand where you are," the professor told Janis. "I may have special instructions for you later. Keep an eye out for my signals."

Once Dr. Wythy went to work, Janis was impressed with the way her persona changed from someone with a weird gait to her gallop, to a professional exhibiting deadly serious dignity. Her diminutive stature became more commanding. Even Millard Thorpe sat where told.

"Normally, I use a channeler," Dr. Wythy commented, "but I had no time to arrange one."

Janis didn't dare smile. Dr. Wythy had known the time she might have to get her ghost was apt to be cut short if the board members' less than wholly enthusiastic cooperation was changed by unexpected negative pressures.

"I'm sure one isn't needed," the doctor said airily. "Paranormal signs are terribly strong both in Underwood and Wharton House."

Paranormal signs at Underwood House? Janis frowned. She made the third attempt of the day to correct Dr. Wythy's misconception. If it did not change Dr. Wythy's mind, Janis would at least have registered facts in front of her two docents, one of whom — Millard Thorpe — was also the Association Treasurer and the Vice President of the Board. She had twice already told the psychologist that Underwood House couldn't possibly be haunted.

From her student days at Claremont, where everyone called the eccentric psychology professor, "Dr. Maggie," Janis knew she might as well be talking to the wind, but she once more repeated, "Underwood House is only a *reproduction* of Old Town San Diego's first hotel."

The original Underwood had been razed well over a hundred years back, but the plans had survived, and Janis had found them uniquely suitable for the Association's future needs. A museum, library, and book shop were slated for the ground floor. The second floor would display typical mid-nineteenth century hotel rooms furnished with vintage items from Old San Diego's early days. Her father had provided for the museum establishment in his will, particularly to house his own extensive collection of what Janis' brother called "junk." Millard Thorpe had been an ally for the extensive project because of his vision for utilizing the still unfinished third floor as Association office space.

Janis disliked stairs that carried her higher than a second floor and shuddered at the thought of an office on the third floor, but finished her firm denial to the psychologist. *"No ghosts."*

Dr. Maggie serenely arranged her seance table. "The workmen said some of the bricks they're using for facing came from the original Underwood Hotel. I took crumblings to serve as focals."

Janis had to admit they had utilized bricks from many of the oldest structures in the city. The likelihood of bricks from the old hotel was about as likely as Dr. Maggie recognizing one when she saw a crumbling bit in the work area. Even if possible, one brick did not make a ghost.

Arguing about it was futile, though. Dr. Maggie was only too well known to Janis, a Claremont grad who in her salad days had taken a required Psychology 101 course from the professor. Once the campus character captured a bee in her bonnet, there was no way in the world to make her let go of it. Janis could not deny that everyone who visited the Wharton House complex hoped to see one of the numerous ghosts it claimed.

What Dr. Maggie would write about her experiments was sure to bring in more tourists and more income. Nevertheless, Janis could not help balancing the risk of becoming a laughing stock after all the energy and effort she had expended during her first year as Director to put the Association on a forward track.

Dr. Maggie placed a box shade over her lamp. Shadows deepened and writhed along the walls. In the center of the table, she positioned the crumbs of the brick she insisted after hours of prowling about the Underwood House construction site that afternoon was authentic salvage from the original Underwood site.

"Place your palms flat on the table," she ordered Nancy and Millard Thorpe. "Be sure all our little fingers are touching. Don't break the circle!"

At Dr. Maggie's pre-arranged signal, the three at the table, and Janis, obediently standing by the iron parlor stove, began to hum steadily.

Because each participant chose whatever note seemed most comfortable, the effect of their humming resembled a sustained, dissonant organ chord. Dr. Maggie called it her *mantra.* Janis considered it inexpressibly silly.

She suppressed an impulse to giggle. At thirty, her giggling days should have long faded...if indeed she ever had such inclinations even before her marriage to Dexter Carter. Nevertheless, the giggle tickled in her throat, the result of nerve-wracking concern about publicity that could go awry.

She hummed away with the others, observing as best she could, what with the shifting shadows, that Dr. Maggie was not in a trance.

"Spirit, are you there?" Dr. Maggie asked in a hollow voice. "Spirit! We call you forth!" Still a third time she commanded, her voice changing to peremptory. "Spirit? Show yourself!" If Janis had been a ghost, Dr. Maggie's order would have made her put in an appearance on the double.

After an unproductive interval, Dr. Maggie's voice shifted into monotone. "We. concentrate. on. the spirits. of. these. historic. buildings. We. call on. a. particular. un-named spirit. for. any. message. to those. who guard. these. houses. Spirit! show. your. presence."

Dr. Maggie stopped and sing-songed in the same pitch as the mantra's hum, "Janis, go to the piano in the music room and play—ah— *'The Ash Grove.'* " She opened her eyes wide and stared at Janis as though she had never thought of naming that particular tune until it issued from her mouth. "'The Ash Grove!'" she repeated in the same chanting rhythm.

Janis silently snorted at Dr. Maggie's blithe assumption she could play the piano, though such assumption didn't take any psychic intuition. In her long-gone and unlamented childhood, like any other little girl growing up in culturally and financially top-drawer Mission Hills, Janis had taken piano lessons. Her father, Ocho (he always insisted she and her brother call him by his nickname) expected them both to become accomplished. No lack of trying to please had kept

Janis from becoming a world-class pianist, although Keith never liked his violin. Their skills never came near Ocho's expectations. Janis had been disappointed when Ocho canceled her piano lessons, but Keith gleefully smashed his violin.

Janis sing-songed back at the seance leader, "I can't play without sheet music. There is none here."

Dr. Maggie responded, still sing-song, "Fa-a-ake it."

The optimistic parapsychologist might well get a one-finger fumble, but Janis obediently passed under the music room arch on which spot one of Wharton House's reputed ghosts, an ox-cart thief, had been strung up in the bad old days. Little more than Mrs. Wharton's great black piano, one supposedly played by Jenny Lind on tour, furnished the music room. The moment Janis sat on the piano bench a sharp gust of cold air came through the pierced wood divider screen across the office door to the back hall. She ought to have reminded Millard Thorpe to shut the back door window screen after bringing in the chairs.

From her central position, Janis could see through to the back hall door of Nate Whartons' office without moving her head. She could also see the others at the seance table in the parlor. Her fingers hovered over the keys while she summoned recall of "The Ash Grove" and surprised herself to find she could actually play it—and not one-finger hunt and peck—even if far from concert caliber. She must have played the piece at an early piano recital, and on demand the memory unexpectedly returned.

The draft from the back door grew colder. More than cold—her left arm and shoulder sprouted goose pimples. Oddly, her *right* side remained warm. She wondered if she might be suffering a mild delayed reaction to the car accident that morning. Even as she attempted to ignore the draft, an icy hand grasped her left wrist.

Instantly she stared down. Everyone known to be in the building was accounted for, and all were in her peripheral line of sight. Her stomach went into free-fall. *Someone had sneaked in through the back door—?* But all she saw on her wrist was her Rolex watch.

Nevertheless...*Someone* had a grasp on her just short of pain, certainly impossible to discount as anything else but what it was—a masculine grasp...A female or child's grip would have been lighter, less authoritative. She could see Millard Thorpe with the others at the seance table, still humming.

The increasing pressure of what was definitely a thumb over her pulse point caused it to hammer. The noise was surely loud enough that the group had to hear it and be as alarmed as she was. A great deal of time seemed to pass during which she was aware of many irrelevant details—yet paralyzed.

This is no wandering spirit. There's a rational explanation.

She stared at her icy left arm, unable to breathe. Her visually unencumbered arm. Her fingers, flexed in the chord position, frozen momentarily just above the keys. Panic rose and choked her.

She whipped around again to call for help. Dr. Maggie sat immobile, her head up and back, facing her, but with closed eyes. The other two at the seance table hunched around the table rim, concentrating on the flat necklace of their six hands circling the table top.

I'm having a hallucination...or something...can't the rest of them tell? Help me, someone!

Instinct for self-preservation kicked in. She twisted her arm frantically to break the grasp. Out of control, she thumped the piano with her right elbow.

A decidedly dissonant chord issued. Dr. Wythy cried out and fell from her chair with a resounding crash.

The others interrupted their humming with cries of confusion. Mr. Thorpe overturned his chair in his rush to turn up the wattage of the lamp. He and Nancy stared at Dr. Wythy sprawled like a rag doll on Mrs. Wharton's much-prized oriental carpet.

Nancy hit the switch on the hall side of the parlor door. The parlor rooms flooded with light. Nancy returned and bent over Dr. Maggie, uttering little squeaks of distress. Unnecessarily, Millard Thorpe announced, "This seance is definitely *over.*"

The invisible grappler no longer held Janis. *She wouldn't*

think about him...it...whatever seemed to have happened.

She massaged her wrist while maneuvering around Mr. Thorpe to help revive Dr.Maggie. Mr. Thorpe knocked over one of the folding chairs in his haste to move in the opposite direction. He returned with a paper cupful of water from the discreetly hidden cooler behind the hundred-and-sixty-year-old elephant's foot umbrella stand in the hall. When Janis leaned over her, the parapsychologist's eyes fluttered open. "Have you eaten today, Dr. Maggie?"

"I was so excited, so busy—" Dr. Maggie ineffectually fluttered her hands. "Blood!" she said faintly. "I smell *blood.*"

"You smell engine exhaust from the street."

Dr. Maggie struggled up. "*Something* happened. I know *something important* happened."

Nancy said, "Jan hit a clinker? You fainted? I'm real disappointed because I hoped for something well...more." She chafed Dr. Maggie's hands. "Ladies our age shouldn't go without regular meals, you know. We'll take you across the street to the Jalisco Cafe and see to it you eat a nice, substantial supper. This excitement certainly made *me* hungry."

Dr. Maggie allowed herself to be gathered off the rug, brushed off, and reassembled.

"Tell The Jalisco to put supper on my running account," Janis ordered Mr. Thorpe. He was the dragon guarding the Association's treasury, but half of the Logan millions were hers to spend as she pleased.

She needed to be *alone.* She needed to examine the perfectly reasonable and ominous reasons she had experienced the episode at the piano. She might even call her doctor. He had been the family physician all her life, and would know she would never call on him after hours unless it was an emergency. She could explain that it hadn't seemed necessary before, but..."While you all eat, I'll stay here, record the day's receipts, and set things in order. Dr. Maggie's Astral Photography session can wait until tomorrow."

No purpose could be gained by upsetting them with the idea that the morning's auto accident might have included a concussion and consequently malfunctioning Executive

Director.

Millard Thorpe turned to Nancy Rogers and thundered, "You, Ms. Rogers, will say nothing about this seance. No press releases to the newspapers to make us a laughingstock! No more seances *ever.*"

Amen to that. Janis rubbed her arm, and wished them all across the street and out of the building as fast as they could move.

She gathered to herself what control she could salvage. *Not* that there was a ghost, but if impressionable people did hear of the interrupted seance they could imagine all sorts of things. Mr. Thorpe was absolutely right. Figuratively she kicked herself for her own undeniable surge of imagination at the piano. Dr. Maggie had pushed all the right buttons, and Janis had reacted like Pavlov's pup. If her ex-husband was around, he would say it was because she was basically suggestible and easily manipulated. She said, "Nancy, be a dear and get Dr. Maggie's cloak?"

Dr. Maggie was not to be so easily derailed. She grasped both Janis's hands and let out an explosive sigh. "I knew it. I knew it!" Her head bobbed and her green eyes sparkled. "You were touched by the spirit, Janis! Admit it. Your skin is icy."

"Not at all!" Janis denied—absolutely denied—her first impression that someone unseen had grasped her arm while she was at the piano. She had manifested a *neurological* problem, hopefully minor.

She pulled away and briskly rubbed her hands to return circulation to her left wrist and fingers. "There was a ghastly—not ghostly—draft from the back door window you left open, Mr. Thorpe. Sit at that piano, and you can feel it yourself. It blows right through the pierced wood screen. That's the only reason my hand and arm seem cold."

"You were touched by a spirit, and he had a message!" Dr. Maggie insisted. "Tell me, quick!"

"No message! No spirit." Janis was thoroughly embarrassed at the implication she had succumbed to the power of suggestion for even a moment. "Go to supper, all of you. Before I change my mind about it being my treat."

Nancy Rogers peered at Janis with near-sighted concern. "You look awfully pale, Jan. Is Dr. Wythy right? About your having seen or heard something odd?"

Janis gritted her teeth. The last thing she wanted was revelation of her strange moment at the piano. She refused to put into words what she for a moment *thought* had happened or she as well as the Association might end up as laughingstock.

"I told you, you shouldn't try to work another of your long days right after wrecking your car," Nancy scolded while wrapping Dr. Maggie in a flamboyant purple cape. Nancy was probably right. If Janis had allowed the Auto Center owner to take her home instead of insisting he just give her the loaner car and cart her Lexus off to be repaired or totalled, the whole silly business might have been averted.

She had gone through a long day, including the Altrusa meeting where she had barely touched her lunch. Pure hunger and shock explained her muddling at the piano, not insidious brain damage. Pure wishful thinking and hunger explained Dr. Maggie's aberration. Janis brightened. "I'm fine. Someone bring me back a takeout Gordo Combo Plate and plenty of diet soda."

Frantic to get rid of them all, she physically pushed them out of Wharton's front door and locked it behind them. Immediately she felt calmer...until she thought of Dr. Wythy versus Mr. Thorpe on the validity of contacting spirits. She envisioned the possibility of flying tacos as the weapons of war.

Holy smoke, I should have gone with them. Sat between them to head off fireworks. No, they could jolly well fight it out themselves. She would do the day's receipts and not have them to do later in her home office. The sooner the day was over, the better she'd feel.

She checked the back door—properly locked, though the screen window *was* open to the night air. The relatively minor discovery reassured her, even though the night draft blowing through that back door window screen was nowhere near as cold as it had seemed when she sat at the piano.

She retrieved her briefcase and papers from the credenza

in the dining room, hit the switch on the wall that wired the period chandelier over the dining room table where she was going to work, and turned. In the great oval mirror framed in ornately carved wood on the room's east wall, she caught a glimpse of herself and—

Behind her stood a naked man, streaming blood from a hideous pattern of stab wounds in his chest. Though he was losing quantities of blood, he showed no inclination to collapse. His opalescent blue eyes were fierce with determination, the eyes of a man who refused to die no matter how ghastly his injuries. Before Janis had any opportunity to break her paralysis, the stab wounds—she was sure they were *fatal* stab wounds—faded before her eyes until there wasn't a mark on his body.

Those blue eyes gleamed in the intruder's lean, tanned face. His thatch of blond hair glittered in the light from the chandelier, but she particularly—and inanely—noted his eyebrows, sideburns and body hair, dark with golden highlights in a masculine pattern of triangles that could awaken the libido of a stone.

She had no control over filling her eyes with all of him, even with the sight of herself in the mirror, practically enveloped by him, her face unnaturally pale, her eyes darkened by shock.

His glowing blue eyes on hers in the mirror, he reached to grasp her left wrist. She knew that touch instantly from when she had been at the piano across the hall. This time, his grip was warm, but still demanding attention.

More adrenaline coursed through her, preparing her for flight or fight. She whirled and slammed her Italian leather briefcase...into thin air.

Her defense stopped her in mid-action, facing the dining room table. No one had stood behind her—she was quite alone in the room, lunging at nothing!

But the strong, warm fingers still gripped and twisted at her left wrist, and the coiling heat which had somehow overjoyed her was replaced by utter terror.

I don't believe this. I won't believe this.

If she wasn't hallucinating, she faced instant changes in the way she looked at life, heaven, hell, eternity— Halloween!

It had to be a delayed reaction to that morning's accident. The thought comforted. She must have struck her head. She ran her free hand over her skull, but found no swellings, no evidence of any bruises.

Only one option remained. She was definitely off her rocker.

With a gasping intake of breath to fortify herself, she turned toward the mirror again. The naked man still stood behind her. Wings of dark blonde hair channeled down his chest and muscular torso to below his navel, where it widened again. In a room illuminated clearly by the antique chandelier, a room without shadows, the mirror image was wildly erotic. She couldn't believe how susceptible she was to the—hallucination.

Her head came only to his shoulder, and she was taller than average. When she compulsively twisted to see him directly, the warmth of him remained, the pressure on her wrist was firm, and she had every sensation of being pulled back against that strong body. She could only see the dining room table, set with the Wharton family's antique silver.

Bloody stab wounds? Gone. Image in the mirror. There. Man behind her?

She twisted helplessly, trying to make sense of it, but oddly enough her panic faded even though her blood continued to heat with excitement. This...somehow...must be Dr. Maggie's predicated spirit.

There were no such things as ghosts!

In Millard Thorpe's words describing Dr. Maggie...she was unhinged.

She said the words aloud to the mirror. "I'm unhinged."

She trembled, unable to take action to free herself. For one thing, the image wasn't ghostly. It was totally, shatteringly physical, and not only could she see him via the mirror, she could feel his body heat and sense the additional essence of him—rubbed sage, a hint of old brandy and fresh-shaved tobacco on the warm exhalation of his breath. A smaller chill raised the hair on her neck. How would she know it was *fresh-shaved* tobacco?

The opal blue eyes mesmerized. The masculine essence entrapped. "I won't believe this is happening. Nothing can make me believe it!" she tried to convince herself in the mirror.

For the first time, the apparition seemed to see himself in the mirror. He moved expeditiously behind her mirror image, but spoke. She shivered from nape to knees and was sure her toes were curling. His words emerged, heating her neck. His voice, though a little raspy, as if it hadn't been used for a hundred years or more, melted her bones still further.

". . . someone wants you dead," the apparition intoned.

"She managed to croak, "W-wha—?"

"Wants you very dead."

She shut her eyes. His breath continued to puff, warm and steady, against her neck. She remembered her collision with the tree, the crumpled metal hood suddenly adorning her practically new car. She once again heard the Auto Center Owner's declaration that failure of everything—brakes, gears, the works—couldn't be his mechanics' fault.

"The descendant of my enemy is your enemy," intoned the solid apparition. "I'm here to warn you. He's going to kill you."

TWO

The visitor's words did not register with nearly the impact of the recent phenomenal change of gory mess to well-set-up, buck-naked male physical specimen. Janis stared in awe. He was so close to her she could smell the masculinity of him—pure musk and male, with a whiff of pine needles—which was of course ridiculous.

His hand gripped her shoulder. His body warmth went right through her suit jacket and blouse to skin and bone. She wanted to wail like a banshee. Her back sprang goose-bumps as cold as the ghostly grasp on her wrist had been at the piano. The intruder tripped a toggle in her and heat raced in widening circles from her center until even her fingertips and toes burned and tingled.

In consternation her gaze fled upward to meet his. While her first impression had been horror at the terrible wounds, she became weak in the knees with his sensual impact. She had less armor against him than she had ever had for Dexter Carter...and she had once been so lovestruck for Dexter, he could have chopped her into little pieces, and she'd only have been pleased to be of assistance.

Until the day she found he had betrayed her. Betrayed and betrayed and betrayed. She had no certification the betrayal included every nubile female who had crossed his path, but he had certainly worked his way through her considerable list of bridesmaids.

She wavered between the reality of her eyesight and other senses, and the illusion she was experiencing. The apparition's words made no more sense than the seance.

Hoarsely she said, "I'm definitely hallucinating."

The hallucination said pleasantly, "No, you're not."

Her interior coils began heating again. Not only was this nonsense, it was dangerous nonsense. He might even be someone escaped from the county mental hospital only a few blocks west.

She fiercely embraced the idea of a hospital escapee, somehow to be preferred over a serious head injury and consequent hallucinations. She could cope better with either of those explanations than with the warm, breathing nothingness behind her. Desperate, she pleaded to no one in general, "Tell me I'm asleep or in a coma."

"Not that I know of, Ma'am. But I beg your pardon for offending you. I had no idea how grossly indecent I looked after the assassin got through with me. I happened to be wearing not a stitch when the bushwhacker sneaked into my room at the hotel and knifed me. I meant no insult appearing so indecently. I swear it."

His incredible baritone voice held a faint half-British, half Deep South inflection that poured over Janis like molasses.

"Accept my apologies, Ma'am. It seems I come from limbo without luggage."

The effort not to fill her eyes with the more intimate physical details in the mirror was monumental. She said faintly, "I don't suppose you could...cover yourself with something so we could have a rather more civilized conversation? The lace tablecloth will suffice."

"If you will but excuse me briefly, Ma'am, I will attempt to do better than a tablecloth."

The mirror image faded in jittery stops and starts, finally leaving only the after-impression of opalescent blue eyes, which in turn faded.

Moaning, Janis leaned weakly on the table, knees shaking worse than they had that morning when she staggered from her badly dented car. "You're—excused—" she muttered. In the mirror she saw herself wobbling like a rag doll. Nothing else. "Are you there?" she squeaked.

No answer.

Again she pressed trembling hands to her cheeks, forehead,

nape. Still she found nothing out of the ordinary. Maybe it was last night, and she was still asleep in a bizarre nightmare. Today had never happened. Any of it.

She moaned again. Everything had to be perfectly simple and explainable. Laws of nature were involved here.

"It's all inside my head," she muttered, and was again horrified to be disappointed in that perfectly logical conclusion. Did she want him to be real?

Was she so repressed, so hungry for an encounter with such a physical man in spite of the humiliating knowledge she was a failure as a woman, that she could hallucinate a ghost in revealing detail just to experience such reactions? If he really were a ghost, should she not be terrified out of her wits instead of disappointed to be in one way or another out of her mind?

I really am terrified, she told herself severely. *The impact simply hasn't arrived yet.* Her hair was undoubtedly turning white with terror as she stood undetermined on her next move. She glanced at the mirror. Her hair was still brown. The mirror wasn't to be trusted any more than her mind was.

Even as she waffled over whether she wanted a ghost to return or to cope with a hallucination from a concussion, a man in the uniform of a Confederate major abruptly materialized with a crack of sound like crisp, faint thunder. He was close enough to block out most of the view in the mirror, but only his back was visible from that source.

The uniformed man was every bit as solid as Millard Thorpe, but with several exceptions. The major was decidedly younger than Millard Thorpe had ever been, and devastatingly attractive, which Millard Thorpe, in his decidedly less authentic-looking costume as a volunteer, certainly had never been.

As a Civil War era officer, Janis's apparition was easier to confront objectively than when he had first been viewed in the mirror. She forced herself to breathe calmly.

The Confederate major turned to inspect himself in the beveled glass. He flexed his fingers, slapped the officer's hat on his thigh, nodded in approval, snapped to attention, and gave Janis a sweeping bow.

"Your servant, Ma'am. Major Benjamin Blair, late of the Virginia volunteers, mustered out at Appomattox with Lee and party because I was one of the remaining officers with a uniform fit for parade duty. Turned soldier of fortune after. And finally, victim of murder most foul. And now you have the advantage of me. To whom do I address myself?"

"Janis Carter," she said, inexplicably fluttering. "Ms.Janis Carter, rather than 'Miss' or 'Mrs.'" She stopped abruptly, aware she was babbling. She frowned. "If you know someone wants to kill me, why don't you know my name?"

He studied her warily. All the time he had been trying to reach her, he had not expected his responsibility to be what she turned out to be in the flesh. He had no memory of her name. He had never had any difficulty with names previously. But this was the first time he had seen this twenty-first century woman, and there was nothing particularly odd in not knowing the name of someone who was after all a stranger to him. Except that he had been sent to warn her and to carry out a mission that would also affect himself.

Nothing surfaced within him to tell him what she wanted to know. The woman quite disoriented him. "The name evidently isn't as important as that I reach you with the message."

He narrowed his eyes at her, wondering if indeed the way he perceived her was some quirk of being materialized. He was seeing double. Two women, one superimposed over the other, and both strangers.

He rapidly shook his head to clear his eyesight, but the anomaly remained. Aha! There might be a reason. "You have a point, I admit. No...I do not find the name familiar. It does however seem appropriate. J-A-N-U-S, from Janus the two-headed god of the Greeks. It fits you."

He wondered if his already skewed fate was playing another trick on him. The basic point was not to be ignored, and seeing double was only a minor matter. "The faster you come up with the name of your killer, the safer you'll be, and the more easily I can take care of the paramount problem."

"There are several ways my name can be spelled, depending on who owns it," she said in the severe way of a schoolmarm. "I spell my name J-A-N-I-S, as did my maternal grandmother. My mother is supposed to have said that, since I was born with Grandmother's Italian nose, I should have her name. And I may have my faults, Major, but no one has ever called me `two-faced' before."

Bemused in spite of his intent to ignore the cosmic peculiarity before him, he said, "Nevertheless, I see two faces when I look at you. I note that one has a fine, strong nose, and one has a nose some would call charming, but I call insignificant."

She instantly cupped a hand over the feature under discussion. "You *don't* see two noses!" Her reaction was sufficient to tell him there was a reason he could see two faces, one superimposed on the other, with the one he preferred the image behind the other.

He walked around the table, took her chin in one hand and tipped her face up toward the lighted chandelier. His touch feathered over her features; his fingers also detected the two faces. A decidedly unusual experience.

"Two noses," he said firmly. "One as smart as a fresh painted wagon but bland. Under that, the nose you were born with, I presume. Your grandmother's delightful Italian nose, perhaps?"

"Dexter insisted," she said in a small voice. "My ex-husband's one of California's leading plastic surgeons. He said my nose belonged on Mrs. Gargantua. He'd always called me 'Beaky,' and the name stuck all through school. So once we were married, he operated on that and a few other items he thought were in need of being improved. Suddenly everyone was calling me a beauty, which I know is ridiculous. I know I'm still the person everyone, even my father, Ocho, called `Beaky.' I wonder why it doesn't bother me that you can still see me that way. But why not, if you're a ghost?"

He ran a lean forefinger lightly down what she supposed was the feature under discussion. "The most beautiful women in the history of the world have Italian noses. Too big? Indeed not! It's absolutely magnificent. Take him to a court of law for destroying a masterpiece. Better, force him to replace it!"

A small, childlike laugh escaped her. "I don't think anyone's *that* good a surgeon. But the minute we were married, he insisted on making me over and explained the wonders it would do for his reputation. Before and After shots, you know. He called it, `making a dud into a delicacy.' I never fooled myself that I wasn't plain as a fence post. Even plainer," she said apologetically. "I should have had to be stupid not to know he was only telling a bald truth. He said plastic surgery was no more superficial than having my teeth straightened."

"Your teeth weren't all that crooked." The major checked her teeth the way he would a skittish filly's. "But I see what strides dentists have made in this last century. Once upon a time I knew a number of ladies here and there who would have been pleased to consult your husband on the matter of teeth. I can't fault them, but he should have left that beautiful nose alone!"

She laughed again. The sound seemed to startle her. He gathered she was not someone to laugh much, and that was a pity. Both faces were quite marvelous in the midst of a laugh. "I just don't understand why you want to look like a pretty porcelain doll," he said.

"If you'd come around before the great make over, I probably wouldn't have listened. I wanted to please Dexter. And I don't know *why* I'm talking to you like this. I've never unloaded on anyone else. Never. I have to be fair to him. This `doll face' has been photographed for *Vogue* and *Harper's Bazaar,* among others, as evidence of perfection. Dexter probably is Beverly Hills' premier makeover man now because of it. It seems disrespectful to denigrate his skills, no matter how I despise his morals."

Really, Janis thought, her apparition was having a bizarre effect on her. She had been plain, but aside from having her teeth straightened, she had never seriously thought of tampering with what nature dealt her—until Dexter pushed all her buttons. She hadn't had to have a dermatologist when she was an adolescent. Most of her peer friends had Dr. Cook or Dr. Silverstein, but she had never needed to weigh the abilities of either one because her own complexion remained fresh and smooth even when other teens had faces like relief maps. Some of them had undergone nose jobs. She had balked when Ocho suggested the operation. He had pushed it long before Dexter persuaded her.

"If this Dexter person didn't like you the way you were, why did he fall in love with you?" the Major asked, genuinely curious about this strange girl who was the focal point of the mission he had momentarily forgotten, but reminded himself to reintroduce as soon as possible.

"When all's said and done, I suppose he fell in love with the clinic my father offered to build for a talented son-in-law who would upgrade a plain daughter who showed no signs of blossoming any other way. Dexter needed someone to bankroll his specialty. Ocho knew I had a crush the size of Mt. Everest on Dexter. As his wife, I could be persuaded to be the great `before and after' ad, the `dud into delicacy' bit. He leaped to the bait of a wife with social and financial clout, who wouldn't object like an ordinary patient to being used as a tool in his trade. What did I know? My own father always was embarrassed by me. Any attention from Dexter thrilled me, from the first day he joined my brother's poker club until I figured out what a fool I'd been. And before that, Ocho said the clinic was cheap at twice the price when he considered the results."

She subsided, annoyed with herself for being so forthcoming. She really didn't blame her father. Ocho had been...Ocho. He was notoriously handsome himself, from a long line of handsome forebears. He had married only beautiful women—eight of them. It must have been a burden for Ocho to display a daughter who'd inherited every recessive ugly gene in the family.

Keith wasn't a throwback. He was his father's son, the image of Ocho except for being blond like his mother who had run away with someone she met at the race track long before Janis was born to Ocho's fourth wife. Keith was only her half brother, but the two of them stuck together during her childhood because they were all the family support either had ever had.

"You hate your husband for leaving you," the Major said. "That's natural."

"Your ghostly powers aren't perfect. I left him. And it will probably amuse you to know that while I went along like a sheep as the great display in Dexter's test reconstruction project, I've never gotten used to seeing men's eyes light up when they see me across a crowded room. No one's eyes ever lit up when I was `Beaky.' And being an acclaimed beauty didn't make him love me. He wasn't true to me for a minute. Getting a divorce made me feel better about him. Lots better."

"How did your father feel about the divorce?"

"Ocho could not have cared less. He thought I would shortly marry someone high up in politics or commerce. But he fell ill just after the divorce and needed someone to lean on. His eighth wife died just when he needed her to take care of him. She was gorgeous, and she was a nurse. The priority on his mind after that was that he needed a nurse, and I was elected. There you have it. The story of a mess. I can't hide a thing from you, can I? You really must be a ghost. But I'm probably talking to myself in a delirium, certainly not to someone real."

"Think what you like of me, but you were beautiful to begin with and never should have been butchered."

"I must defend the man on that point. He really has talent."

"But the rotter abandoned you," the Major protested in a voice with undertones of a thunderstorm approaching.

She glared straight into the wonderfully blue eyes. "He didn't leave me. I found my pride and left him. I saw a lawyer the morning after my maid of honor filled me in on details that couldn't be disputed. I said if he tried to stop me I'd make the divorce public and messy. Though I don't suppose I would have, if the chips were down."

"That's an interesting point about this era. A woman needn't put up with being humiliated by a publicly unfaithful husband. Glad you got up the gumption." He gave her a rakish salute.

She squinted at him suspiciously. "And how, coming from the past as you claim, can you know about this era?"

He grimaced and bit on his thumbnail in intense contemplation. "Hmm. Odd, indeed. I don't seem to know the answer to that!" He looked at her with all the appearance of candid surprise at his own gaffe.

"And you seem to have a modern way of speaking," she pursued.

"Just because I've been restricted doesn't mean I've not kept tabs with what's going on. How else would I know about that blasted son of an assassin?"

"Couldn't be the son of. Anyone born within fifty years of your supposed death would be almost a hundred years old himself. "

"Don't quibble," he advised her. "Any descendant of that assassin is heir to the same proclivities. Thievery and murder."

"Let's get back to the bomb you exploded regarding someone wanting to murder me, shall we?"

He pursed his lips consideringly and took stock of their surroundings. "First, orient me. I collect I'm in the Whartons' home, but how did I get here?"

"I'm not sure. But we had a seance led by Dr. Maggie Wythy, a parapsychologist. I think she managed to call you up. Unless you're a figment of my concussion."

"Now I remember! I opened books at appropriate pages and directed night winds to blow old newspaper clippings off her desk, somewhere in a musty tower room far from here, and into her lap. I did everything but write the letter for her to the President of the Historical Association here."

"You did that to get her attention?"

He brushed the lapels of his uniform coat. "Whom do you suppose earlier managed to pull that rolled up blueprint parchment out of the Whartons' upstairs press so you would conveniently find it when you came to work the next morning?"

"What did you do that for?"

"I had no better way to start my plan of warning you. It worked. I seemed to be hemmed round with barriers to climb over before I could warn you."

"Why you? Why not Nate Wharton or Mrs. Wharton or—" she shuddered, "—the town boozer who was hanged on the beam smack over the heads of everyone at the seance table, but more than a hundred and seventy-five years ago when Wharton House was being built?"

"So you know the story? The old boy rode off late of a Saturday night with Mr. Wharton's new oxcart and two prime oxen. Gomez told me about it himself. The lawmen apprehended him bawling a lusty ballad while weaving down the road toward the bay. His fate was to be the salutary example of the city council's first `zero tolerance' ordinance."

"You're using an expression new to the late twentieth century and saying the old drunk told you the story himself?"

"Just because I had a problem reaching you doesn't mean I spent all my nights in solitary confinement. I had company of sorts on occasion. Not necessarily the company I'd choose, but there are artifacts stored in that warehouse from Wharton, too. And with the antiques sometimes come the spirits to go with them. Like the stool pulled out from under Gomez when they strung him up."

"Really?" Janis hoped she would remember, when her bizarre brain fever burned itself out, to check the warehouse for the stool. Such items should be in their rightful place on display for tourists' benefit. "What else is there that belongs to Wharton House?"

He dismissed the warehouse with a careless wave. "Only a few old nails and such. Nothing you don't have plenty of already."

"Then the ghosts we advertise really are haunting our complex like we say?"

"What do your advertisements say?"

"That the aroma of Nate Wharton's cigars wafts through the halls from his office, and people have seen Mrs. Wharton sweeping the steep back stairs. Some say they have seen the ghost of Wharton's little girl who supposedly romped the paths of the garden with her dog. Why didn't one of them come to Dr. Wythy's call for a spirit materialization?"

"They have no wish to be called. I did because I'm looking for a murderer. I've been patiently waiting to get my hands on my murderer's last descendent since the date of my death on January nineteenth, 1869, at a little after midnight, and a hell of a way to celebrate General Lee's birthday that was! I'm here to be at your service because you need to beware that descendant of the man who murdered me."

"I don't mean to sound indifferent or insensitive, but even if you *were* murdered in Underwood House, you can't be wandering around here. Underwood House was more than two miles away, and what's left of it, if anything, is under Mission Bay with tourists sailing or waterskiing over it."

He looked at her with a pitying expression. "You don't reside here, either, but I'm not making an issue of that. I gather you're employed in some way here at the Wharton home? As a housekeeper, I presume."

"You could say that. I'm the Executive Director of the Heritage Homes Association, of which Wharton is the headquarters—or flag ship, in a San Diego Navy Town manner of speaking."

"You therefore are often ordered about by a group devoted to remembrance of local things past, and direct campaigns to raise funds and so forth?"

"I am, but what does that have to do with my being a target for murder?"

"I'm not sure. Except that's the way I was able to put myself in the position of talking to you right now."

"Who's the murderer, then? Someone in the vicinity, I gather? Surely not someone on the Board of Directors. One of my volunteers? I'm the only full-time paid staff."

"You're the director of a tourist attraction that invites visitors to come see ghosts who haunt the place, and you don't believe in them?"

"You're right, I don't," she said. Her words weren't as certain as they would have been a half hour earlier. "I don't believe in ghosts for a minute."

"Boo," he said. "You're dealing with one."

"I prefer to think I'm suffering the effects of an automobile accident and am a little bit concussed."

He grinned amiably in spite of her denial of his existence. "You ought to believe even without a confrontation. I imagine a lot of your business comes from a public dying—excuse the phrase—to see a real ghost."

She could hardly argue. Although no one in the Association ever claimed Wharton was haunted, there was no discounting how disappointed most tourists were when they secretly hoped their two dollar tour ticket would deliver a bonus ghost and didn't.

The most important part of her job in preservation of landmark homes was marketing the historical group sufficiently to cover all costs. The possibility of a ghostly confrontation had an undeniable bearing on the gross receipts. "I can't discount the value of ghostly legends, but I didn't set out to sell legends. I set out to sell the Board on the idea of a professional salaried director to make this previously ignored tourist attraction a paying proposition so we could buy more landmark buildings and preserve them."

"Why this association? There are others in a city this size."

"It was the natural one for me to target after I earned my graduate degree in non-profit agency management skills. Our family has supported the Association for three generations. As for experience, I've been an Association volunteer since my Junior League days."

Her fingers itched to reach up and touch one of the brass buttons on her apparition's uniform coat, or even to touch his tanned cheek. She splayed her palm lightly over the apparition's uniformed chest. "You can't be a ghost. You're as solid as I am. But of course I'm in the midst of this wildly complex hallucination."

"I'm a ghost all right. From sunset to sunrise, anyway."

"These buttons are genuine antiques. I'd stake my...well, I'm sure." She fingered the material of the coat sleeve. "The uniform's in exquisite condition. You might just have had it made except that there's a feel to it that today's materials simply don't have." The fine, tailored wool was so well-preserved it should have been in the Smithsonian. She shivered at the rasp of it under her fingertips. Real. Very real. And under it, warm, hard muscle and bone. She shivered again—whether in sensual pleasure or at her audacity—or because of the general situation—she couldn't decide. "No matter how cleverly you talk, you're not a ghost."

His blue eyes flashed. A definite dark cloud floated under the chandelier and darkened the room. Thunder rattled at the windows. All but the blue eyes disappeared. They remained like jewels in the dark.

"Be a ghost if you insist," she croaked. "Just don't give me a heart attack on top of a concussion!"

He instantly reappeared. "I would not have you devastated, Ma'am. I apologize for taking umbrage." He neither looked nor sounded apologetic, but pulled out one of the high-backed antique dining room chairs for her.

Janis dropped into it, glad of support and remembering a semblance of manners taught her by her favorite step-mother. "Thank you."

He seated himself in another of the carved chairs and stretching out one long leg clothed in Confederate gray, examined the toe of one polished boot. "I wish I had my orderly here, but haven't seen him since Appomattox. I'd have liked him to use one of the sadirons in yonder kitchen to put the uniform in better state. Best I could do was find where someone had placed it and rid it of dust."

"When you went for it you were gone from this room only a matter of seconds."

"A few seconds, a few hours, a few hundred years. I'm out of practice in referencing time at this point."

"And just where did you find this?" She leaned forward and fingered his sleeve.

He stretched. "In a glass case in a museum of some sort in what appears to be a large park somewhat southeast of here. The uniform is mine. No question. My name, stitched by my orderly, is still inside the coat collar if you care to see proof."

He rapped tentatively on the Wharton's dining room table. The sound was solid. He held his hand up to the chandelier light. "I'm not transparent. I don't carry chains or moan. I wonder if I walk through walls?"

He stood, adjusted his uniform and walked straight at the wall between the dining room and the granary, turning slightly at the last moment, which kept him from crashing into it head-on. He rebounded and rubbed his shoulder.

"I don't go through walls," he said with a surprised frown. "I wonder how I managed the clandestine requisitional sortie? Aha! I didn't think about it. Just went where I had to, and did what I had to do to obtain what was needed. Well, well. My so-called renaissance is as much a puzzle to me as to you. Or perhaps not. In any case, here I am. More or less decently attired."

Janis had a twinge of alarm. "In the morning there's sure to be a TV news flash about theft from the museum."

He grinned. "The moment the sun peeks over the hills to the east, my uniform will be back in its sealed paper casing. They should have no complaint about my using it when they're closed for business. Nor I for their display of it when I have no need for it."

"But what will you do for clothing in the morning?" She didn't really mind if he showed up naked around her, having gotten over the initial shock, but Nancy Rogers or the morning tourist visitors would undoubtedly undergo heart attacks.

"I shan't need it, ma'am. I shan't be around come morning. The minute the sun comes up, poof, I go. Forward? Backward? Where, I don't know. It may be a condition of my ghostly penance, I have no idea. No one from whatever administrative system is in effect has explained it to me. Perhaps it has to do with my goal, or punishment for my sins. Your guess is as good as mine."

"People who believe in this kind of thing say vampires exist at night and burn up in the light of day, not ghosts."

"I do not `burn up' in the light of day," he said with dignity. "I simply do not exist during the day, unlike some other phantasms haunting this facility. Since there is nothing painful, terrifying or destructive about it, I see no point protesting. And you, Ma'am, have no proof of any of your theories that will hold water even as well as a sieve does. Especially in view of my presence here."

He tested his eye teeth with his thumbs. "You suggest I am a vampire because I am not around in daylight hours? I confess I find myself uncommonly hungry. More than a hundred and twenty-five years between meals has made me work up a powerful appetite that grows more demanding by the minute. While I was making myself decent for this conversation with you, I took the liberty of helping myself to coffee and tasty cakes I found yonder." He gestured towards Badger House to the rear, where the Association staff used the kitchen as a staff lounge. "Alas, what I found only whetted my appetite. And now I detect the aroma of refried beans and chorizo. I do believe I smell hot and sour pork, and sharks' fin soup. The Whartons' Chinese cook must be hard at work in the kitchen of this house at present, but no one was on the job in the spot I found those light refreshments."

"The Jalisco Mexican Restaurant is across the street. One of the best Chinese restaurants in the city is just around the corner. You smell their cuisine of the day."

"What a relief to know, Ma'am. I thought I was hallucinating."

"Very funny, but I'm not convinced I haven't gone around the bend. Your story of why you are here, for example, has holes in it."

Exasperation sparked from under his hooded lids. "If there are non sequiturs, I'll explain as soon as the powers that be enlighten me on the gaps in my memory. I am dead as a doornail, even if I can feel the bruise I inflicted on myself with the wall." He rubbed the shoulder which had taken the brunt of the confrontation. "And I came specifically to warn you via the means of the seance I organized."

"You?"

"I certainly did. Although I could have materialized nightly, over the years since the razing of the old Underwood Hotel I've done so infrequently. One night's much like another in a warehouse. The effort of arriving here in my present state took considerable conniving, effort, and determination. Perhaps more than I realized, since I see you as you were and as you are, at one time. The effort it takes me to focus may be disturbing my equilibrium."

"You needn't look at me at all if it bothers you."

"Madam, will you listen to reason? You remind me of the *sublime Mona Lisa*, or one of the Raphaels I saw on my earthly travels. If that isn't beauty then the acknowledged connoisseurs of the world are in error. And that, Ma'am, is the last we will debate the question, for I will firmly instruct my brain not to recognize your husband's execrable judgment as executed on your person. Now to the matter of my assassin and his descendant—"

"Why haven't you revenged yourself on him long ago?"

"For three generations I was marooned on the mud flats of False Bay before coming to my senses one night to find myself in the locked warehouse, and bound to its perimeters. I made my escape via Underwood House bricks."

"That must have been when the Association began to salvage usable materials from old buildings, bricks, moldings, ironwork . . ."

"Whatever. About a year ago, I became aware of your presence here in Wharton House. And your danger, but you're a difficult woman to communicate with, and I'd fallen out of practice. I tried to contact you by calling your attention to the hotel blueprints. Then by drawing your attention to the bricks and ironwork from Underwood Hotel, stored in the warehouse."

He stretched again, and she winced at the decidedly un-ghostlike sound of crackling joints. She was hemmed in by nonsequiturs, oxymoronic circumstances and peculiar evidence that forced her to consider at least some of his story. For example, the great find—the old Underwood blueprints when she was going through cubbyholes throughout Wharton House gathering all kinds of memorabilia untouched and unclassified for so many years. The blueprints had fallen from a niche and literally hit her in the head. The Underwood, razed long before the turn of the Twentieth Century was exactly what the Association needed in the way of a compatible structure for accessory purposes.

With money earmarked from Ocho's estate for that purpose, Underwood had since rapidly risen to within weeks of completion. The Board was happy with her first year on the job. *But someone wants to murder me?*

The information and the impact from the Major's opalescent eyes made her dizzy. Especially did his eyes confuse her with their incredible dark lashes that any girl would die for. She regretted the metaphor the moment it occurred to her.

"The murderer's plan is at explosion point. This morning disappointed him unduly, because he had it so well planned."

"What do you mean `so well planned'? *My accident?"*

Her automobile's misfunction could have been fatal to herself and others, but she couldn't go into paranoia about it without a lot more evidence than the protests of the Auto Center owner that it couldn't have been their mechanic's responsibility.

Her entire day had been weird, beginning with the incident a few blocks from work, on Juan Street, San Diego's steepest thoroughfare. When the auto's highly complex system malfunctioned, she had managed to stop the vehicle with relative safety by steering it around Heritage Homes Industrial Park until the momentum slowed. The car stopped against a young liquid amber tree. Unfortunately for the car and the liquid amber, neither could claim a victory. Fortunately, she was only shaken up. At least she thought that was all, until the ghost made his appearance.

When Janis finally had arrived at work, she'd found Dr. Maggie's arrival totally unnerving the goggle-eyed visitors until she reminded the staff of the rules of courtesy to researchers and bustled Dr. Maggie off to the monthly Altrusa luncheon meeting with her. Dr. Maggie no doubt was a zinger to the Altrusans as well. Such an eruption of burgundy and gold tie-died gauze cotton, impossibly high heels, and plethora of bangles and beads was an awesome view.

Even from Janis's undergraduate and graduate studies at Claremont—in a practical field far from Dr. Maggie's sphere of influence—the emeritus professor's reputation for endless enthusiasm and eccentricity was legend. Janis found Dr.

Maggie interesting, if off-track. To be in many ways like Dr. Maggie at seventy, which was forty years in Janis's future, was a prospect not without a certain charm, but Janis doubted she would still be around at Dr. Maggie's age with her family's penchant for popping off prematurely. Their record of early deaths from unheralded heart attacks and strokes or bizarre accidents was legendary.

Given her workaholic habits, Janis did what she could to ensure a normal life span. She was also fussy about keeping her car in tip-top working order. Yet the electric system of a top of the line luxury car had winked out going down Juan Hill. Had her driving skills not been a paradigm, she surely would have become a statistic that very morning.

The Major was saying, "The varmint will shortly be near enough for me to get my hands around his throat at last. And at last I'm solid and he can't escape me. You're in luck I'm assigned to be your bodyguard. As for me, getting rid of him will be well worth a little heat of hell due me."

"No one can be popular with everyone, but there just couldn't be anyone who would seriously want to kill me." Even as she firmly expressed that belief, she knew there were a number of people in her circle who did fit the major's criteria of descendants from early Californians.

...and could have had a vendetta against Ocho that she had unwittingly inherited.

"Everyone is on the wrong side of at least one person, and you had best figure out who's turned sour on you, Ma'am. That will help me get my hands on him, even with my temporary ghostly amnesia. We'll start with your ex-husband as prime suspect."

"Dexter has no reason to murder me! He got everything he wanted out of our marriage and isn't the one who has any reason for being offended. My brother and I are the only ones left in my family, so he isn't the last descendant. As the younger, technically, I am. You wouldn't be on a mission to save me and get at a murderer if I were the one. Keith, who has as much money as I do, has always relied on me as much as I've relied on him."

"Keep going. My ghostly amnesia will clear up when you get to the party. You're thinking along lines that will give a clue to the villain sooner or later."

"I just can't believe it's anyone who has to do with the Association, but many of them also trace their roots back to the beginning in this part of California. If it is one of them, well...it's a big list of unlikely suspects just in their area."

The list of her acquaintances who fit the Old San Diego forebears criteria was equally numerous and unlikely. "Good heavens, put all but one of my bridesmaids on the list...although I'm still the one most likely to have a grudge."

"If you were in my shoes, blue thunder and lightning would be flashing," the major empathized.

"I've done my best to restore my perspective on life and come out pretty well, considering. I refuse to turn into a suspicious, bitter woman when the mistake in judgment was mine to begin with."

"Dexter was the fool, not you," he said so softly that she heard his words only through his breath against her cheek. *"Quanta cion che perdo pete. Famm'adurmi, Abbracciato nu poco cu te!"*

The major's words might have meant anything, but enveloped her in a kind of steam. Faintly she said, "Very impressive. But in spite of my Italian grandmother, I understand only the words `Ciao' and `Arrivederci.'"

He was practically touching her lips with his while saying, "`Why do you tease me when your kiss can do so much for me?'"

She backed away. "You mean if I allow you to kiss me, you'll turn into a frog?"

"Cruel beauty! Kiss me and we can both become frogs."

With that, and no opportunity to sidestep or backstep further, she found herself being kissed.

Granted, the assault was meant to be comic relief, the way she was seized, turned sideways and backward in a parody of an old movie on late night TV with Clark sweeping Myrna or Lana or Vivian into a blockbuster kiss with a full orchestra playing in the background. Stagy and improbable as it was, she had once dreamed of being kissed that way. No longer naive, she realized she wasn't yet immune. The Major gave her a devastating idea of how short her fuse could be if she ever let it be lighted again. She had studiously avoided all opportunities to make a fool of herself ever again, and this should be no exception.

She not only didn't want him to stop kissing her, she wanted the kiss to go from there to wherever, with nothing else considered. She heard someone moaning. Not the ghost. Her.

He broke off abruptly and set her away from him. "What the devil am I doing!"

One moment she was hanging in his hands like a demented rag doll, absolutely drunk with bliss, wanting more, more, more. The next she was staggering back against the Victorian sofa.

He stood a good six feet away, looking surprised. "I apologize for getting carried away. I hope I didn't alarm you."

In light of her roiling reactions, Janis steeled herself to give him a royal setdown—as soon as she could think of one.

"You, Ma'am are quite the most ravishing woman I have encountered since 1869. But no future in it, so I must focus on our problem." A distinctly cold atmosphere emanated from his vicinity. "I will not be guilty of a second such offense."

Janis scraped her dignity off the floor and wherever else it had been shed in the absolutely mindless indulgence, and wrapped tattered virtue around herself as armor. "I'll thank you to wink off before I punch you right between the running lights!" She attempted a tone as cold as his aura and winced to hear how childish she sounded.

"A show of simple disinterest is sufficient." The air warmed in the room. He said cheerfully, "I am beholden to you for letting me know that just because I am part of the vastly complex spirit world does not mean I have lost my interest in the ladies. I make no apology for ability to enjoy an encounter with a charming lady, but I must recall my situation as a transient spirit. Taking advantage of an attractive and susceptible woman is quite unacceptable when that attractive woman is also vulnerable. You are of course off limits."

"Thank you for clarifying the parameters." She hoped she sounded as freezing as she wanted to, but wished she weren't so devastated.

"You are extremely attractive," he said firmly. "But I am and must remain a traveler with a mission. In any case, I am not insensitive enough to allow you to fall in love with me only to find I, like your abysmal ex-husband, have abandoned you. That is exactly what will happen the moment I take care of my business and am able to retire from the premises. If there is one point on which I pride myself, it is that I never in life, or out of it, disillusioned any woman. You may be sure I will not begin with you."

Janis did not know whether to laugh, cry, or kick him in the shins. She rather favored the last, having seen his confrontation with the wall. Bad enough she had revealed her emotionally messy hangups to this hallucination as if she were an adolescent. She now found he had a colossal estimate of his effect on women. The discovery was the perfect chiller for her initial hormonal reaction.

"I trust I have not been too forthright for this era, but ghosts can be nothing else, and I never was one to dissemble. For the last time, I never meant to distress you."

She was still breathing hard. "I'm...not at all distressed."

"Not even a little?" he asked in what she thought was a rather wistful tone. "I admit to having momentarily been totally seduced by that gorgeous Italian nose. Too bad the owner must be off limits. Well, to the business of finding an assassin."

THREE

Janis reminded herself to be tolerant of the major. He was acting as little like a nineteenth century cad and as much like a gentleman as one could expect of one in his circumstances. She forced herself into a mood to listen to anything he had to say about her earthly problem as he saw it.

"I hope your ex-husband's family is on the list of one locally going back four or more generations?"

"As a matter of fact, his forefathers were either among the Spanish land grant families or among the first Yankees in Southern California. But, trust me, he's not the one you're looking for."

"I'll be the judge of whether your ex-husband is my target or not. He's obviously a sadistic monster to have put you through horrors no better than the rack just to satisfy his own monstrous aims. I have seen sufficient agonies of battlefield surgery to know what you went through, and the thought that a delicate flower of womanhood has deliberately been put through it makes my blood boil."

"He gave me a mean time with his insults and his women, but this modern age has anesthesias and techniques that make any operation bearable. Remember, I could have said no. On the other hand, he did wring me out and hang me to dry, which depressed me for a time. I promise you I'm quite recovered, and he has gained a brand new clinic off Wilshire in Beverly Hills, with entertainment stars of both sexes as well as aging wealthy industry wives beating a path to his door to create for them the illusion of youth and beauty. I hardly ever want to boil him in oil any more."

"I was never before considered a violent man," the major

stepped closer. "However, the prospect that he is the man I seek fills me with pleasant anticipation of any retribution I can heap on his head. He deserves every bit as bad as he gave you and intends to give you in the future."

Alarmed at the possibility the major would act on knee-jerk conclusions, she assured him, "My father settled everything on Dexter that he's ever going to get from our family. Believe me, he has nothing to gain as the villain. As soon as you remember who your assassin was, we can go from there. I happen to be in the best possible situation to trace him to his present-day counterpart."

"It's—" The major stared at her blankly again. "The bastard's name was on the tip of my tongue once more, and it's gone."

"I should expect the name of your partner and murderer would be the last thing you could possibly forget."

He delved so deeply into his memories that his face turned mahogany-colored. "It will come to me," he promised, and withdrew into a heavy scowl.

"Considering the fact you don't know where you go during the day, or why you're limited to what we can call your `half-life', as well as other missing items in your half-omniscient existence, you seem to me, if you don't mind my saying so, a considerably flawed ghost."

"I *know* that. Stop hammering me with it."

"I don't even know the right questions to ask that could trigger the return of your memory."

"Whoever or whatever is pulling my strings sees fit to deprive me of the name at this time. So, back to your husband as a prime suspect—"

"Major, I'm still one of his prize guinea pigs. For free he can hold me up as the worst possible `before' and most improved `after' image in his portfolio, except for those few good-deed patients who suffer from serious birth or trauma disfigurements. He's generous with serious reconstructive surgery and very good at it. His practice lets him balance a few million dollars a year earned from aging, wealthy women's vanity against a fair donation of skill that ends real tragedies."

"Gracious of you, Ma'am, to forgive and forget how he treated you. I personally like thinking he is the polecat in the brush pile. Whoever the villain is, however, he will not try to bushwhack you tonight, though certain to try again soon. I can tell you I am heartily tired of sitting around tied to bricks and a dreary night existence and wish to put this matter out of mind forever."

"What I do not understand is why you pursue his unfortunate descendants."

"I swore with my dying breath not to rest until his last descendant is in his or her grave. It was foolish of me, but I was not in a mood for being gracious about it at the time. If I had known then what I know now, I would have confined my judgment to him alone, but we die and learn. You are the means to my peace, Ma'am. I tell you, I truly could love you for that if you were as plain as my aunt's picket fence."

"Thank you very much." Janis hoped her voice dripped with icicles.

"Don't put me on the defensive. Your era allows full indulgence in the admiration of neat ankles and the other revelations of attractively scanty clothing."

His leer was delivered politely enough for her to ignore, considering the provocation the last of the twentieth century provided someone whose lifetime had been spent in a time when ankles never showed. He would have a real shock if he hadn't already seen his first girl in mini-shorts or micro-mini skirt. Janis was herself clothed in a conservative navy blue Donna Karan power suit with considerably longer skirt than worn by most women with legs as good as she happened to have. "And you evidently are attracted to women with two noses, if I understand you right," she reminded him.

He sighed. "There is not an ounce of flirtation in you, is there? Just as well, I suppose. I shall soon be gone forever. `Gone forever' should sound as good to you as to me, considering it means in this instance that you will no longer have to look over your shoulder for what dangers lurk. I'm sorry circumstances don't allow me to give you a few lessons in regaining the self-confidence your former husband took from you."

"Thank you, I have all the confidence I want."

"Liar," he said with a smile.

Unfortunately, he was right about that, but she intended to keep that to herself. Except that she went right on talking as though her tongue were unhinged at both ends. "My father undermined my self-confidence long before Dexter did. Ocho didn't mean to be cruel. He could only relate to women who were great beauties, and I was anything but a beauty, even as a child."

"Not that again! You were a beauty from the start."

"You're the first to tell me so while apparently looking at the old Janis, though I've heard it many times since my numerous hospital procedures. At least I'm as aware as you that what I am now is an illusion."

Major Blair snorted.

"I'm still the same person I was when no one gave me a second look unless they were looking for an heiress."

"With your prickly nature, I am surprised they came within twenty leagues of you even for money."

"Exactly. And that suits me just fine."

He regarded her thoughtfully. "Tell me about your father, Janis-of-the-two-faces."

She thought unwillingly of Ocho's pride in her manufactured good looks and how he had failed to realize he had also fathered a *cum laude* daughter, a daughter with a community conscience, a daughter who loyally supported all his most cherished interests. That daughter he never acknowledged had created herself. *That* daughter hadn't counted with Ocho until she was attractive enough in his estimation to be paraded about on his arm and introduced to friends because she looked like a credit to him.

In the end, though, she actually had become his right arm. He had truly depended on her the last two years of his life when he was so sick.

The reasons Ocho despised Keith were no more rational than despising her for being plain. She still winced under the suspicion she had progressed to being in Ocho's good graces only by virtue of his estimate of her looks; but Keith's unsettled life and his relationship with Ocho remained in chaos to a certain extent even after Ocho's death.

Keith had also needed Ocho's attention and love, and when he couldn't get attention any other way, he forced Ocho to pay attention to the way he behaved. Outrageously. Conversely, since his little sister admired and adored him just the way he was, he hated to admit to her when he was in trouble again, hated to let her know until he had worked his way out.

"Ocho was a man who knew how to use money to make money. His hobbies were the Heritage Association and nineteenth century artifacts found locally plus being a serial monogamist."

The Major raised his eyebrows in sudden interest. " Your father was a kind of criminal unknown to me."

"He was legally married, one after the other, to six flawless beauties. His name being Henry—Henry Logan—After his sixth marriage, people began calling him Ocho. For `Henry the Eighth.' But his first six didn't go, divorced, chopped, died, divorced, chopped, survived. They went, `divorced, ran off with his Super, crashed in a plane, divorced, divorced, divorced. Seven and Eight were, divorced, died. And in between that impressive list, he was San Diego's King of Construction and principal owner of County Beach Front Properties."

"A land baron of sorts who liked being married even if he chose for the wrong reasons?"

"I suppose. My poor brother and I neither one of us ever knew our own mothers. Keith's mother ran off with Ocho's Project Super and just left him behind with never another word from that day to this. After that it was five divorces. One divorce is all I'm going to go through, and you may be sure that is a sacred vow. Keith's said often enough he'll never be caught in the marriage trap even once. Ocho's eye was on his ninth when he died. Neither Keith nor I have had promising looks at family life. And I certainly had enough marriage with Dexter to last me more than the rest of my lifetime if I live to be a hundred. According to you, if you can't prevent my murder, that lengthy a life isn't likely."

"What a recitation." The Major didn't sound as though he carried an ounce of sympathy around with him. He yawned.

"We've eliminated Dexter as my would-be assassin. He left me free to move towards being a damned good Association Director. I'll give you a list of my bridesmaids and the Heritage Homes Association to see if any of the names ring a bell with you."

"You should have married again." He ignored, for the time, what would be a totally useless list except for old California names with a long local history.

"Did I mention anything to you about fish needing bicycles?"

"Getting away from a bad marriage is much like being thrown from a horse. You should have been wed again before you became so grim about your work habits. But far be it from me to argue with you the case for marriage."

"I'm married to the Association."

"Go ahead and coop yourself in a haunted house, if you want to. Raise funds to buy the ugliest pieces of old furniture you can find. Spend your nights doing books and your days sitting on community committees." The Major lifted a shoulder. "I still fancy seeing your ex-husband receive comeuppance for addling your brain and being unfaithful in the bargain. If a man has no intention to remain faithful, he should stay single. Now, I had a roving foot and an appreciative eye for the ladies from the time I was thirteen. Never fooled any woman that I meant more than a good time. Never fooled myself or anyone else that it was love. Didn't even fool myself that I was in love when I decided it was time to settle down. Just as well, because I could have brooded about it all these years, thinking about how she married my ex-partner indecently fast after my demise. Actually, I figured if she picked a husband with so little deliberation, she deserved what she got."

He still had Janis's hands in his. He didn't allow her to pull away, and she had too much pride and liked the feel of his hands on hers too much to struggle. Especially to struggle with a ghost.

"I understand you were hurt to have your father be so delighted with your remodeling results. But that was *his* problem, not yours."

Janis had never thought of Ocho's rejection of her before her "transformation" as his problem. She had always been sure it was hers. The Major's words shed new light.

He moved still closer, and since he had her cornered, she could retreat no further than the Wharton's dining room wall and the end of the sofa's carved armrest which jabbed into her thigh.

"I do love your Roman nose and the freckle right at the tip." He thoughtfully nibbled at the end of her nose. She hesitated to slap him away because whatever he was doing tickled deliciously and she was distracted with his comment about the freckle. He couldn't have known about the currently non-existent freckle that Dexter had declared an impediment easily erased with his trusty laser.

The Major said sternly, "Stop feeling sorry for yourself!" He added a quick shake to ground her.

"I don't. Do stop the nibbling. I want you to tell me how you were murdered. Maybe that will bring back the name."

"Let me make myself comfortable," he said. "It's something of a story." With that he removed the velvet rope that discouraged Wharton House visitors from resting on the antique maroon velvet sofa, once Mrs. Wharton's pride along with the oriental carpet.

"When I was twelve I ran away from a great aunt who took me in after my parents died. Went to sea. Saw the world. Educated myself. Picked up trinkets here and there along the way to hedge against a poverty-stricken old age. I kept most of them in a strongbox in a vault at a San Francisco bank. `Twas the strongbox led to my downfall."

"The thief who stabbed you was after the strongbox? Why didn't you leave it in the vault?"

"I needed what it contained. My partner and I were each going to buy into a more profitable business. The thief was my partner."

"Oh, dear!"

"I met him after the war of secession, when I came west again and he was in the wagon train. We hooked together on a profitable business of shipping supplies from the east out to the Coast. This far south we sold to Wharton's Merchandising and Mercantile. When we had the big opportunity to buy into another promising business, I went to 'Frisco to get the strongbox out of the bank for my share. I never guessed my partner meant to take my orphan's mite for himself."

The Major's eyes literally flashed sparks. Janis had the impression distant thunder rumbled again from a dark cloud forming above his head.

The impending storm faded. "We were going in with Don Carlos Zuñega to do business clear to Mexico City, with partnership levels determined by initial investment. My partner deduced I could buy in to the level of the most senior partner. I came back from the Presidio of San Francisco to port of San Diego late on the nineteenth day of January 1869 with my nest egg."

"Why did you let *anyone* know you had the fortune in the strongbox with you?"

"My partner only guessed, and he had a good idea of the strongbox value. You see, when we were first on the trail, before we were partners, I'd told stories around the campfire connected with particular jewels I'd acquired, the good-sized gold nuggets and such. Every one of the gems had a story that went with it—some of them funny, others to curl your hair. He didn't know the half of it, but it was enough to trigger his greed and doom me. I never did know how he managed to arrange an unscheduled bank holiday so I couldn't put the box straight into the bank in Old Town. I found I'd have to wait from Friday until the following Monday to do business with the bank."

"And your partner killed you for the strongbox? You're right. It's worse than if it were some unknown cutthroat!"

Major Blair put his arms behind his head and crossed his boots over the sofa arm. "He and I were due at the Estudillos for dinner and the nuts and bolts business dealing with Don Carlos and Estudillo. My partner figured if the box was stolen by persons unknown, I would be unable to buy in, and he saw himself becoming the richest man on the Coast. Getting hold of what was in that strongbox and cutting me out added up to more temptation than he could resist."

"There was *that* much in the box?"

"Oh, yes. He thought I'd taken the box back to my hotel room, but I had made a little side trip before going to the room. I climbed Mission Hill and buried the strongbox under a young pine tree."

"How did he finally find it? By following you?"

"He never got his hands on it. Coming down the hill, I ran into a little Mexican lad nipped in his bare heel by a rattler that had crawled out from its winter nest when the boy went out to the family privy. I sucked out the poison and carried him to his family *casa.* His folks were grateful and pressed *pulque* on me in a way that was hard to resist without being rude. Besides, the *pulque* killed the taste of the snake venom. I could have done with a little less gratitude because by the time I stumbled back to the hotel I was three sheets to the wind, but had to get out of my dirt and change before reporting for dinner at the Estudillo's house. The *pulque* on an empty belly had hit me hard. I stepped out of my clothes and succumbed to the need for a nap.

"My killer thought the strongbox was in my room and I was on my way to Estudillo's. He climbed in through the window and began ransacking the place. I woke up. The first knife wound was enough to bleed me out. Second and succeeding thrusts were merely insurance. While I lay there with my life draining into the mattress, the assassin tore the room apart."

"And I thought Dex was a snake in the grass! If you can remember all these details, Major, why can't you remember your partner's name?"

The question twisted his eyebrows. He finally said, "I have *no* idea! I simply draw a blank when I think about it."

"Who knows—I could be a descendant of the man. My father's family was here about that time."

"Maybe your family could have been, but since I know

I'm here because *you* are definitely the target of a man who's already tried once to kill you, it couldn't be your family, or my vendetta would go into operation on any well and truly cursed descendant."

He sat up. "To finish my story, I remember my attacker adding insult to assassination when he cleaned himself up at my washstand with the water the maid had brought upstairs for me. Then he left the same way he came, through the window and over the roof. Not before I cursed him and his progeny to the end. He made a big thing out of coming in the morning to find why I had not shown at dinner the night before. He and the room clerk found me cold as the Sierras. You should have seen the crocodile tears and dramatic promise of a huge reward for the arrest and conviction of my killer. They never found him, of course."

Janis gazed at him in open horror. "That's the saddest story I ever heard."

He stood. "Not sad. Infuriating. But the aromas from the restaurants are making me as hungry as a catamount. I detect dozens of savory edibles cooking nearby. I can think of nothing more at this moment than breaking my long fast properly. What I found in yonder kitchen wasn't near enough."

Lowering though it was to be dismissed in favor of more prioritized pursuits than her potential murder, Janis acknowledged her peculiar ghost had a right to break his hundred-and-thirty-year fast. Her good sense told her to caution him. "You can't just walk off to a restaurant. Ghosts can't wander the streets. They're bound to the place where they die."

"If that were true, I could not be here in Wharton House. You were the one who mentioned my murder took place over a mile away. Besides, you told me about brick from the Underwood on the parlor table. By those rules I just stick a crumb of brick in my pocket and go wherever I please. I presently am pleased to follow my nose to the Chinese restaurant you said is nearby."

Janis protested. "I'm not exactly telling you, `you can't,' but—you'll frighten people, and you haven't any money."

"Why would I frighten anyone? Do I frighten you?"

He had a point except that he tended to swell and create thunderstorms over his head when upset. "I shudder to think what patrons in a crowded restaurant would do if you behave like the Cheshire Cat in *Alice in Wonderland.*"

"Whatever zoological creature that is. Very well, you can be assured I will be completely discreet. No lightning flashing. No swelling myself out of proportion to those who surround me. I just want a decent dinner. Will you join me?"

"My staff and Dr. Wythy will be returning any minute from the Mexican restaurant across the street. They're bringing back my dinner."

"I've already discovered I can telescope time when I'm by myself. I should think we could both fly to the Chinese place, eat, and be back in a trice."

Janis experienced real alarm. "I don't climb *ladders,* let alone fly. All my life I've been terrified of any heights at all. I don't fly in *planes,* much less without one. I think it's because my mother was killed in a commercial plane crash. In any case, I certainly wouldn't fly with you. You can't even go through a wall properly."

"I managed to find my uniform and get back without a bit of trouble, didn't I? Come on," he coaxed.

"No flying for me. No compressing hours into trices. It could disrupt metabolism!"

"You don't take risks, do you?"

"Not with ghosts or hallucinations—or flying. And—I have all of today's bookkeeping work to do, with time not telescoping for me that I know of, though it's a trick that has its temptations."

"Your problem really is you don't want to take chances with men any more, either. Good, that will keep you out of trouble to an extent. And you will be safe for the rest of this night and I can whisk about exploring."

"How do you *know* I'm safe?"

He frowned for a moment. "Although I have no clear picture in my mind, I am quite sure. Almost sure. At least if I am wrong, I promise to show up in time to avert any serious problem."

He rose and straightened his coat. "Each to his own pursuits. You put your nose to your business grindstone. I bid you good evening and mean to have a fine time for the first time since I left life so abruptly. The aroma from the Chinese kitchen reminds me I last ate a really first-rate Chinese feast when I was twenty-two and in China's Celestial City."

"*If* you can leave these premises, you'll need money."

"I shall dig up my strongbox and use the gold."

"You can't use gold for cash in this day and age. The economy is based on gold, but not as legal tender. If you tried to pass it, the restaurant would probably call the police. I can't answer for what else might happen. Wait—" She rummaged in the inner pocket of her briefcase and handed him her mad money, a one hundred dollar bill folded into a tiny square.

"I intend to repay you. Tomorrow night, I'll give you gold or jewels, or whatever, and you can exchange it."

Sure he will. Not. If he was what he said he was, she could chalk it up to bodyguard expenses. If he wasn't, she would have learned another lesson about *trust* being a synonym for *stupid.*

"I'd go tonight for it," he explained, "but right now I truly cannot think past my stomach thinking my throat has been cut. Which it was, literally. There must be at least a couple of hundred dollars' worth of gold in the chest. One of those nuggets is the size of your fist."

She stared. "If so, the gold is worth a *lot* more than a couple of hundred!"

"Well, then. Your loan is safe enough. Now to see if you are correct in that I must remain locked to these premises, or if my premise stands and I can go anywhere." He strode through the dining room arch and down the hall towards the front door.

Janis hastily followed, warning, "Don't try to walk through our antique glass door!"

She unlocked it, and they stepped out on the porch.

"So far, so good," the major said cheerfully. He stared into the street. "Good glory! If this don't beat the Dutch!"

She supposed he meant the traffic. “They’ve replaced horses and wagons. We call them `cars.’ Or `automobiles.’ Or—”

With an airy gesture, he dismissed the cars going by on San Diego Avenue. “I’ve seen automobiles previously, though primitive compared to these. Those produced in 1925, if I recall. Certainly not in such numbers! My amazement is at the way everyone goes about virtually naked in the public streets.”

“Don’t judge *anyone* by what they wear. You’re hardly one to talk, the way you’re dressed to match the era of 1865 or thereabouts.”

The Major grinned. “I’m off to enjoy what I see. As for being shocked, the last time I remember that sensation I was no more than fourteen. An *houri* palace in the port of Ifni in Morocco. This street in front of your establishment was merely a bit of surprise.” He patted the pocket containing the brick crumb and marched down the porch to the sidewalk. Nothing untoward happened. He looked back with another grin. “So far, excellent.”

A girl in red leather micro-mini came around the corner on Harney, accompanied by two young men in torn jeans and leather jackets. As they passed by Wharton House, one of the young men pointed at the major. “Is the South going to rise again, man? Or are they shooting a movie in Old Town tonight?”

The other young man whispered something to the girl, and all three looked back laughing.

The major scowled. An ominous thunder clap sounded in the distance, and hot on its rumble came a dancing flicker of lightning.

Janis ran down the steps and grabbed the major’s arm. “Whatever you’re thinking of doing, Major, don’t. Consider *tempora et mores,* please!”

“The times and the customs be damned, you’ll excuse my language, Ma’am. I’ll allow no one to insult this uniform. Too many brave men died wearing it.”

“They aren’t insulting the uniform. *Every* American agrees

they were brave soldiers who fought nobly for a lost cause. Those kids just think you're going to a costume party or you're an actor."

"I may have been hasty," the Major acknowledged.

He marched her back into Wharton House. "I saw a closet in Underwood, when I was prowling about looking for my own things. It had various bits of clothing. Some of it looked about like what I just saw passing by."

"Underwood workmen's, I expect."

"If you have no objections, I will gather what I need and see you again after I replace my currently inappropriate attire."

"Don't forget to take the uniform back to the museum!" she called into a void as he vanished.

He was back almost before she had time to blink. This time he wore a gleaming white tee-shirt that smelled of being freshly washed and ironed, and over his boots a pair of denim pants. They fitted his lean, muscular thighs like second skin and left little more to the imagination than when he had worn nothing. "Will I do?"

"Oh, you'll do!" she said. He looked every bit as dashing in the bits and pieces as he had in the Confederate uniform—rather more so because the Confederate uniform made him look more like a ghost, and what he had found made him look wickedly irresistible.

"I thought I ought to look like any of those passersby, but I prefer to be cleaner than the three who annoyed me."

"Did you return the—?"

"Right and tight, to the park museum." He hitched up the jeans as though accustoming himself to them. "Since I have no idea whether I'll have another free night to roam, I'll be off to enjoy a bit of exploring. Too bad you won't trust yourself to fly with me, but you tend to be restrictive and would undoubtedly hamper my intention to encounter adventure if the opportunity presents itself."

"If I'm murdered while you're taking advantage of opportunity, I guarantee to haunt you."

Unrepentant, the Major dropped a kiss on her nose. "You will be safe until tomorrow night, *Bellissima.* We have an appointment when the sun sets." He sauntered to the front door, opened it—and bumped right into Mr. Millard Thorpe and his dinner partners.

FOUR

The major stepped back, politely saluted the incoming three, and held the door for them. He sauntered onto the porch and down to the sidewalk, as if he were the leftover from the project crew his clothes indicated. Nancy Rogers and Mr. Thorpe lifted eyebrows. Dr. Wythy frowned after him. Mr. Thorpe handed Janis her enormous food order. "Never a good idea to let the workmen through the building after hours," he cautioned.

Janis mumbled, "You're probably right." She determinedly led the conversation in other directions, fending off any pointed questions she could see festering in Dr. Maggie that would require her to dissemble.

***

On the ride up the hill to *Rincon* in the luxury end of Mission Hills, Dr. Maggie spoke philosophically of the destruction of her seance and astral photography shoot. "Things happen when ghosts do not wish to be called up." She looked hopefully at Janis, who concentrated on driving the rental car. "How perfectly lovely of you to invite me to be your guest, Janis. You've made it so convenient for me to handle the Wharton project the same week I was asked to address the California Parapsychology Foundation convention here at the Convention Center."

Janis hoped Dr. Maggie would not press her further about the seance and also hoped when she was Dr. Maggie's age she might still be going at such a rate. She activated the electric gate opener and pulled into *Rincon's* circular drive. "My pleasure. Mrs. Cadigan and I rattle around in this old mausoleum. She's delighted at the prospect of someone to fuss over."

"When I contacted the Heritage Homes Association I had no idea you were not only an alumna of Claremont, but had been one of my students. I confess I wouldn't have recognized you, but I remembered you well. Always wished you were more interested in exploring the paranormal. I thought you had a certain... well...that you could be an adept. But you were targeted to your own choice of studies, and that's always encouraging to see."

Janis mumbled politely.

Adept? Is that the reason my ghostly visitor has so particularly targeted me? Naah. She refused to think about her weird evening or mention anything about it to Dr. Maggie.

"You were such a shy girl when you were undergraduate Janis Logan. I can still see you as a freshman in Psychology 101, in the front row, third seat on the window side, looking serious and making straight A's on the tests. I'm not surprised one so young has achieved the directorship of an agency."

"I doubt I'm the youngest agency director in San Diego...."

"And I was delighted to find you receptive to my request for access to Wharton for my parapsychology projects."

Janis, considering what she had just been through, wondered if at some later date she might have to apologize to the emeritus professor for her one-time skepticism. Meanwhile, she showed Dr. Maggie into the primary guest suite at *Rincon*. "Would you like to see the library tonight? I told you in my letter my father could have old reports of interest to you. I recall papers having to do with origins of our local ghosts. Wharton House, of course. And documents on your other target sites."

Dr. Maggie's green eyes sparkled over rainbow-striped half-eyeglass frames. "Do you suppose I could take just a peek at the library tonight?"

Janis led the way, her mind still tied to the confrontation with the Major. Now that she was safely home, she could tell herself the incident had definitely been the result of getting her brains scrambled when the car plowed into that liquid amber in Heritage Park, and also convince herself a call to the doctor would wait until morning.

Dr. Maggie and she were on the landing when the front door quietly opened. A man wearing black, from knitted cap and sweater to boots, slipped in and closed the door behind him, so carefully maintaining silence that Dr. Maggie and Janis both froze. Only when the man turned from the door did Janis breathe. "Keith! You gave us such a start!"

Keith Logan took an abrupt step back against the door and stared up at them on the landing. Janis's heart, which had begun to thump at the thought of interrupting a burglar, recommenced its regular rhythm.

All the Logan family's looks were his—the naturally up-cut nose, the cleft chin, curling coal black hair, the charm of a dark angel all in black, even to his running shoes. However dashing, it wasn't the smartest outfit to be running about in at night, Janis considered. He could be run down while crossing a street, invisible to headlights.

"You scared us to death!" she scolded. "Next time, call out, `Jan, I'm here!' We thought you were a burglar jimmying the front door and about to murder us, ransack the place and carry off the television remote." She was a little shaken from the fright and a little annoyed at the Major for putting her in the notion to jump at shadows.

Keith flicked the nearest light switch. The Waterford chandelier blazed. Prismed light flooded the hall and staircase. He flashed the grin that always melted Janis and her housekeeper. "I haven't seen you since—we talked about putting the house on the market. What *have* you been up to?"

"I've called and left messages."

"Sorry I didn't get back, but I bring good news along with intent to take a half-dozen bottles of wine from the cellar. Give me time to get them, and I'll fill you in. Didn't want to wake the ogre—Mrs. Cadigan complains every time she sees me—and I thought you'd still be at work."

Janis ran down the remaining stairs. "She isn't complaining. It's just her natural curdled disposition. You're welcome to all the wine you want. I won't have room for a wine cellar in my new pad." She hugged him.

He frowned. "Can't think why you haven't pensioned Cadigan off or pushed her down the back stairs."

"Dr. Maggie will get the wrong impression of both of you," Janis protested, laughing.

"She allows you to occupy space here as long as you don't disrupt her blue laws," he grumbled.

Janis linked arms with him. "This is Dr. Maggie Wythy. She's staying with me a week or so, doing paranormal research."

He reached around Janis and offered Dr. Maggie his hand and a warm smile. "I'd think you'd find more excitement at Winchester House in San José. Lots of rooms, and a different ghost in every one."

"I've already covered Winchester. Now I'm working on San Diego's ghost colony. I'm fairly sure—" and Dr. Maggie shot a look at Janis, "—that I've already discovered a new and hitherto unknown spirit inhabiting the Wharton complex."

Janis gritted her teeth. She might eventually have to buy into Dr. Maggie's obsession, but not without a struggle.

Keith asked, "Just how long a project do you plan, Doctor?"

"Claremont will think I shriveled up and died if I stay away too long. They'll shovel out my traps and calamities and give my office to another emeritus. I must return the first of next week."

Keith smiled at Dr. Maggie and turned to Janis. "I need the wine because I'm poker host to a bunch of bachelors. Thought you'd still be out, so I scribbled a message about taking the wine." He held out a folded sheet of paper. "I knew you wouldn't mind."

Janis stepped back and looked him in the eye. "You aren't...gambling again, are you?"

His black eyes were steady. "This is just fun and buddies."

She continued to look searchingly at him. He had always looked innocent while avoiding answers. "Is everything all right? *Really* all right, I mean?" She swallowed down embarrassment at having thought he was a burglar bent on murder. That doom-prophesying ghost had thoroughly sandpapered all her senses. The ghost said Keith wasn't being targeted. If she told Keith her story, Keith would call men in white coats for her. Or laugh her to death. In any case, she did not want to alert Dr. Maggie to her confrontation with "The Major"—if indeed she really had confronted anything other than an incipient concussion symptom.

Keith returned his attention to Dr. Maggie. "You'd best use the library while you can. Jan's going to hand it over to the Historical Association. They'll dither around for a decade before they decide how to handle it, and no one else will get at it until after their act's together."

Janis squeezed his arm in a warning not to speak rudely of the Association. "The Historical Association is the safest place there is for the collection. And we'll have a very large donors' tax exemption, which ought to please you."

"I'd have sold everything in this house, and the house, at auction the minute Ocho left for the ultimately hot climate."

"We might have made more money selling everything piece by piece, but Dad and I both agreed his collection should remain a unit. That's why I chose to do the Underwood Project the way I did."

"So, how much of Ocho's money has already been poured into the shrine to the old robber baron?"

Maggie looked uncomfortable with the mild brangle. Janis was used to it, though she wished Keith would be silent in front of Maggie about his annoyances with their father. "Only the amount he designated in his will. Anything more comes from my share. After the building is operating, the Association will maintain it. I'm sure Maggie isn't interested in all these technical details. I'll show you the Underwood budget another evening."

"Don't defend Ocho, Jan. You were never his fair-haired girl any more than I was favored son. I don't care beans about pleasing him and can think of a million better uses you could make of your share of the estate. I could also put you into investments sure to double and triple it in less time than you think possible."

She smiled. "Thanks but no thanks. My money's earning

more safe income where it is than I could ever need if there were three of me. You ought to know, Keith. Your income is from the same source."

His lip curled. "But you have control over your capital. Mine's doled out with bonuses only if I'm a good boy." He patted her hand and threw a twisted grin at Dr. Maggie. "You might as well know—everyone else does— our daddy considered me once a wastrel, always a wastrel. He has a watchdog doling out my share until I'm sixty-five. Twenty-five years to go, on a leash. So, let me go get the bottles and then we'll celebrate the good news that lifts his heel off my neck. A little."

"We'll be in the library," Janis said. She led Dr. Maggie into the enormous library that had been Ocho Logan's pride.

While she kindled a fire in the stone fireplace, she directed Dr. Maggie's attention to the layout. "The literary classics on the north wall and best selling novels in the double-sided, free-standing case are mine. I'm a fiction addict. To make space for new ones, I weed them out regularly for elderly Edgemoore Farm patients. The rest is early Southern California, already well catalogued."

The question of whether there might be uncatalogued references within Ocho's collection about one Major Benjamin Blair was foremost on her mind. She had never noticed the name, but it would now leap out at her from even the smallest news bit of its day. His murder would have been a headline in the newspapers back then. She cast a thoughtful eye at Ocho's prized collection of early San Diego documents. "Make yourself at home until I come back with cheese and crackers."

When she returned, Dr. Maggie was flitting from one section of the library to another making ecstatic little noises.

Janis arranged three raspberry, cut-crystal wine glasses on the sterling tray containing a round of Edam and water biscuits. "My job makes huge demands on me, but before the collection leaves my hands, I want to go through everything once more. While you're here will be a good time for me to do that plus look for any specific material you might particularly want to see." She could ask Maggie to keep an eye out for the name *Blair.*

"You are incredibly generous, my dear. No wonder I always had a soft spot for you in spite of your dim view of astral life."

Keith sauntered in with bottles dangling from between the fingers of both hands and clasped with one arm to his black-sweatered chest. He eyed Janis at the open file of early newspapers. "As a functional illiterate, I ask you, why would anyone other than an economist care about reading the price of eggs in 1840?"

Janis clucked in disapproval. "Just because your interest lies elsewhere than historical trivia and antiques doesn't mean others can't be fascinated. You love giving people the wrong idea of you. So behave, Keith, and do tell us your news."

"Compared to *your* many public accomplishments my news is trivial. But hard work's paying off. I've not only earned the trust fund bonus, but was just promoted to project supervisor which doubles the bonus. How's that for reason to celebrate?"

Janis gave a joyful shriek. Dr. Maggie asked, "What does a project supervisor do?"

"The on-site foreman's in charge of each job, but the project super roams around checking to see crews aren't using sub-standard building materials or paint. An undercover aspect is looking for guys keeping one eye on the foreman and one on the work. It usually means the foreman's a loose cannon. They'd like to report higher up but don't dare. I'm supposed to get those complaints out in the open, and if necessary get rid of bad foremen."

Janis said, "I never heard Ocho describe project foremen that way."

"Because Ocho never delegated authority he could hold onto. He had his own system of getting rid of people."

"His men were always loyal to him."

"Yeah." Keith's tone was bitter. "With one or two notable exceptions."

He was referring first to the super who had run off with his own mother. Janis quickly shifted the subject from Ocho.

"It sounds as though you're just a couple of steps away from becoming big boss by working from the ground up." She beamed at him. Ocho had been unfair to Keith, even when just before his death he relented and changed the will that had cut him out ten years earlier. His lack of confidence in Keith was no different from selling the company and related business to the employees because he hadn't believed his daughter could continue the company successfully.

Keith scowled. "Save the kudos, kid. I'm still small potatoes, even if I just scooped up three years' income instead of one."

He uncorked one bottle and poured a glass for Dr. Maggie. "When I said I was illiterate, Dr. Wythy, it wasn't that big a joke, y' know. I was thrown out of all the best schools in five states as incorrigible."

"That's why you were promoted on this new job, of course. And do call me Maggie. You, too, Jan. Everyone does."

"I actually did flunk out of every school that didn't toss me out on my ear. Would you believe we're celebrating the first job I ever kept for more than a year?"

Again, Janis shifted uncomfortably. "Now, Keith—"

"Come on, Jan! You were always the one with the brains, talents and discipline. I was always Ocho's rotten kid."

"Mother Ann said you'd be a late bloomer." Janis turned to Maggie. "Mother Ann was Ocho's fourth wife. She practically brought us both up."

"Until Ocho dumped her. Speaking of ex-spouses," Keith said, "Dexter's been in town all week."

His words brought Janis up short. "All week?"

"Since last Thursday."

She shivered.

"He's part of the poker party tomorrow night."

Keith had continued to buddy with Dexter, which wasn't surprising since they'd been friends from childhood. Men and women didn't see friendships and loyalties in the same way. Janis couldn't fairly expect Keith to treat Dexter like an outcast, even though she wished Keith had a little more sensitivity.

She glanced over at Maggie, poring over the closest items

in the Logan historical collection. "Dexter's skills as a surgeon are almost equalled by his acumen as a real estate agent. Does he have anything to do with the call about your having had a nibble on this house?"

Keith frowned. "Well..."

"That answers my question. Dexter glories in getting a bargain that's more like a steal. Put that with what friends of mine in whose knowledge of real estate I have complete trust say—including your boss, Keith—it's *not* a good idea to sell *Rincon* now. The market's depressed and will be until late spring. I'm holding out."

Keith set the antique wine glass down too hard, and for a moment he and she both mopped at the splash of wine on his black jeans. "You were the one who wanted to sell," he said. "You complained about rattling around, and the place being draughty. You wanted a view of the skyline and the Bay and living accommodations that don't take two full-time gardeners. What changed your mind?"

"I haven't changed my mind, but I'm not going to give valuable property away. That's what Dexter would want me to do."

"If you hate losing money on the house sale, what makes you give Dad's library to the Historical Association? You could have sold it for a whopping piece of change."

"Only in pieces. That's the way for everything to really get lost."

"Dexter mentioned a fair price to me for *Rincon.*"

"Dexter would *never* mention a fair price. If we wait until spring, your half of the sale proceeds will be half again as much as if we sell now to the best offer."

"It's not as though you need the money, so what does taking a few thousand less than top dollar mean? You should get the place off your back. A-agh, it's your funeral."

She laughed at him, but his words brought to mind someone walking over her grave. "Lordy, Keith! I'm not anxious to stay here, but there aren't many homes south of Beverly Hills, except in Rancho Santa Fe or La Jolla that can touch it. A reasonable sale would realize more like another *million,* not change. I promised to share the profits, so you should be just as interested as I am in getting every cent...unless you need money right away? If you do, I could advance—"

"No! Do whatever you have a mind to do with the old dump. You don't even need to go halves. Things are looking up at SunSol and with the Trust, too. Don't worry about me."

"You're sure?"

"I'm sure. I'll tell Dex he'll have to come up with a good offer, or you'll spit in his eye. It's just that I know you've felt tied down by this place, and I'd like to see you out of it and into a pad that's not such a white elephant. A place with good security. This place is wide open. I don't want you to find it out the hard way. Look how I walked right in on you tonight."

"You have the right to walk in, and you have a key. Don't make a deal out of it."

He appealed to Maggie. "Talk some sense into Jan. I think she should unload this white elephant to the first bidder."

"Tell Dexter if he wants to pay the appraised value, I'll think about it instead of waiting for someone who appreciates the value of turn-of-the-century architect Irving Gill's first masterpiece. That's worth more to many buyers than the appraised value."

The ten-foot-high Tiffany clock by the library door sounded its rich four-note melody. Keith stood. "Time for me to be going, ladies. I may have become an upper echelon employee, but SunSol expects me to be on the job at 6 am tomorrow, nose bent to grindstone. Unlike you, Jan, with old Cadigan in your kitchen, I still have to pick up my poker party fixings at an all-night Deli and play cook as well as host."

"I'll just see Keith to the door, Maggie," Janis said.

On the portico, she hugged him goodbye. "I know you're not a wild boy any more. You're standing on your own two feet, and doing well. But I can't help remembering when Ocho bailed you out of that awful scrape in Reno. Is there any chance someone in—that kind of crowd—might, you know, have some kind of grudge against either of us?"

His laugh was boisterous, but stopped abruptly. "What's given you such a wacky idea?"

"Nothing. Just be careful, won't you?" She thought she had felt him flinch when she spoke about Reno. "Put it down to my being silly, but be extra careful." Even the rudiments of her confrontation with the Major were too much to tell Keith without making her seem truly off the wall.

He backed from her embrace. "I'm always careful. Watch out, Beaky. You'll have me breaking six expensive bottles of wine before you know it."

"—Sorry." Watching him disappear down the drive and get into his sports car, she wished she'd had enough guts to tell him about the Major. She wished he hadn't flinched when she referred to Reno, where men in black shirts and pink ties had threatened in the none-too-distant past to break his knee caps if he didn't pay his gambling debts. That was the time Ocho had almost permanently disinherited Keith after bailing him out. Keith, after the fright of his life, had been on the straight and narrow ever since.... Hadn't he?

The image of enforcers with uzis, or whatever, possibly coming after Keith—and herself—was scary. The thought of the Major was suddenly very comforting. He wouldn't let anything happen to either Keith *or* her.

She took a deep breath and went inside to Maggie in the library. "Would you guess Keith's twelve years older than I am, Maggie? To me he's always seemed rather like Peter Pan."

Maggie looked at her a long moment over her granny spectacles and the book she was examining. "He has a certain...ingenuous air."

"Forever young, you mean? He's had an awful time of it, Maggie. When his mother left him and never looked back it really affected him. He's just now growing up."

"I gather you lost your mother when you were a toddler, but you don't seem to have been affected in the same way."

Janis bristled. "I wouldn't bet on it having hit me hard in other ways. I've grown up. Ocho was a lot harder on Keith than he was on me."

Maggie looked skeptical and Janis added, "—Riding him all the time, I mean. Ocho was determined to break him. He disowned Keith for almost ten years."

Maggie's sharp eyes regarded her steadily.

"Keith was given to wild pranks in those days," Janis admitted.

"Let's see if I understand. Your father died less than two years ago, so Keith would have been close to thirty when he was disowned? Are you sure it was a case of 'prankish'?"

"Ocho had this *thing* about Keith, probably because of the way he felt about Keith's mother. Ocho became paranoid about—well, about whether Keith was really his son. Every picture of Ocho is as good as a DNA test. Keith looks more like Ocho every day. Ocho was wrong. Keith turned out great. You didn't pay any attention to Keith when he joked about being illiterate, did you? It's true he didn't want to go to college. Ocho forced him, so of course Keith didn't do well. Finally Dad took him into the business. Keith wasn't suited, and—" she stopped. "I'm sad Ocho didn't live long enough to see the change in Keith. He would have been proud."

"Maybe your brother is one of those sons who do better away from the family business," Maggie suggested.

Janis agreed. "The new head man at SunSol always liked Keith and gave him the job last year. So now he's had his first big promotion. He'll end as President and owner, just like Ocho once was, believe me."

Janis picked up a silver-framed picture on the desk of Keith as a child in the pewter-blue military uniform of one of the schools where he had temporarily been boarded. "Keith's climbed out of his penchant for trouble. I grew up after the mess with my ex-husband. For a hundred and fifty years the Logans have *been* San Diego. `Logan's Empire'—that's what the media used to call the area from Mission Hills through Old Town. The Logan and Douglass combination—Malcolm Logan was my maternal great-great grandfather's partner—were the first go-getter Yankees here. Earlier than Horton, and contemporaries of Wharton. They passed their savvy down. Real estate. Construction. Building a beautiful community. Neither Keith nor I has to lift a finger the rest of our lives. We're both Logans who work because we love what we do. See how it's paying off for Keith who was hired on as a laborer?

Promotion to project super after one year, and *no* Daddy in the wings orchestrating it!"

For all her confidence and pleasure in his promotion, she wondered if Keith was into gambling again, and that was the reason he was pushing the sale of the house. Surely he surely would have told her on being questioned bluntly. He had sworn syndicate-types had nothing to do with anything. She believed him.

At the same time her prickling neck told her she had reason to be concerned. If only the Major could remember more of his pertinent past!

FIVE

On the table in the staff kitchen, Janis put a carton of three dozen doughnuts as an offering to the double crew starting work that afternoon. The crew and the staff had come to expect the greasy treats, and luckily she had brought them in because the big glass doughnut locker was empty. Having replenished the goodies only the day before, she marveled at the appetites of the work crew.

In bold black, she marked a paper sack with "BENJAMIN" for the Major and put in a bottle of California premium wine pulled from *Rincon's* wine cellar. At the back of the refrigerator, she stored it, the labeled sack prominently facing front. She felt a little foolish. She probably was in need of a shrink herself, for bringing a friendly gift to a ghost. No doubt she'd have to lug it home again unclaimed.

Since the thirty-cup coffee pot was dry as a San Diego stream bed during the summer, she started that on its way to filtering.

In Wharton House she found the takeout Mexican food cartons from the Jalisco stacked neatly at one end of the dining room table, eaten to the last bit of salsa. Both giant-size soft drink containers were empty. The night before, she had been much too disconcerted and confused by the evening's confrontation to eat before leaving, and had totally forgotten what the others had brought back at her request. Obviously *someone* had enjoyed it.

No one would have been inside Wharton since she had locked up...unless...

She muttered, "In the unlikely event the so-called ghost ate all those mysteriously missing doughnuts, emptied the coffee pot in our staff kitchen, and ate at the Chinese Gardens too, he's twins!"

Considering how well she felt physically this morning, she shouldn't have been hallucinating the night before. She told herself her confrontation had been with one of the construction workers with a Puckish sense of humor and an advanced skill at conning gullible women like herself. She refused to consider all the non sequiturs involved with her theory. Instead, she stowed the evidence of someone's powerful appetite in the Dempsey Dumpster and said a silent goodbye to the hundred dollar bill she had impulsively loaned "The Major." *"A fool and her money...!"* she muttered.

Sunlight spotlighted the strides the Underwood crew had made in the external facility painting project. They arrived at seven, but she usually came in before they did. The docents arrived at nine-thirty to prepare to open the doors of Wharton and Badger to visitors. Badger, the smaller house in the rear, now faced Underwood. Badger was named for the parents of a captain in the battalion at Fort Rosecrans who had come out to California in the eighteen-seventies and built the charming old cottage elsewhere. With all its original furnishings, right up to Mrs. Badger's crocheted antimacassars, and excepting a few utilitarian modern kitchen appliances, the house had been moved to their Wharton Property when the freeway went through the original Badger property. Between the two buildings was now the wheel garden and the pattern of brick walks lined by low ornamental hedging. Janis did much of her office work in Badger's kitchen, next to the coffee pot.

She had been working less than an hour when Marvin from the Auto Center barged in. "You'll wanna know what I found under the hood of your car!"

"Un-reconnected wires?" she asked without masking her irritation with the careless manner the Auto Center had conducted her first ten-thousand mile checkup. "The reason had better be good!"

"As to that, I can't answer, but you better find out. I only know for sure my men weren't responsible. The electric was cut or re-wired and deliberately made to malfunction. Better bring the police back in on this."

She just stared at him and tried to make sense of the words.

"Someone *wanted* you to have the accident. The car was rigged to malfunction the first time you stepped hard on the brake. The system went when you put the brake on at the top of Juan Street Hill. You always go to work that way, don't you?"

"Any other route would take at least a half-hour longer." She considered his message. "I won't believe it. Marvin, I didn't touch my car from the time your man left it in my secured driveway until I drove it to work. I personally closed *Rincon's* estate gates and locked them as soon as your man left. Actually, he must have seen me do it before he drove off in the company truck with the other driver."

"He says you didn't put the car in the garage."

"My garage is temporarily full of old furniture stored for the Heritage Homes Association. But the car was as secure as if it were in the garage!"

Marvin wasn't satisfied. "Someone may have known exactly where you would most certainly trigger the rigged mechanism. Loss of control on that street ought to have been a death trap."

Janis remembered exactly how she'd felt when she realized nothing was working.

She had pumped the brakes. Buildings flew by. She switched off the ignition, and the car accelerated anyway. Ahead of her she could see traffic streaming by on Taylor, perpendicular to Juan. Across Taylor, at the end of Juan, squatted a concrete warehouse. If she survived that distance, the stop was bound to be sudden and make a lot of noise. She frantically attempted to steer, which was all she could do until halfway down the hill, the park area began where housing ended.

She managed to jump her speeding car over the curb, between knots of children ambling down the sidewalk on their way to school. The car plowed over the Heritage Village park lawn, showing no inclination to stop. She circled the Lexus up, around, and down, avoiding the cluster of relocated

Victorian homes that housed arts and crafts shops. She spotted the liquidamber tree, big enough to stop the car, young enough to be springy and give hope of a less drastic stop than the concrete warehouse across Taylor Street.

The impact slammed her hard against her seat belts. Breathless, she stared blearily at shopkeepers streaming toward her out of the storybook village of renewed buildings. Technically she was their landlady, but their surprise to see her drop in was nothing to her own surprise at being alive.

Even though the Lexus' vaunted air-bag did not inflate, she had been only a very shaken-up landlady. Afterwards, she accused Marvin of conducting criminally inadequate quality control and shook him up.

Here he stood in her jerry-rigged office telling her it had nothing to do with his mechanics' quality control. "The tampering was done some time *after* they returned the car, Ms. Carter. One of my men drove the car to your house specifically as a test run. If the trouble originated with us, he would have been the one to trigger it."

The Major had said something about her potential assassin having planned a disaster on Monday night that hadn't worked out. Meaning the car was rigged?

Marvin was still talking. "...Maybe some car-jacking punks got annoyed because they couldn't steal it because of the locked gate, Ms. Carter. Tell the police. I'll show them the evidence. They even disconnected the air-bag. Couldn't have been an accident. Your guardian angel must have been on duty for you to get out alive!"

What Marvin didn't know was her guardian angel didn't exist at eight-thirty on Monday morning with the sun shining bright.

She thought about it all day while running herself ragged arranging for the old hotel furniture to be transferred from her garage to provide security for her car when returned. She supervised the final setup of her temporary, if show-case, working quarters which were disguised as a mid-nineteenth century hotel office. At the same time she directed where the Spanish, Mexican and California Bear flags were to be displayed, while counting display cases for the museum section of Underwood.

She wondered if the Major would find Underwood House a comfortable place to haunt.... The idea she was worried about being a good hostess to a ghost amused her after a fashion, when it didn't remind her she had to be mentally unstable if she were worrying about making Underwood attractive to a ghost.

The idea reminded her to find a bed for Room 201 large enough for a tall man's comfort, instead of the skimpy iron cot that had come from old Boulevard Inn, recently razed. His room—*the* room—also ought to have a desk and bookcase.

She made a note to add items to the list being circulated through the Antique Dealers Association. If she was able to complete only one typical hotel room on the second floor this year, it was to be 201. *Was she actually planning how to lure her ghost into staying?*

Yes.

When the SunSol Construction crew chief checked in with her, he said the antique light fixtures were scheduled for installation later that day. "As soon as the electric's ready, you can work there if you've a mind. Take a look at the staircase, Miz Carter. You were right. It's gonna be great."

"Will the Otis be ready to use when the draymen come?"

"We'll have it operating temporarily for them, but off afterwards until sometime next week. There's more finishing to do in the shaft. With luck, by Christmas you can celebrate your grand opening with everything in A-Number One shape. Except the third floor."

"I seriously doubt we'll be doing anything to that for a year or two. It's final use hasn't been decided...and the Association needs to raise the money first."

She had promised herself to go easy on pouring Logan money into the project other than that earmarked in Ocho's will. For its own health, the Association should not depend on one donor family's largesse, but on many avenues of funding. The original blueprints showed hotel rooms on the third as well as the second floor, but until the Board made its decision between more museum space or Association offices, the third floor was to remain a shell.

"When you're ready to decide, Miz Carter, SunSol will give you a competitive bid plus a generous non-profit agency discount to keep Association costs low."

When she stopped in Badger House kitchen for a cup of mid-afternoon coffee, Millard Thorpe rose from the work table at the back of the room, looking more than ever misplaced in time. In his Civil War Yankee officer's uniform, he—not the Major—seemed unreal.

"I didn't think we'd see you again until Thursday, Mr. Thorpe."

"I—ah—thought I might be useful here, packing these old files in readiness to store on Underwood's third floor. And I—er—thought you might need someone to steer Dr. Wythy about so you wouldn't be kept from your routine."

"How thoughtful of you to give up your day to her, Mr. Thorpe."

"I—er—received a direct impression last night she needs someone to keep an eye on her. Also, the docent staff asked me to make an official complaint about workmen helping themselves to all of our coffee and doughnuts. Last night, I noticed before we locked up that they ate every last one of them—and drank an entire thirty-cup pot of coffee which we volunteers pay for."

That major and his fleshly appetites! Well, the workmen would have to bear one-time blame for the Major's gargantuan food binge. She soothed Mr. Thorpe. "I brought in enough for everyone this morning, but I'll take care the problem doesn't happen again."

Nancy Rogers' cheerful voice came over the intercom: "Ryan Aherne, ConVis, reminds you about the Chamber of Commerce dealie this afternoon. Said he'd pick you up at a quarter to five."

Nancy's voice trilled with coy notes. She had more than once commented what an attractive man Ryan was and that he and Janis would make a "cute couple."

Janis cast about for a legitimate reason to call him and

cancel, and perhaps see the Major again the moment the sun set. Duty to the Association's networking opportunities won over temptation. "Call Ryan back and say I'll be ready, but I need to leave the Chamber get-together early because of my house guest."

She was certifiably crazy to believe she might see her ghost again...but she anticipated it with every tick of the clock.

At a quarter to five, she climbed reluctantly into Ryan Aherne's red Porsche and took an obvious look at her Rolex while reminding him she had to return as soon as possible. Ryan agreed there never was time enough in a day, and on the way to the Chamber do they amiably contested which was most pressured by projects. He, of course, had a high-tech office and two full-time, well-paid, secretaries to keep on top of his paper work. Most of the Association's volunteers came from socially prominent backgrounds and had never held a salaried, white-collar job even in their youth.

Ryan also piled on so much sugar she began to feel cloyed.

"You look gorgeous as usual. Escorting you around to these functions sure gives me points. If they ever hold a national contest for the most beautiful agency executive, you'll win hands down."

Janis murmured something non-committal and wished he could give her some reason for existence other than being an ornament. She only half-listened to him cast out lures to help him "check out" one or another local watering spots. Fortunately she had job-connected commitments every night of the week for a couple of weeks ahead, and he did not pressure her further into the future.

With spaniel eyes, Ryan looked sideways at her. "I was hoping to take you for dinner tonight at The Hotel Del or at the Top of the Cove."

"Friday night we'll be going to the Civic Center. That will have to do. I'm busier than one of Santa's elves with Underwood's grand opening coming up." She thought it expedient to cool any more intimate expectations of the Friday night event. "I know you won't mind that I'm inviting my house guest and the vice-president of the Association to join us."

The annual Civic Center gala was for her a serious community service obligation as well as the Salvation Army's cultural fund raiser of the year—a first night theatrical opening benefiting the homeless shelter. She, as was Ocho before her, was one of the major sponsors. She also was having second thoughts about having invited Ryan to be her escort. He obviously took it to mean a green light for other moves.

She managed to get back to Wharton House by a little before eight. At the Chamber "do," Ryan had introduced her to three out-of-town people active in funding projects for non-profit corporations dedicated to community betterment. She had also, at Ryan's suggestion, found the new head of county libraries—a gold-mine of sources for rare local historical material. Ryan's possessive air and pride in escorting a woman declared to be San Diego's premium society beauty was far too obvious. A woman needed a lifetime of practice to handle being a so-called beauty, and she simply didn't have the time to deal with his open homage except to armor herself with the Heritage Homes Association first, last and always.

More prominently on her mind was the projected discussion with the Major on whether that Monday morning "accident" had really been an accident.

Ryan wanted to come in and play bodyguard until she left. She assured him there was absolutely no need, and managed to get rid of him.

The Wharton House staff had zipped off as soon after five as they could manage. She beelined into the dark dining room. "Are you here?" she called softly.

No answer.

"Major Blair? It's me, Janis Carter. Janis Logan Carter."

Still no answer. She went across the hall to the parlors and switched on the lights. The rooms were disappointingly empty. She sat at the Jenny Lind piano and played "The Ash Grove" three times. The peripatetic major remained absent. Embarrassment set in. There was no ghost. She truly had been the victim of temporary brain dysfunction.

More disappointed than she wanted to admit even to

herself, she retrieved her briefcase, a carton of correspondence waiting for attention, switched off the lights and struggled to balance her homework burden while unlocking the back door. Her loaner car sat behind Badger House. Before she stepped outside, she inhaled hopefully. Not the slightest hint of Nate Wharton's cigar smoke or Mrs. Wharton's bread baking came to her.

She was destined to be peculiar, like her paternal great-great-grandmother who was supposed to have chattered incessantly about ghosts and spirits influencing her life. The family had always acknowledged poor old great-great-grandmother Cirenia to be dotty but harmless.

The Wharton garden, by tradition mainly herbal, filled the night air with the scent of marigold, verbena and rare diosma. The Cleveland sage had been badly trampled yet again. Crushed leaves sent into the night the heady scent of their wounds.

Janis secured the door and wound her way through the box-hedged brick path connecting to Badger House. Though shadows puddled under the oaks, Old Town's lights illuminated the low, planted area sufficiently to see without difficulty.

Rounding the path to Badger House she heard quick footsteps behind her. Before she could react, a hard, acrid-smelling hand clapped over her mouth and pulled her backward.

A cold band of sharpened metal pricked her throat. Brute strength wrestled her off the path toward the deeper shadows of the trees. Her Gucci heels beat a fast tattoo on the bricks before the attacker dragged her into the herbal ground cover, where she dropped the file box and briefcase.

That someone should have been waiting for anyone at all to come out of the house so long after closing was odd, except that her loaner car was still on the lot. Either her attacker had been waiting for whoever owned it...or preparing to break into one of the buildings...or had seen her re-enter Wharton and knew who she was...

All possibilities jumbled through her mind in a flash. The hand over her mouth and nose stopped most of her breath.

She had to occupy herself solely with breathing. A low, mean giggle sounded in her ear. The dreadful creature whispered hoarsely, "You and me's goin' to have a party. If you're real nice maybe I won't cut you up in li'l pieces so they'll have to put you in a body bag to carry you away. Keep thinkin' about the fun we're gonna have in just a minute, soon as I..."

She didn't have a prayer of preventing whatever he had in mind. She was beginning to blank out from lack of breath. *I'm going to die!* flashed through her, a sharper thought than the knife at her throat. On the fringes of her awareness was knowledge that he ultimately meant to kill her...but not immediately.

The odoriferous hand, the cold steel, the rasp of her attacker's fetid breath, her paralyzing terror were not as strong as one small seed of hope.

If the ghost of Major Benjamin Blair had any reality at all, he would show up to protect her, *now!*

Where was he with his claim he had materialized because she was in danger?

With a roll of thunder came the words, "Let her go!" clapping over her head. No one could imagine such an unearthly sound, nor the rush of relief it brought her. The hand over her mouth and nose abruptly dropped away, allowing her to gulp in air.

"What the sh—" her attacker hissed, and she, arms viciously twisted behind her and the knife still at her throat, saw the Confederate major again, only not exactly as she had seen him the night before.

This time he was quite transparent, like an enormous video image played against a scrim, garden behind him, and all the more visible because he glowed. His image changed the area he occupied to a hole in space almost like daylight, with muted colors shifting and roiling within, shimmering and unreal. The space grew. Major Benjamin Blair grew. She had never seen anything so awesome. So perfectly beautiful.

A knight in shining armor could never compete for effect with a monstrous, angry, Confederate major revealed in a thunder cloud, eyes literally sparking shafts of blue lightning.

In Major Blair's hand flashed an enormous Confederate army sword, its glow radiating from the honed edge as he cut a swath with it that lopped a twig from a rose bush and scattered the leaves. He might look like a horror film special effect, but that sword was reality and meant business.

The mugger dropped Janis.

Major Blair advanced within his own tornado. The creature who had attacked Janis, with another of his shrill giggles, pulled a gun from his dirty rags and waved it. She heard the tiny click of the hammer being pulled back.

"Look out!" she cried at the same time the mugger discharged the gun.

He could not miss, and she, even suspecting the shot could not damage Benjamin Blair, uttered a little scream, for Major Benjamin Blair simply disappeared.

"What th—" the mugger whirled as though he expected the terrifying image of the Major to have somehow flanked him. He waved the gun wildly.

Though Benjamin Blair could no longer be seen, his voice came from in front, from the sides, from behind the mugger and Janis. The Major might have been many men with identical voices blending into a mighty battle cry. "If you're looking to be sent to hell, you've come to the right place!"

While she lay gasping for breath in the marjoram, the ghostly major materialized again, surrounded by the glow and shimmer.

The mugger howled with the accelerating volume of an approaching siren. He backed away and scrabbled for the wall. He scaled it more nimbly than she would have thought possible.

Benjamin Blair's Rebel yell at the disappearing creature was enough to frighten bears. Her attacker dropped over the wall and pounded, still howling, up the alley.

Benjamin lowered over Janis. "Perhaps this may change your mind about not being the target of someone who means you harm?"

She groaned. She could still smell the mugger, and the things he had said to her began to make the belated impact that she hadn't previously fully absorbed. Her stomach churned. Her bones turned to jelly. "You're giving me a crick in my neck, and I don't think I can stand up," she said in a small voice.

"Did he hurt you?" Benjamin condensed into normal size, sheathed the sword, knelt in the herb bed, and ran his hands over her face and neck. She found nothing ethereal about the sensations they caused. His touch was a line of tingling hot and cold fire along every nerve, and rough in its concern. "You are bleeding. Let me carry you inside."

Inanely, she said, "A volunteer watered the garden today. You'll get your beautiful uniform and boots all muddy kneeling here."

"To hell with muddy," he said pleasantly. He scooped her up as though she were a rag doll, into arms strong enough to lift a burden twice as heavy as she.

He strode straight at the closed and locked outside kitchen door to Badger House. She ducked her head into his chest and, a moment later, they were inside the kitchen.

Their entry in retrospect was as simple as their progress over the hedges rather than winding down the brick path. Instantaneous and physically impossible though it was, she had never felt so safe in her life, never so protected, never so comfortable. Her nose tickled in the worsted of his uniform. He smelled clean, herbal like the garden. *She could feel his heart beating!*

Definitely, he was solid. Her own heart beat in the same rapid tattoo against his chest. His breath was warm against her cheek. They had gone through solid wood, but he exhibited all the signs of a living, breathing man. She gave in to the irresistible impulse to pinch his arm, the last test of solid flesh and bone.

He stumbled against one of the three utilitarian green vinyl-padded kitchen lounge chairs and set her down with a decided thump.

Leaning over her, imprisoning her in the chair, he scowled down in shadows lit only by the rising moon. "Why the hell did you do that?"

She shrank back, expecting him to again become the avenging wraith at any moment. "I needed to know how real you are. After the horrible demonstration outside—"

"Dammit, woman, I could have dropped you! What does it take to convince you I'm a ghost? I've been practicing fading in and out, even perfecting how to walk through walls. I managed quite nicely once I put my mind to it. Do you need more proof? Where do you keep the candles?"

"The electric switch is by the door," she told him loftily. "That metal plate with a toggle."

The moment the light went on, he disappeared. Again only the opal-blue eyes were left as an after image.

"Don't *do* that!" she protested. "It's gross.... Or are you cranky because I pinched you? I'm sorry! Come back, please?"

He walked through from the exterior kitchen wall, appearing first as an amorphous extrusion on the cabinet face, oozing through as though being screened. Finally, he stood looking perfectly normal and gorgeous in front of the cabinets. She squeezed her eyes shut, opened them tentatively. He was there. She shut and opened them again. He wasn't. A moment later, he slowly materialized, blue eyes first, over by the door.

"You see? I've mastered the technique. Now to understand these miraculous lights." He flipped the switch once or twice. "Marvelous." He returned to stand over her and examine the scratch on her neck. He reached across her to a glass which stood on the table with the opened bottle of wine she had brought in that morning.

Evidently he had explored the kitchen's facilities thoroughly without the need of light, for he pulled out the dishtowel drawer behind him, removed a clean cloth, dipped into what was left in the wine glass and sponged her neck.

"Ow!"

"Sh-h! I am relieved beyond belief to see the bushwhacker's knife barely broke the skin."

She eyed evidence he had been sitting in the kitchen enjoying a drink while she had been vainly calling for him over at Wharton House. "If you'd come when I called, that nasty little recent confrontation might have been avoided."

Unfeelingly he said, “The incident served to get your attention, so it wasn’t wasted.”

“You let him *cut* me so I’d know my life is in danger? You let me ruin a perfectly good, new, pair of Christian Dior panty hose? You let me muddy an ash rose silk suit that I paid a great deal more for than was sensible, and you probably ruined your uniform—it has blood on it—and let your murderer get away in the bargain? Just to prove to me you’re a *ghost?”*

“He’s no ghost and was given *carte blanche* to do with you what he liked to do, paid with his favorite drug to make sure you didn’t come out of the experience alive. Everyone was to think the incident was just another sign the police and their maintenance of public safety aren’t doing their job to control the growing number of criminals who inhabit the night. Your murderer doesn’t care if his minion is caught. No one would believe an incoherent story from a certified asylum patient. Hold still.”

He dipped his head, and his lips touched her throat, sucking at the stinging little spot near her jugular. Her heart nearly stopped of its own volition. If he was a vampire, she was about to lose her soul and her mind.

She didn’t care. She owned to the insane desire to feel his lips on hers. To that goal, she twisted around until her face was squarely a breath from his.

“Don’t wriggle about so. There. If there was any poison on the rusty blade it’s gone.” Benjamin patted her on the head as though she were a recalcitrant child and sat back in one of the other chairs. “Our mutual friend doesn’t care to be on scene himself, so hired a crazed pervert to do the job.”

The major’s words made her shudder, but in spite of her shock, she was fascinated by the sight of stains on his uniform fading as she stared. Fortunately, his attention being on the primitive first aid he had practiced, he hadn’t noticed how he bedazzled her. She had to stop fighting the evidence he was a ghost and be more alert to how vulnerable she was to him.

She squeezed her eyes tightly shut and held her breath to the point of pain. The resultant roaring in her ears forced her to forget the pure sensuality of his impersonal act of charitable concern. She concentrated on his having known whereof he spoke when he warned her of danger. He was here on a mission, and when it was accomplished he would vanish into limbo or heaven, whichever deserved.

She opened her eyes. "You seem well acquainted with my murderer's plans, Major. Tonight I hope you have a better clue as to *why* he wants to kill me?"

"Let me rescue your papers and your suitcase, and we will ponder the situation."

"What's to think about? Either you know or you don't.... What if that—monster—comes back?"

"He is now a mile from here and still going. I doubt his feet touch pavement more than once every other running yard. Shortly he will be found deep in blithering idiocy and be taken to the nearest lock-up. He is of no consequence to your future."

With that, the Major stalked out of the kitchen, using the door in an everyday sort of way, and she remained at the kitchen table, casting frantically about in her mind for any enemies she might have made all unaware.

Once the Historical Association made its choice, the only other applicant for the job of director of the Heritage group had immediately taken a job in Ukiah as head of their Chamber of Commerce. Cutting him out had not created an enemy, but had done him a favor—his salary was twice Janis Carter's because non-profit groups didn't command the same salary scales as Chamber of Commerce Executive Secretaries. *No.*

If Dexter had wanted to kill her, he could have done so with relative immunity any one of several times when he had a scalpel in hand and she was on the operating table. *No.*

Sheryl, her bridesmaid, had maliciously told her Dexter was having an affair with her. *Naa-ah.* Although Sheryl obviously held no affection for Janis, if for some inexplicable reason Sheryl wanted her dead, Sheryl wasn't bright enough to find someone who could deliberately disable a car. Nor brave enough to find a man like— ugh!— the man in the herb garden.

Dexter being a doctor, and a doctor in town for a week at that, could have managed both situations. Perhaps she could not completely dismiss Dexter after all. *Outside chance.*

Thugs from a gambling syndicate! They were going to greater extremes this time to show Keith they wanted their money. *The only reasonable explanation!*

The shock of thinking about Mafia types who wanted their gambling debts paid and would kill her to convince Keith they meant business gave Janis a headache she didn't need.

Benjamin returned with the file box, scattered papers—somewhat the worse for wear—and her briefcase, which would be good as new once wiped down. "I've already told you the murderer is a descendent of my partner. Since he could be descended through the female side, even his name isn't necessarily a gauge. Though I still can't remember. I don't need to. I *know* I'd know if I were within a mile of the fellow."

"How?"

"Just would. My few advantages are like wild cards. Since I materialized at the seance, when I 'exist,' I appear to function blindly in certain areas."

"You're still sure the murderer is a man, not a female?"

"Quite."

"I *do* believe you...because—" She told him about the accident that Marvin said was no accident. "...You were right about plans being laid the night before you showed up. Ocho made sure I was a good defensive driver, and that probably saved my life."

"Your murderer is going to become bolder and more desperate," Benjamin warned.

Plaintively she asked, "Can you pinpoint his next move better than that?"

"*Mi bella Italiana,* you hold the key to the clues and have not spied them as yet."

"I hold *what* clues?" Her brains itched ferociously with the effort of trying to shake any keys loose. "All my bridesmaids have connections to old California except my maid of honor, Sheryl. I don't think the others...but one of them *could* harbor a few mean thoughts about me because of Dexter, I suppose..."

"Now we are getting somewhere," Benjamin said most

unhelpfully.

Dexter's face kept surfacing on Janis's brain screen, in spite of her insistence he couldn't be the one. He could certainly throw his family's Old California clout and connections about like confetti. His father had three times been president of the Association, and his great-grandfather had founded it. Dexter wanted *Rincon.* And *Rincon* was valuable. "Why doesn't he just *buy* it, if he's the one and that's what he wants?" she wailed. "He can afford it!"

"You're apparently more valuable dead than alive, and you're keeping something from yourself or from me. Out with it."

She said angrily, "Money. I have half of a very large fortune. My brother Keith has the other half. Neither of us can spend all we have, and can never run out...but neither of us can get at large portions of it easily. Major Blair, what if my brother were in some kind of financial trouble with thugs from a gambling syndicate? He was once before. And suppose *they* won't wait for the next distribution of the trust fund and are stalking *him* through me?"

"Unless the murdering thug is a descendant of my assassin—which I suppose isn't beyond the realm of possibility—why would I know only you are in danger? Of course, if your brother's running from a gambling debt, he is no man of honor, and not someone on whom I feel compelled to spend my energies. That could, I suppose, be the reason I don't see him in danger. At least, it's the reason I have no interest in his danger."

"How can you be so heartless!" Her head hurt with the struggle to deal with conflicting concerns. "You obviously don't understand Keith has faced awful problems ever since he was just a little guy. Only since Ocho's death has he been able to climb over them and find a good stable life. He needs support and compassion, not the same kind of punitive rejection Ocho always slapped him down with. I'd think better of a spirit. I'll never turn my back on Keith in trouble."

Callously Benjamin said, "You experienced a lot of the same problems he did with your father and his succession of wives, and you seem to have conquered them."

She recalled Maggie saying much the same thing. "Keith's been on the straight and narrow for over a year."

"Then why think of him connected to Mafia?... but never mind." Benjamin raised a peremptory hand. "Your loyalty does you justice just a hair beyond good sense. My good sense says you are not yet facing facts about your brother even if he has nothing to do with this. When you do begin using your common sense, we can talk again. Meanwhile, watch your step. Look over your shoulder during daytime hours when I am unfortunately unable to be of useful assistance. Surround yourself with persons you know could not wish you into the next world prematurely. Give me a call when the sun goes down if you need me."

"I've heard you say that before, and I *did* call and you *didn't* come."

"When you were simply prowling about wanting company, I was otherwise occupied in enjoying myself. I came fast enough when it was important."

Grudgingly, she had to agree.

"Incidentally, I'll report my whereabouts last night after I left. I ate at the Chinese place and the Mexican place. Then I whisked about looking at the way things have changed since the sixth decade of the last century. I spent all of the hundred dollars on food, and discovered I needed either ten times the amount of cash to cut a real dash, or something they call `plastic.' What's that?"

"Rather like a letter of credit in your day. I tried to tell you."

He shrugged. "Thanks for leaving the snack in the dining room and here in the kitchen for me. I appreciated that."

"Er—please don't eat the staff doughnuts again?"

"They were stale and I thought they were probably meant for pigs or chicken feed. After this, I won't eat or drink anything else left in this vicinity without my name on it." He gestured at the bottle of wine.

"The doughnuts are there for the staff. *One* is all right. Even two. But have some consideration for all the others. Three dozen at a gulp is not considerate! And thirty cups of coffee isn't considerate, either. You were welcome to the Mexican food I forgot to eat. Or was someone else responsible for doing away with it all?"

"On a scale of making up for starvation for a hundred and thirty plus years, I didn't eat that much, but I apologize and won't do it again. However, if you and I are to get along, you will refrain from correcting my manners unless I request it, which I believe will happen when hell freezes over."

"You needn't be testy," she said. His scowl warned her he was barely beginning to be annoyed again. Hastily she changed the subject. "I happen to have gone to an ATM today and can give you two hundred more for walking around cash."

"The money, Ma'am, would not be a gift but a loan. If I had no means, I would not have been assassinated by my partner, damn his eyes. My strongbox contains plenty of gold and an assortment of good gems valuable in any era. I don't have it with me only because I have had a bit of difficulty remembering exactly where I buried the blasted thing. The terrain looks vastly different from my day."

"You'd have to know where to exchange such items for true value, anyway. You can't barter a little gold dust or a pearl to do business just anywhere in this day and age. I do know of one way to arrange a responsible exchange of gems and gold after nine in the morning and before five o'clock, a time of day you say you're unavailable."

"I thank you for the assistance. I don't know how much time I have to exist. I do know I have no wish to sit around and do nothing. Last night I knew you were safe and enjoyed myself. I don't want to miss any possible additional adventures."

"I warn you, I could get only a few cents for any denomination of currency. They're only a curiosity with no real value. Gold or jewels I could convert."

"Excuse me," he said. "I'm going to fade away. I have another idea where that burial spot is."

In the nature of the Cheshire Cat, only the memory of opal blue eyes remained glowing above the chair, but shortly he faded in again holding a dirty metal box approximately as big as one of the workmen's smaller tool boxes. It appeared to have been buried for at least a century, and definitely under a tree, for one end of the rusty container was crushed by a portion of root still curled about it like a hungry python.

"As I was saying—as a ghost I suppose I could manage by my wits, but I like to pay my way. I buried this box the evening I met my untimely end, and it was still there after all that time. Whatever you can spare at the moment to lend me, I promise you'll not be left holding the bag—er, box, later."

He wrestled with the root. "Within this container is the ample wherewithal, and I leave it to you to find a gemologist who appreciates quality."

He wrenched away the rest of the root, opened the lead-lined container and began to unfold oiled cloths. "Never locked it. Felt at the time if anyone found it before I retrieved it, they would simply smash it open anyway."

Janis gaped at the treasure revealed. Multi-colored glittering gems tumbled out. "Are those *emeralds?* I can't believe my eyes!"

"Picked those up on the banks of the Putumayo River in Colombia. Had them cut and polished in Rangoon, where I got two of the rubies."

"May I?" She pointed at a cabochon ruby with magnificent star fire.

He handed it over. "From Siam. Chanthaburi. And this one, from Ceylon. Note a certain difference in color in those from Rangoon?

"They're all absolutely breathtaking!"

"This diamond is nice." He held it up, big as a crystal drawer knob, glittering, even though unpolished. "A gift from a native up the Zambezi for whom I did a favor in...let me think...fifty-four, if I remember rightly."

She shook her head vigorously to clear it and remember he was talking 1854 not 1954, ancient as 1954 seemed to her, since it was years before she was born.

"Now, these black opals I won from a rotten poker player in Denver on one leg of a trip across the country with a wagon train of supplies. He claimed to have found them somewhere in the Antipodes. You think you could rustle up cash for them?"

"I wouldn't be a bit surprised," she assured him faintly.

He sorted items one after the other, each more priceless than the last. "...And finally, these gold nuggets from the 1849 goldfields to the north of here. In their original state. Ought to be useful for small change."

"Small change!"

"You could tell the buyer you've decided to cash in unnecessary gew-gaws which have been in your family a hundred years or more."

She gulped. "I'm no expert, but I'm sure any one of these stones would keep you for a year or more in the style of an oil sheikh!"

"My wants are simple. Convert three of them to start. Keep a commission as a donation to your pet project."

Stiffly she said, "I'll bring you full value and a receipted account from the most reliable jeweler in San Diego."

"Don't go out of your way to get affidavits. I trust you. Mind you, I was once or twice disappointed by people in my former life, but as a ghost I think I know whom I can trust."

She said stiffly, "I am bonded by the Association for a million dollars."

"Only for your agency's business dealings. Don't sputter like that. I perceive your own trust instincts have been badly battered, except for your lamentable excuses for your brother—but you knew at the outset you need not mistrust me. I will never speak anything but the truth to you."

"How did you know I'm not bonded for anything but the agency's business dealings?"

"I don't know. When you said what you said, I knew what the details of the facts were."

"More of your wild-talents?" Janis fingered the spot on her neck, which no longer stung from the knife's scratch, but was warm with the lingering memory of his lips.

"I cannot blame you for being cautious. If I had paid more attention to caution, my own circumstances would be different." He poured himself a reasonable portion from the wine bottle. "I didn't realize my partner wanted my little collection for himself so badly—until it was too late."

Thoughtfully, he juggled three rubies the size of jawbreakers before tossing them back into the box. "I discovered last night that I need a more extensive wardrobe. Nothing in the museum where I found my uniform will suffice. Though my workaday buckskins wouldn't be impossible even today in many quarters, they've disappeared. Disintegrated to dust, I suppose. From what I saw on the streets, work pants like old Levi Strauss made in the goldfields are still being worn by men and women today, but with rivets. A good idea. Old Levi ought to have known about the rivets."

"He did," she said, automatically pulling out information on items of the late nineteenth century West. "After you were dead and gone, though."

"I'll search out a new pair of jeans for a start."

"You can find them in just about any store selling men's clothing," she advised him.

"I went about extensively last night. The central shopping area of the high rise city, the beach shopping areas. But it was after shopping hours."

Janis left off admiring the crumpled box full of gems. "How in the world did you cover so much ground in one night?"

"I flew. Or floated? Or sailed? And I wasn't the only item in the sky, either. A monstrous machine came down with a tremendous roar, lights blazing. It nearly ran me down."

She shuddered. "A plane landing at Lindbergh Field. I don't suppose you could have anticipated anything like that in your day. I do hope no one *saw* you flying or wafting?"

"I may have arrived in this era an anachronism, but I use good sense and have no intention of creating an uproar. I even discovered a mammoth library doing business. Unable to prove myself a resident, I had to be content with browsing. In my day I often enjoyed a good book. I find I still do."

"I expect I have many authors from your era in my own library at home. I could lend you some."

"I had rather see a representative sample of what people

are reading today. Anything you choose will do. I could catch up while marking time. I doubt there is any point in looking for our murdering friend in the small hours before dawn when the living generally cave in to their need for sleep. Why not leave the books for me in Room 201, Underwood? By the way, I was up there last night while you were closing up. Maggie came in and prowled about. She did not see me, however."

Surprised at the familiar way he tossed out Maggie's name, Janis asked, "Have you had previous dealings with her?"

"I put the bee in her bonnet to come here and do the seance."

"The room is not ready for occupancy or display. She was definitely out of bounds."

"Leave the old girl alone," he advised.

"CALOSHA has fits about the public wandering around without hardhats in the midst of a construction area. I'll have words with her—"

"There was nothing there to hurt her and nothing there she could hurt. Her very good instincts told her to go take a look. Having satisfied her curiosity, she won't have any reason to go back."

In spite of Benjamin's indulgent attitude toward Maggie, Janis made a mental note to have words with both the workmen and Maggie about safety regulations. The Association's insurance rates could soar with one accident determined to be from careless attention to the laws. A major settlement from negligence could shut the Association's doors. No one but workmen in hardhats were supposed to be anywhere inside the yellow cautionary tapes with *KEEP OUT* warnings printed continuously on them, and large signs to augment.

"She's got the Gift of Sight," Benjamin Blair said. "And she's perfectly safe. She won't get you into trouble."

Janis's mind did not change in regards to having a word with Maggie, but she said, "I'll see you get both new and familiar books to read in your no doubt copious spare time, Major."

He leaned toward her. "Having rescued you once and

warned you twice, I believe I'm entitled to be called by my first name. `Major' is far too formal. If you could print it on a paper sack, you can say, *Benjamin* or *Ben* or anything but *Benny*. My Aunt Bess always called me that, and it sticks in my craw. Last night while exploring, I met delightful women in pleasant social circumstances, who advanced to first name basis in less time than it takes to tell you about it."

"I see. And exactly what were these pleasant social circumstances, *Major Blair?"*

"A wedding reception at the hotel next door to the upright shopping center in the center of the city. One of the bridesmaids broke the heel of her shoe, and I was able to save the evening for her with a quick emergency mend—which made me a welcome if officially uninvited guest at the reception."

"A heel? Wedding receptions?" she said. "Why do the two elements seem to be perfectly combined?"

"Tut-tut," the major reproved. "This was a happy event. Quite informal, even though a bishop was present, and a senator from Washington, D.C. The bridesmaid was a guest at the hotel and invited me to see the hot tub in her suite. Marvelous inventions, hot tubs."

"And very informal," Janis said dryly.

"I made an interesting discovery—a number of the women present had two faces, like you do. In some circumstances are such operations considered rites of passage? For most of the ones I noted, their first faces were, well, to put it bluntly, elderly."

"Probably a great many years older than you might guess. Women outlive men by six or seven years in this century, and routinely live well into their eighties. They like to prolong the appearance of youth even more dramatically than is possible with today's cosmetics."

"Ageless beauty, if you like it that way, but nary a one with the tiny waist women had in my day." He put his hands on Janis's waist. "Not one could I span with my two hands. Not even your second waistline. And not a corset on one of them, any more than on you."

She stepped back as if his hands had burned her...*Second*

waistline? she flushed at the realization he could see she had been downright chunky before Dexter had insisted on diet and liposuction. “You look right through their clothes? How rude!”

He protested in hurt tones, “It doesn’t take ability to see through layers of clothing to tell a woman isn’t wearing corsets. I am not in favor of the old-fashioned infernal cages, but I would think all of you would die from pneumonia, even in this mild climate. You go about with bare legs even with December coming in a day or two. Surely they don’t dress like this in November back in cities like Boston?”

“They do.”

“I have no objections to short skirts. But along the Zambezi, I saw women wearing very little less than the women wore at the once very respectable Casa Bandini which seems to have been refurbished and turned into a noisy eating place. Do you know of it?”

“It’s primarily for tourists,” she said.

He forgot his tourist restaurants and examination of scantily clad ladies for a moment and fixed her with a reproachful glare. “You, who vow you care so much for landmarks, should never have allowed such a thing to happen to that gracious *hacienda.* Old Don Eustacio must be turning in his grave!...Though perhaps the old gentleman would enjoy seeing such a lively parade of humanity. He always gave a good party. Last night, one friendly young woman waiting with her friends for a table invited me to join them, bought me drinks. She invited me to her hotel and later begged me to stay for breakfast. She handed over not even one piece of silver for her favors.”

“You mean she—? You’re as much of a tom cat as Dexter! And anyone who has promiscuous sexual encounters these days is out of his or her mind.”

“Oh, come, now,” he said mildly. “I’m a free, un-wed and uncommitted spirit. Dexter, on the other hand, was a married man. You may have a legitimate complaint where he’s concerned, but not with me.”

“Indelicate though it must sound to you,” she repeated

for emphasis, "carousing around can expose you to all kinds of social—er—diseases. Not just the two simple ones you knew about in your day, that you probably called `French pox' and 'clap,' but a dozen other really awful ones, including one that is as far as I know invariably fatal. Any sensible person—"

"I," he said, "am a ghost. What will a pleasant slap and tickle do to me? Kill me? or vice versa? I am not subject to any earthly cautions and neither, may I add, would be any one I dally with. Who am I hurting? No one! What harm can be done me? As a matter of fact, the young woman last night invited me to visit her at her lanai in Hawaii any time of my choosing. Not that I could or would take her up on the offer, but obviously I didn't make her unhappy with my attentions. I told her frankly that I would be moving on shortly, and we were merely ships that passed in the night, and so on. She had no objections. Why should you?"

Janis set her teeth so hard her jaw ached. "Do whatever you like. It's *no* business of mine."

Still, she frowned over the conviction that he was *her* ghost and supposed to be devoting himself to *her* welfare. Not that she would ever want to be a playmate, in spite of how attracted she was to him.

He lit a cigar and puffed on it complacently. "Shame on you, Janis. You're *not* being truthful. Now if you had a hot tub and invited me into it, I should be pleased to accept, even though I am quite aware you are not disposed to be as friendly as either of the young women last night. Then, there's your houseguest. I daresay Maggie would pounce on me and nail me to a specimen board before either of us could relax in said hot tub."

Janis stared at the cigar and realized she might be inhaling her first awareness of one of Nate Wharton's legendary cigars which others had claimed to detect. "I do not have a hot tub to share with you or anyone else," she said coldly.

He studied her. She was a nice enough girl, though as prudish as any to be found in Boston in 1860. If he must be around young ladies who were not amorously minded, he would choose an early California girl who might be guarded by a dragon of a chaperon at all times, but had a native instinct for romance and a store of ways to dodge the chaperon if she were really inclined. On the other hand, his prudish responsibility had that sensual Italian nose, and he felt a certain personal duty to let her know he appreciated it.

"Who knows what that would do to my ability to cope with your problem? You could come with me and explore the city, no hot tub activities attached. I would then not be lured into passionate encounters with strangers, and your sensibilities unaffected."

"I have piles and piles of work," Janis alibied. "We're opening Underwood House before Christmas if I can possibly manage it."

Ben thought she looked and sounded wistful, which was a good sign. "All work and no play makes Janis old before her time," he warned. "You could stand a relaxing evening at one of this city's lively night spots. And if you've never seen it from the sky...well! I tell you the place is a sight to see from a couple thousand feet up. Every color of jewel scattered on dark velvet as far as the eye can see."

Janis shuddered. "I told you I'm terrified of heights." She suppressed the temptation to offer herself in spite of her phobia as guide to his discovery of a San Diego quite different and certainly more worthwhile than the one he had aimlessly blundered around. She was also embarrassed by her suspicion he was enjoying himself entirely too much when supposed to be guarding her. "—But I wouldn't go flying. Even being on a step-ladder makes me dizzy."

"Janis, you're a lost cause who doesn't know how to enjoy life. When you are old and dried up, remember I invited you, and you missed the memory of a good time. Drive your machine on home, but use caution, or you'll put a nail in one of the tires. You're otherwise safe for the night and for tomorrow during the day, which is as far as I can see. Until tomorrow night, then. I'm off on more adventures." He rose and stretched.

Before he could desert her by fading, she rose too. Obviously he was only interested in her company when she was in danger. He bent briefly over her hand in an old-fashioned, gentlemanly gesture. She swallowed the impulse to tell him she had changed her mind.

Whistling the tune, “The Ash Grove,” he disappeared, leaving the last few notes hanging on air.

SIX

Janis put the box of books with other items slated for Room 201. At Underwood House, the construction boss said, "Good thing we finished knocking the wall out between room 201 and 202. Gives room for all the stuff you decided to cram in there. But Miz Carter, the walls is still raw wood. Don't you wanna store the stuff on the third floor until the room's finished?"

"In its time that room wouldn't have had finished walls. I wanted it double-sized so the space insures good brochure photos."

When she called Mrs. Cadigan to see if the draymen had arrived at *Rincon* to transfer furniture and collection items, they were there and loading.

"You had a call from Mr. Carter," Mrs. Cadigan told Janis. "He said he's been asked to go to the Association meeting tonight and wanted to take you with him to supper at The House of Hospitality in Balboa Park."

Whether he was or wasn't her potential assassin, he was probably up to no good. But her common sense stepped in and assured her he was too status-oriented to stoop to murder for any motive when any number of other options would suit better. So he wanted *Rincon.* Killing her would not achieve the ownership unless he paid her estate administrator a fair price, and if she knew Eli Simonsen—and she did—Eli would administer the estate administration with every financial safeguard.

Nevertheless, Dexter was a genius at taking cars apart and putting them together again. Dexter, like Keith, had been wild during his high school years. Even as a doctor, Dexter was a loose cannon except for his undeniable skills. He would also have known right where to look for a mentally deranged creature willing to do a dirty job. But why?

She didn't want to think about it...but had to.

Mrs. Cadigan gave her the still familiar number Dexter had left, his original clinic for reconstructive surgery in La Jolla.

When he came on the line and heard her voice, his voice became ingratiating. Had it always sounded so oily? She was impatient, too, with the little *heh-heh-hehs* with which he sprinkled so many statements. They telegraphed when he was not being forthright.

She must have been incredibly naive to find him devastating when she was young and green. Sweetly she inquired, "How's Sheryl?"

"Sheryl went her way. I went mine. You know how those things are."

"How nice for her," Janis said, not without malice.

"I was talked into attending the Historical Association meeting, and thought it would show a friendly attitude if we showed up together."

"Stories of your family's early days in San Diego are always interesting to those who haven't heard them overly often."

For the first time since she was ten years old, she had needled him instead of the other way around. She experienced no triumph. He was actually rather pathetic in spite of his mile-long list of degrees and his obsession with perfect appearances.

"I know you have to be there, Janis. We might as well show we're on civil terms. I'll even make a small donation to the Association."

All this conciliatory manner and the pile of "hehs" punctuating his every sentence was like him when he wanted something—*Rincon,* or worse, his need for her permission to promote more of his surgical skills. The prospect of a ghost watchdog and her curiosity made her say, "I have a houseguest. You'll have to include her."

"Keith told me an older woman was at the house. She no doubt needs a face peel, or a bit of sculpturing? I'll mention the clinic. Our specialty is nose jobs. Or the new sculpted lip lines that don't require fat injections. She'd be in fine shape for the holidays. So would you, for a nip and a tuck. I'd make it worth your while."

"Never again. Haven't you been able to find any guinea pigs since me?"

"No subject so clearly progressing from a `dud to a delicacy.'" He had used that awful claim in the publicity that had given him his big jump into prominence, and the words made her see red.

"If I were you, I wouldn't mention plastic surgery to my guest. She gave me an awful scold when I reappeared on campus for graduate school after our divorce. Couldn't fathom why I had done it. At the time I couldn't explain it myself."

"Now, Jan, you know you were as delighted with the results as I was."

"No doubt at the time. But now delight and gratitude somehow elude me."

"Your houseguest may be more appreciative."

"My guest, Dr. Wythy, a parapsychologist from Claremont University is around seventy years of age. She probably never was a beauty as you define it, but she flaunts her wattles, wrinkles and the bags under her eyes as honestly earned. Suggest erasing them, and she will shoot you down with laughter. Or clobber you with her parasol."

"Parasol? You're kidding."

"Not at all. She has a parasol for every single one of her ensembles. Today she is wearing pink, orange and saffron yellow."

Dexter audibly winced. "She sounds like a sunset. But drag her along anyway."

He must *really* want *Rincon* badly. Her curiosity got the better of her. "What brings you back to town?"

"The clinic here needs me on premises temporarily. I heard you have *Rincon* on the market, and I might be interested."

"I might sell it to you, too. At the right price."

"You won't get a better price than from me."

"I'll turn over the keys to anyone who makes the best offer over the appraised value."

Dexter knew real estate. He would know that appraised value to the penny.

"The real estate market's way down," he said. "It's going lower in the spring, mark my words. You stand to lose more if you wait."

Her lips curled. He knew spring held better promise than winter did. He had no intention of making an offer anywhere near the appraised value, but was his interest in her real estate evidence of hostile intentions?

"I rely implicitly on Attorney Eli Simonsen's advice regarding all my financial affairs, up to and including the disposition of my estate should the need come up. You remember him?"

Just mentioning that Eli Simonsen would handle her estate was enough to put Dexter on notice, whether he was murderous or merely a con artist.

She still thought Dexter an unlikely suspect as her potential murderer, no matter how willing he would be to legally steal her property. She would rather suspect Dexter than anyone else she knew, but she couldn't. He was as transparent as a glass of water.

Her curiosity about his motives for being nice had almost certainly been answered. Beyond that...he bored her. But she could tolerate the supper meeting. "Dinner at The House of Hospitality is at six-thirty. Why don't you meet Dr. Wythy and me at Wharton House at five-fifteen?"

Since the Major was sure he would know the murderer, she would have Major Benjamin Blair evaluate Dexter. The time of the year, rapidly approaching the winter solstice, brought dark by five. Her arrangement for Dexter to arrive at Wharton was enough for the Major to take a good look. He said he would know the killer if he saw him. She flashed an image of the major with his strong lean hands around Dexter's neck, throttling him, and was shocked at the pleasure the idea still gave her. The next moment, penitence overtook her. She was sure Dexter didn't deserve ultimate vengeance from the grave. A good tweak, maybe.

Dexter said amiably, "Lord, let this be the last of those Association meetings I shall ever need to smile through. *Heh.*"

The *Heh!* erased her penitence. She glanced at her watch. Only nine o'clock in the morning. She had a mile-long list of priorities to handle before sunset.

***

She headed straight to Badger House kitchen as soon as Ryan Aherne dropped her back at Wharton after the Chamber of Commerce luncheon meeting. There she found the truckload of furniture and files being unloaded and Nancy brandishing a wad of phone calls to be returned. Afterwards, she set to with a pair of scissors and the afternoon edition of the newspaper in her daily task of scanning for materials of every kind that should be part of the Association files.

A photo and item in the second section caused her to jump up in shock. "He ought to be kept mummified in a tightly wrapped strait-jacket shroud," she said aloud.

The previous evening, a person or persons had vandalized two fir trees in Mission Hill Park. Each venerable tree was over a hundred and thirty-five years old.

In the news photo, a groundsman pointed to signs of digging having been done under the roots of both trees. The article concluded that if it wasn't senseless vandalism, the perpetrators might have been interrupted while doing "early Christmas tree shopping."

As if anyone would dig up a seventy-foot tree to decorate for Christmas! Room dimensions aside, long before anyone could saw through the trunks and load them on a major flatbed truck, an entire National Guard unit would be aiming bazookas at them.

She knew she was looking at the one of the trees under which the Major's steel and lead box had been buried. A wave of guilt washed over her...as if she could have been the one digging under the old fir herself. She certainly knew the culprit. *I'll take this up with you, Major Blair, ASAP!*

The Association staff and the Underwood construction

crew left at five. Janis searched out Maggie and found her sitting in the granary, evidently communing with the Wharton children or Mrs. Wharton's ghost, at least taking advantage of the quiet time before they had to leave for the Association's annual dinner. Maggie had been doing her astral photo shoot and seemed quite pleased with the protoplasmic signs. "I have an errand and will be back shortly," Janis told her. "When my ex-husband arrives, would you let him in?"

That would keep Maggie out of Underwood House for a time. With her briefcase which she had clutched in a death grip since her errand to Horton Plaza earlier, Janis slipped into the empty interior of Underwood and called tentatively into darkness, "Benjamin?"

The major was as independent as a contractor and just as casual about appointments. She sat on the bottom step of new staircase, her back to the spiraling height that could trigger her vertigo with even a close-up examination and the *idea* of ascending. She hoped her rushed schedule and impatience were being transmitted to the Major wherever he was dawdling.

"Now, what?" His crossest voice came from behind her.

She twisted around and squinted up the dizzying whorls of the free-standing circular stairs. Only because he looked so gorgeous could she ignore the usual waves of dizzy nausea triggered by looking at height from below as well as from above. He wore a pair of stone-washed blue Levi jeans and was barefoot. His ecru silk shirt, open to the waist, revealed great pecs. His blond hair dripped.

"All the way from La Jolla I heard your voice nagging at me. My head might as well be an echo chamber. Everything was pointing to a great evening, but I no sooner jumped into the jacuzzi with this girl I met the other night, when I had to climb out. Now stop yelling at me like a fishwife."

"You aren't here to go hopping into jacuzzis with every girl who wants to get a better look at all your muscles."

"Let me worry about that, my prudish little obligation. Has anyone tried to murder you today?"

"You know they haven't. But the loaner had the flat tire you predicted last night. You could have let me know it was bound to happen."

"I was kind enough to warn you. I'm not here to rescue you from nuisances, only from murder."

She seethed. "I can't compact my time like you can yours. Waiting for Triple A cost me valuable time last night."

"If you had come with me—" the Major began, but she cut him off.

"Furthermore, today, on the *time-consuming* trip for your *trivial pursuit of pleasure,* the jeweler asked a great many difficult questions about the origins of what I was selling *for you.* Also my ex-husband is in town. He's apparently been here several days, and as far as my property goes, he's up to no good. I'd like you to take a look at him and either take measures or cross him off your list."

Major Blair raked his fingers through damp locks that curled in silvery blond ringlets around his ears and down his neck. He hunkered beside her on the new circular stairs. "His presence must explain your crotchety behavior. Where is the bounder?"

"I told him to meet Dr. Maggie and me in Wharton House just ten minutes from now...And I think it's *disgusting* that the very second the sun sets, you're into a jacuzzi with any bimbo who comes along."

"My dear, I can tell from your sour tone that `bimbo' is not a compliment. I assure you Libby is a lovely, lively person in addition to being delightfully hospitable. I hardly think she deserves to be called names."

He shook his head in a parody of sorrowful protest. Drops of water sprayed the area. "The paltry amount of paper money you gave me didn't go far last night. Prices these days are shocking. Worse than in the South in `66. Were you able to get a fair price for the baubles?"

"I said I would and I did, but—" She brandished the newspaper clipping. "—first, you were responsible for this, weren't you?"

He scanned it. "I told you time dimmed my memory of under which tree I buried the box—had a devil of a time finding it, but the tree is all right. What is the fuss all about?"

"You left a mess," she scolded.

"A couple came down the hill, and I had to leave in a hurry."

"You told me you can compress or expand time. Surely you could have covered your tracks."

He looked embarrassed. "I forgot to go back...Now, about the jeweler?"

"I thought his loupe would pop right out of his eye when he saw the first emerald. Then I couldn't breathe for a while after he made his offer. My family has always had money, but I'm a conservative buyer and spender. He gave me a certified check. When I took the check to my bank, they tried to argue me out of taking it all in cash. I've tried not to think about how much I've been carrying all afternoon. You can't carry all this money around with you, either. Let me set up an account."

She opened the briefcase, packed with currency, and turned her purse flashlight on the stacks. "Take my word for it, there's enough to keep you in style for an eon. We don't bury assets any more, so if you don't want an account, at least let me put it in my safety deposit box. The way you seem to get around, you could go in and help yourself to it from time to time at midnight without any problem—unless you continue to leave signs you were there. Isn't there an old saying, `The dead need no keys?'—"

He raised an eyebrow. "No one's going to rob a ghost."

"You really *can't* carry it around with you. I really think you ought—"

"Let me worry." From a packet of hundreds he counted out the money he owed her and began methodically to tuck the rest in one hip pocket of his skin-tight jeans.

"You're not going to try to—? You'll look like an over-stuffed pillow!"

Packet by packet, he slipped the currency into the same hip pocket. Seeing her attention on the tight fit of those new Levis, which were affected not at all by the deposit, he grinned. "Not much like the old canvas we wore in the gold fields when I was a kid. But works better than a bank deposit box, don't you think?"

After a moment of absorbing how devastatingly well set-up he looked in skin-tight jeans, and that he could indeed carry any amount of money about with him invisibly, she wrenched politely from admiring him too blatantly.

From the other hip pocket, he extracted one of the books she had left in 201. "What is being read today is nothing like Dickens or Cooper! The amount of catching up I have to do could over-strain my ability to stretch time." He pulled out another book. "Thanks for this one on politics of the Twentieth Century." He withdrew the big *Time Lines* coffee table book from the same hip pocket. "Fascinating."

"If you really want to have a mind-boggling experience, I'll show you how to use the television set in the staff room."

"I have already acquainted myself with that machine. I watched an amazing outline of world news on a television in the lounge at the Westgate while a young lady and I were taking each other's measure. I think it's simple enough. And I thank you for putting furnishings into Room 201. A man likes his own retreat on occasion."

"I wanted you to be comfortable. I know it isn't the same furniture Room 201 once had, and the room's more than twice the size because I had the workmen take out the partition, but I did as best I could."

"In my day, the hostler divided the rooms into half the size of original blueprint specifications. Barely room for a small iron cot that didn't accommodate my entire length in a straight line, a scrawny chest of drawers and a straight back chair, as I remember. I practically dressed with an elbow out the window. Room 201 as you have reconstructed it is palatial compared to my day. But not as comfortable as the Westgate."

She was unaccountably annoyed by the comparison."I see you've set yourself up as a connoisseur of travel accommodations in the short time you've been back."

"My specific complaint to the management of this one is that, in the absence of a jacuzzi, there should at least be a hip bath."

"I furnished 201 with a chamber pot, wash bowl and

pitcher...none of which I would think you need as a ghost."

He shrugged. "I never was one to walk around in my own dirt when I could clean up, and ghost or not, I like a bath."

That *might* explain a portion of his preoccupation with jacuzzis. "The room isn't plumbed," she said in exasperation.

"I can manage, notwithstanding."

"I'm sorry I questioned you about needing amenities. I'll see about a hip bath. One of the Adams' Avenue dealers has a copper one." She paused. "I wasn't nagging you just because I was nervous about carrying around so much cash. I thought I should tell you about Dexter. He's related to the Bandinis, so his family was here long before ours, and I want to know absolutely that he's not—the one."

"Do I have to inspect him tonight? It shows poor manners to leave a jacuzzi partner waiting any longer than necessary. Besides, she offered to show me more of the area night life which you were ungracious enough to refuse to do. So many exciting projects. So little time."

"My life is supposed to be in danger, remember? And you want to find the descendant of your assassin, remember?"

"I detect no danger tonight. A confrontation of sorts, though I cannot tell if the murderer is involved. If your ex-husband is the one, I can let you know, but I have no wish to waste my existence playing bodyguard unless the matter is a priority."

"The possibility of being murdered is high on *my* list of priorities. How do you *know* no one will try anything tonight?" She might be verging on panic, but she hoped she came across as casual and unconcerned.

He regarded her with a cocked brow. "I either know or don't know. Tonight I know I'm free to pursue my own pleasures. Now, if you have nothing more pressing on your mind, I will be available to look over your ex-husband and then be back to my jacuzzi companion."

He vanished.

Deserted by a ghost supposed to be helping me. So what else is new? Oh, well! I long ago became accustomed to being ignored when I wasn't being useful to a man.

Instantly he materialized, seized her in a backbending embrace, and lowered his mouth over hers for the greatest sample of kissing in the series he'd given so far. Her toes began to steam. Her insides clenched, heated, and clenched again. She could have kept the kiss going forever, but it stopped before she could even completely catalogue it and store it away for future reference and dreaming.

He gave her a pat on her rear. "You are definitely *very* attractive to me, and you already know how attracted I am to generous Italian noses, even when disguised. But, a collateral duty calls. So many wonderfully uninhibited ladies and so little time, as I mentioned. I shall check your ex-husband a little later."

The mocking after-image of blue eyes was all that remained a second later. Janis's self-pity turned to pure embarrassment. He definitely seemed to pick up on what she was feeling, if not what she was thinking. Just as clearly, what she had begun to feel for him was all one-sided. He obviously had no real attraction to her—versus the girls he was meeting everywhere he went—no matter what he said to bolster her admittedly badly wounded self-image. She stalked back to Wharton House.

Maggie came out of the granary and dropped her Queen of England style purse. "The psychic aura in here is simply overwhelming!" She sniffed like a bloodhound. "A spirit recently passed through this *hall!*"

"It's the season they say all the Wharton spirits are most active. Don't stir them up, Maggie. If you do, we might have to shut down to visitors. Tourists are apt to get hysterical when they think they've seen or smelled something described in the literature. It scares them, and they have accidents because they are upset."

"I promise not to stir spirits up, Jan. But I continue to have the most definite impression that *you* are a catalyst for the undocumented spirit we almost reached during the seance."

Nervously Janis ventured, "Exactly what do you mean by 'undocumented'?"

"Why, that this spirit isn't mentioned in any of the records of spirits generally attributed to this trio of buildings."

"Just Wharton," Janis doggedly corrected still another time. "Badger House merely has an interesting *historical* background. Underwood is a *reproduction.*"

"This spirit definitely belongs to Underwood, and is particularly special. I do wonder, though, how I sense him here in Wharton House."

"Never mind spirits for a moment, Maggie. I told you earlier that my ex-husband is picking us up here and taking us to the Historical Association meeting. While I assemble everything I need to take to the meeting, I'd appreciate your showing him around to see the changes made since he saw it before. Could you also trot out your sixth sense and later tell me bluntly how he impresses you?"

Maggie grinned and nodded.

Good, Janis thought. *Let the Major deal with Maggie's sensitivities as well as Dexter's motives for coming around.* If Dexter was the would-be assassin, the Major could take care of him more efficiently than the combined efforts of all of Southern California's police departments.

An impatient rattling at the door proved to be Dexter. She examined him while he waited for her to unlock the deadbolts. He hadn't changed a bit in three years. She had.

She indulged in smug satisfaction at having put her hair back to its original brown, at rejecting *avant garde* styling salons in preference to doing it herself and twisting it into a bun on her nape to anchor it out of her way.

Another sign of recidivism was her conservative professional navy blue outfit with knee-length skirt hem—a far cry from the flashy designer things Dexter chose for her to wear to stand out in a crowd.

That she had completely rejected everything he had foisted on her other than the plastic surgery would register soon enough. She reminded herself not to make it obvious that his little chuckle was quite horrid. She had never even noticed it was annoying until he called earlier that day. The funniest change in her was that she didn't really care if he hated the recidivism, or care if he didn't care.

He entered, the epitome of tall, dark and handsome. Once she had thought Dexter's mustache all that was sexy. Now she thought it rather silly and pretentious looking. He probably considered himself the definitive modern noble *Californio.*

He took both her hands. "I heard about your father. I'm really sorry."

He and Ocho had always been friendly, and Ocho had been sorry she divorced Dexter. With his record, Ocho could hardly forbid anyone else to shed a spouse. She thanked Dexter stiffly, wishing he would release her hands and stop evaluating her for another surgical upgrade.

"Maybe just a little trim on the nose tip," he said. "There's a new technique that—"

"No," she said.

"No charge. *Noblesse oblige,* so to speak."

"No."

He shrugged. "You still look good, except for the mousy hair color."

She snorted. "It's my own, if you can bring yourself to remember. I had it returned to original from that midnight blue-black you preferred on the basis it gave me the look of my Spanish great-great grandmother."

"You may be right. Like an orange bead in an Indian turquoise necklace, it's the tiny imperfection that points up the perfection. And nothing wrong with brown hair in a careless bun. Points up the rest. You really are my star achievement. Would you consider doing another shot for my album to show the improvement as the results mature? With a really good hair style, of course. I just pinned back ears for this terrific Hollywood still photographer who had Dumbo appendages. I think using his skill to show how everything has settled so it's even better than at first would be even more contrast to the before shots and make a tremendous impact for my next article."

She couldn't have asked for a more romantic, more tender compliment from her ex-husband. The light finally dawned on her with regards to his probable hidden agenda. He wanted something, all right. But her death did not enter into it. "Your portfolio, or whatever you plastic men call it, will have to make do without an update on me."

"It's a shame to hide your charms from the world, Janis. You're a work of art."

She thought of offering him a masonry trowel from among the construction workers' tools so he could pile inducements on in his avid desire to exploit her. She wondered how high the pile could grow without making her become hysterical. The answer wasn't worth the bother and, besides, she doubted he would see the funny side.

Her pride wouldn't allow her to pass up the opportunity to bait him. "I met this fantastic man recently who said my nose was much too small for perfection. He saw a picture of me the way I was before the nose job and preferred me the way I was before."

Dexter first looked unbelieving, then annoyed. "He was telling a little fib for his own purposes. I hope you didn't fall for *that* line. Your nose is just right, now. Even without the—"

"But it was a line that worked. I'd follow him anywhere, and he wouldn't even have to whistle."

Maggie Wythy came down the stairs and Janis introduced her. "I still have to pack up the brochures for the meeting, Maggie. Take your time showing Dexter through the house."

Maggie dragged him away. Janis quickly put various materials for the Historical Association Meeting into her briefcase, then concentrated. In a low, firm voice she asked, "Are you there, Benjamin Blair? Is Dex the one? If he is and we're going to be in trouble going with him in his car, would you *please* let me know? If you don't show me a sign, I'll know we're okay for tonight."

Playing cordless invisible telephone games one-way with a ghost must surely be a step in development of a nervous breakdown.

Maggie and Dexter descended the stairs after what she suspected was the fastest tour any visitor ever took. No lights blinked on and off. No thunder sounded in their wake. No chandeliers rattled. No books flew out of the bookcase. Neither did Maggie offer comments on the presence of spirits, either angry or disinterested.

Dexter picked up the box of historical materials Janis indicated was to go. She hefted her briefcase, and Maggie took the smaller box of materials out to Dexter's Rolls Royce Silver Cloud at the curb.

"Classy!" Janis sank into the front passenger seat sure that even if Dexter was the potential murderer he wouldn't attempt a thing in his precious car. "Real Beverly Hills."

"Property of the medical corporation, for tax purposes," he said. "I hope that old clunker you used to drive has gone to the junkyard by now? With all your money, you should have opened the wallet far enough for a Mercedes, or at the very least a Lincoln Town Car."

If he had sabotaged her Lexus, he would *know* what she was driving. Or maybe he was just being clever?

Maggie chattered the whole way to the meeting and all the way back. "There's enough material here to keep me busy for months, if only I could luxuriate in it thoroughly, not to mention your father's library, Jan." She was silent a moment. "Everyone has been lovely to me, even Mr. Thorpe—whose aura is too dark a blue-green, I must say."

Janis winced.

"It's actually an aura that comes from lack of joy, not evil, dear. I must tell you that when I first knew you, I thought your own aura was entirely too indigo for a girl your age. I'm puzzled because it has been radiating a vermilion shade recently."

Janis laughed. "Sorry about that. I like indigo better than vermilion."

"You should be aware, my dear, that though an indigo aura has its strengths—kindness, morality, and a healing ability—it is entirely too serious, too cautious, too intent on materialism and pursuit of profit." Maggie playfully shook a finger at her. "The light, bright reds radiate sensitivity and femininity. They also are..." and she lowered her voice, presumably making it a private observation Dexter could not hear, "filled with eroticism, sexuality, passion and sensitivity as well as love. That nice young man from the Chamber of Commerce?"

"Heavens, no!"

At that point, Dexter—evidently feeling left out of the conversation—asked plaintively, "How about my aura, Doctor?"

"A definite orange-yellow fluctuating to orange-red."

"Good?" Dexter asked.

"Mmm." Maggie murmured. "Sharp intellect, plenty of self-confidence and industry. Also pride and vanity. Every color has its downside."

Janis heard the vinegar in Maggie's voice. Maggie, she had quickly come to realize, was incredibly sensitive to people, dead or alive.

"Heh-heh-heh! Wrong. I'm not the least vain. But you're right-on about the Association vice-president and treasurer, especially if that green aura is also for the color of money. How long has he knotted the purse strings of the Association, Jan?"

"Since I was a little girl," Janis murmured, surprised by how comfortable she had been with her ex- all evening, whether he was suspected of being a prospective assassin or not. Probably that was because the Major was ready to come to her assistance in a split second if need be.

"Actually, Mr. Thorpe's aura has nothing to do with the love of money, which as we have all been taught, is the root of all evil," Maggie said. "Though his report was dry as toast, and he can be off-putting in his handling of people, he has good instincts. Devotion is a strong point with him. But he is too cool and is one for too much solitude."

Janis agreed. "Millard Thorpe loves his docent work at Badger House, and we couldn't do without him, Dexter's snide opinion of him notwithstanding."

"I know," Maggie said, "but you realize it hampers me to be surrounded by targeted vibrations of disapproval."

Janis soothed her. "Ignore Millard's little quirks, Maggie. He took the death of his wife very hard, and he's just coming out of a dark period. That's all."

"He always was a dried old stick in the mud." Dexter handed them from his Rolls into Janis's rented car in the lot back of Badger House.

"I didn't know about his wife," Maggie said, her voice more sympathetic. "I only felt an antagonism."

"You may be seeking those who have passed on, Maggie, but your ebullience is a tonic for him. And let's hope some rubs off on his personality."

Dexter said plaintively, "I wanted a chance to talk to you about the house."

"Why *Rincon?* I thought you were set up in Beverly Hills."

"I am, but one of my partners is going to head the clinic here, and he needs a suitable place."

"We can talk if your price is right. But not before the holidays."

"Jan, there will never be a better time than—"

"Oh, you and Keith! We'll discuss it later, Dex. If an offer piques my interest."

Janis drove out of the lot with Maggie, who promptly spoke as soon as they were on the street. "May I ask what was that all about?"

"He wants to buy *Rincon,* which has been in the Logan family since the original estate in the valley washed out to sea in the flood of 1915. I really do want to sell it. It was too big when Ocho, his current wife, and Keith and I lived there with Mrs. Cadigan, a house man, two maids and a full time gardener. I only stayed because everyone advised me not to make big changes for a year. It's been more than a year. Except for the prospect of Dexter's partner becoming the buyer, there hasn't been a nibble. So far I haven't seen that offer qualify as anything more than an offer to take me for a ride. I told Keith half the profit was his, so it's in his interest to hold out for his share if a million more, minimum. Dexter is tight-fisted. He won't go that high even though the place will eventually sell for what it's worth."

"Where will you go once it's sold?"

Janis shrugged. "A condo somewhere with good security. No higher than the third floor because of this thing I have about heights."

"Have you ever thought of hypnosis to erase your phobia?"

"No. Nor counseling to find out why. I already know it has something to do with my mother having died in a plane accident when I was a toddler."

"Is the sale and your need to move the reason why you're disposing of your father's marvelous historical library and collection of local materials?"

"He left financial provision for that in his will and discussed it with me. Underwood is the ideal realization of his intent."

Maggie's eyes gleamed. "My instincts keep telling me the choice of Underwood was more than coincidental."

Janis laughed. "I found the original blueprints. Ocho would approve completely. The wildest part is that everything about the blueprints could have been designed with his idea of a museum in mind, just waiting for my ideas of what the Association needs, as well. The Association was immediately persuaded to make use of the blueprints because of the money available from the estate bequest."

"Now why should I make a mountain of that molehill?" Maggie mused.

"Why should you put two and two together and get some impossible number except that you naturally thrive on such equations?"

"Moi?" Maggie murmured, but she laughed with Janis.

"Just as soon as they finish painting, Ocho's library and artifacts collection will be moved in. After I've seen the estate matters settled, I'll be champing at the bit to get into a cozy little place of my own."

"I take it your brother doesn't want to live at *Rincon?"*

"Heavens no. He hasn't lived there since he was a kid. Hates the place. Trouble was Keith's middle name, and Ocho and he were like crossed sticks. Ocho even had Keith committed to a psychiatric hospital for a time. They wouldn't keep him any more than the military schools would. Said he wasn't crazy. He just `looked at the world differently than others did.' Ocho said no son of his was going to be labeled a no-hoper by psychiatrists, and virtually disowned him. He relented at the end and divided the estate equally, though he arranged Keith's trust so Keith couldn't throw it away at the nearest gambling establishment. As it is, his income this year will be more than the new SunSol owner's salary. Ten times more than my agency salary, by the way. He's doing beautifully. And he's back in the work Logans have done for generations."

"I gather Logans have built homes here in San Diego since right after the Civil War, and there isn't any part of the county that hasn't benefited from the Logan 'dynasty.'"

"Right."

"But what about you, Jan? Are you *happy?*"

"Me? I do my part as a Logan. Underwood is probably my swan song in `construction.'"

"You'll marry again. Did I detect a gleam in the eye of the man from the Visitors' Bureau? What was his name?"

"Ryan? He just likes to be seen with me. I'll never marry again. I've definitely had enough of that sort of thing."

"It's not far from my being twice your age to you being my age," Maggie said. "You don't want to be like me. I spent the first two-thirds of my life being a professional, too. By the time I realized I was an eccentric, it was too late to be different. I'm a horrible example of old age."

"I don't think you'll ever be old, Maggie."

Maggie grinned. "Then I'm simply a horrible example."

"Shame on you for talking that way," Janis said comfortably.

"Come, come, Jan. All I have is my research. And I'm grateful you let me poke around, even though you say you're an unbeliever."

"I might not be the unbeliever you think." After a moment Janis added, "I did have a strange experience the other night at the seance."

"I knew it! I knew it!"

"I don't quite want to talk about it yet...One day, if I choose to talk about it with anyone, it will be with you."

Eagerly, Maggie promised, "I won't pry. Except...did it have anything to do with leading your ex-husband through that house tonight?"

"Yes and no. Why?"

"When we were passing through the back hall, I briefly felt a strong presence, the presence I've mentioned several times—a rush of— presence —then what I can only describe as...a vacuum. Gone."

So the Major had seen Dexter, then returned to whatever pursuit he was involved in. He would have remained if Dexter was the murderer. "Did Dexter do or say anything I ought to know about specifically?"

"Only that you've accomplished a miracle in making Wharton a tourist attraction, and that we'd be late if he didn't bring the car around."

Janis wished she had an excuse to stay and prowl Wharton's halls—call the Major from his dalliance with that blonde. Though satisfied Dexter wasn't the one she wanted to find, she wanted to know more about the Major. She wanted to know *everything* about him. He had lived a fabulous life, could tell stories for a lifetime of listening. When he discovered his enemy—and hers—and did whatever was necessary...she would never see him again. The hot lump under her breastbone was pure jealousy of the Major's obsession with jacuzzis at the Westgate or the Horton Grand, or...wherever. With whomever. Rational or not, she wanted him to pay attention only to her. She was why he had come. He had no business finding any other woman interesting or intriguing, no matter how dull Janis Logan was. Janis had never been aware of any jealousy in her before, and being bedeviled by it shocked her. She had become too sensible, too practical, for such unproductive emotions.

SEVEN

Janis restrained herself from slipping out of the house late that night and going back to Wharton House to roust the Major. She did not care to deal with someone playing Mr. Macho with the girl at the Westgate and furious with her for interrupting him. She wondered how to work herself up to being able to shame him for his tom-catting.

A ghost had no business being so unforgivably appealing to women.

Worst of all, she ought to have her head examined for being attracted to a ghost. Her best course of action was retirement to a nunnery, except that she felt no calling to a religious life. Perhaps she ought to reconsider that indifference, in light of her evidence of afterlife.

After tossing and turning until three in the morning, she reached the point of determination. She rose, dressed, and left a note for Maggie saying she had to go to work early. Maggie had her own car. so the middle-of-the-night decision posed no inconvenience.

At four o'clock Janis parked and entered Wharton. The building at that time of year was as dark as the inside of her ghost's thunder cloud, and that was truly *dark.* Rather than put on the lights immediately, she whispered, "Benjamin Blair? Are you there? Please, Ben? I want to know about Dexter."

For a haunted mansion, Wharton was singularly inactive at that hour. Not even a trace of unusual chilly drafts blew along the downstairs hall that morning—certainly no signs of any of the many reputed ghosts.

"Ben, if you don't come back where you belong and put my worries to rest, I'll drive down to the Westgate and roust you out. I mean it. I want to know about Dexter!"

The Major appeared with his fists on his hips, bare-legged, wearing a short scarlet satin Cardin robe that molded his body like a second skin. "Woman, you are beyond doubt a number one drawback to my having a romping good time."

Janis stepped back from his annoyance, but bolstered herself with her own. "You have a mission, but you spend all your time chasing women!"

"Temper, temper," he said.

"Was she blonde or brunette tonight?"

"Redhead," he said promptly. "One with the best hot tub you ever saw. Fitted up in an indoor garden made to look like it's hollowed out of one great boulder in the midst of a jungle. All made of plastic, I am told."

"Probably you have seen more hot tubs and jacuzzis in the time you have been with us than I have seen in my entire life. Some of us have no time to loll in hot tubs."

"Poor girl. What you mean is, you have no time for fun. A pity. You're a nice girl but inclined to be grim." He sighed. "At the time you became impatient, I was reading to the redhead from one of the books in the lot you loaned me."

"Steam ruins books." *If* he had been reading, it was probably in a waterbed.

"We were, in point of fact, in front of a fire at one end of the garden room, on a magnificent bearskin rug."

"Bearskin, indeed. Bare skin, more likely. Do you mean I should believe for *one minute* you were simply reading to a woman at this hour of the morning?"

"You may believe whatever you like. The bottom line is that she wasn't complaining. Why should you?"

Janis could think of nothing strong enough to express her annoyance. "You're incorrigible!"

"You, my dear, show signs of being affected by hostility towards your ex-husband's and father's lives to the point of being boring, a nag, a whiner, and a prude. Why I like you, I can't begin to fathom." He relaxed on the sofa, crossed his ankles and yawned. "I'm making the best of my situation in my own way, *piccolo naso Italiana,* and that way is none of your business."

"You're such a philanderer. Just like Dexter."

"Opportunist, perhaps. What do you find wrong with that?"

"What's wrong with—? Spending your physical existence time in meaningless encounters instead of making points toward your eternity? What sort of a man are you, anyway?"

"Actually, I'm not a man, my dear. A ghost gets to make his own rules if they aren't already set out for him. Now, stop lecturing me just because you're personally put out with me."

He sat up, pounced, and she was captured in his arms before she could dart out of his reach. "You wish you could dare me to make love to you. But foreswear that temptation. There's no future in it for you. You should fall in love with a man with a future, and I have none. Not on this level and probably on no other level, either. I don't believe in love for myself. It is enough I wish a fine love for you with all the heart that can beat in my ghostly chest."

She stubbornly thrust out her lower lip. "You hear stories about ghosts and love all the time."

He looked pained. "*Do* you? You don't believe in ghosts. Why would you put any faith in stories about ghosts?"

He delivered one of his maddening platonic pats and released her. "What I suspect is that you have a jealous streak, dear girl. You must work at eliminating it if you ever expect to be in a happy relationship." He yawned again.

She thought of the brazen female or females he had been sporting with since sundown. For him the time span could be the equivalent of hours and *hours* longer than her night had seemed, which was very long and passed in an entirely different frame of mind than his had been. She saw red, not the green of jealousy.

"I have no *reason* to be jealous, but you shock and appall me. And if you don't believe in love, kindly remember, neither do I."

His laugh was rich, genuine, and infuriating. For reasons she did not care to explore, she felt as miserable as he appeared to be genuinely amused with her anger. He pulled her over to the couch and held her next to him—which made it practically impossible to keep her mind on either her anger or what his lecture was all about.

"You believe in love all the way into the face of disaster and disillusion, my dear. Don't fool yourself. But for your information, the lady I visited tonight was married and bored, and bent on being unfaithful to her husband. I did her husband a favor by sending her back to him with a new appreciation of him."

She almost screamed. "Oh, very funny. At least give me the results of your confrontation last night with Dexter."

"The one who looked like an Italian count and smelled like a badly pickled herring?"

In spite of herself, she grinned. "After Dexter went to medical school, I thought the occasional whiff of hospital disinfectant was a badge of his profession. It had an aura of being godlike. It never occurred to me the smell was like badly pickled herring, but you're right. It is. And he does. Is he my murderer?"

"He wants your house at a price I don't think you'd be wise to accept. When you refuse the offer, he'll be mad enough to kill, but will admirably refrain from anything but telling you that you need a bit of trim and tuck on your smile lines. Tell him you don't smile enough to get smile lines and to peddle his skills elsewhere. He only wants you to feel as badly about a wrinkle as he will about losing out on a good steal."

"That sounds like Dexter. But—?"

The major frowned. "Having assessed him, I'm not at all pleased to be compared to him, as you did a few minutes ago."

All she could think was the repetition of her previous assessment that there must be something quite wrong with her for being attracted to men who didn't find one woman enough for them.

"If you still love your `philandering' husband, and are jealous of him because he makes you feel insecure, take it out on someone else," the Major ordered.

"I'm *not* in love with him at all any more."

"Yahoo! Smarten up even more. You are annoyed with a ghost because, since he does *not* believe in love, refuses to trifle with you. You are the kind of woman who will in all your life never sleep with anyone you do *not* love. I do not intend to lure you into a transient adventure with me. I will keep in check any tendency of mine to take advantage of your vulnerability." He looked quite fierce in his intensity.

She couldn't fight that sort of plain dealing. She moved away from him to the other end of Mrs. Wharton's sofa.

"Poor Janis. The sooner we take care of your problem, the sooner I can remove myself as a source of your distress." He deliberately yawned a third time. "Dawn is about to crack. I shall head for Room 201. Thank you for making it fairly comfortable for a bit of reading time before I wink out."

"*Fairly* comfortable? I've spent a lot of thought and money trying to make you feel right at home."

"So you have, and I appreciate it. What I meant was that the best of the Old West is not to be compared to the delights of this era."

"I don't know how else to be a good hostess and still be authentic," she said stiffly. "Suit yourself if what I managed by dint of a lot of work doesn't suit you. I'm limited to authenticity since I plan to set up a sort of museum on the second floor, bit by bit. If you'd rather have other pieces of the furniture from Old San Diego's hotel rooms, I'll make any changes you want."

"Oh? Perhaps I can help you. Now if you will excuse me?"

EIGHT

Still shaken after the Major abruptly disappeared without even an after-glow of blue eyes remaining to tease, Janis nevertheless collared the first of the Underwood crew coming in on their work shift. "The computer goes on the roll-top desk, please. The cabinets to the left."

She placed current files in the refinished cabinet which had once served a hotel in 1850. Soon the remodeled reproduction of an office would be a public fishbowl. Early visitors to Underwood were to come in on a ticket price including all three of the buildings and be channeled past the office at a distance, see only a tantalizing glimpse of the interior.

A semi-fishbowl was better than working at a dining room table or in the kitchen. Eventually, the office was to be a model only, open for inspection at all times from behind a rope; but that diorama for visitors to stare at to their hearts' content at $4.00 a ticket—and cheap at twice the price—was not to be a reality until the permanent offices were ready.

After Underwood's Grand Opening, she would scheme towards those permanent offices where she and administrative staff might work without constant interruptions. By then *Rincon* would have realized the expected sale price; her new condominium would be reality, and her ghost would...

Where would the Major be then? The sense of impending loss was heavy.

She looked up at the ceiling, above which was Room 201. The Major's politely superior attitude toward her efforts to make the room comfortable rankled. If it were truly pleasant as well as authentic, he might be less footloose and reduce his rake-like behavior. Perhaps Room 201 could be made much more comfortable and still authentic. She reconsidered every item in the room. The image dissatisfied even her. With what San Diego could otherwise offer, she understood its lack of appeal to him.

She pictured him ensconced in more Georgian surroundings with the same English flavor that tinged his Southern drawl. He had mentioned his family was once accustomed to such comfort on their Virginia estate. She fantasized a room that said scholar and gentleman and inspired the writing of memoirs. Washingtonian. Jeffersonian. The man...the *ghost*...undoubtedly had a volume of memoirs in him. Probably two or three volumes. One volume for this week so far, with his ability to stretch time when he was having fun. The creation of a gracious Georgian atmosphere was only a fantasy, but the corners of her mouth curved in pleasure as she envisioned it.

On impulse, she left the office with her notebook and keys and crossed the dim, cavernous lobby. The rough pine workmen's stairs were due to come down once the great circular staircase, back stairs, and elevator work was completed. The removal of the rough-hewn pine steps would do wonders for the spacious appearance of the lobby area.

On the second floor landing, she turned left to Room 201 on the south corner, concentrating so intently on how to make the ghost's last mortal address look less rough and ready that she scarcely thought of hugging the wall away from the balcony rails in order to avoid a wave of vertigo at the vista of lobby below. Such sights reminded of what someone else might feel leaning over the Grand Canyon from a balance board protruding out into space. The mental image alone made her lurch and clutch the doorknob of Room 201 to steady herself. When she stepped inside, her mouth dropped open.

Instead of the furnishings delivered from her garage, she saw her own recent lavish imagination multiplied to an extent impossible to find outside one of the national landmark Georgian homes like Monticello, Brandon, Berkeley, or Gunston Hall...gone wild.

The room was centered by a Sheraton bed with finely turned and reeded foot posts. Neatly turned back to show the quality were mellowed linens at least a hundred and fifty years old, including an heirloom wedding ring quilt. The whole was topped by an antique, perfectly preserved, off-white crocheted bedspread that would have made her mouth water if she could have believed what she saw.

The bed stood on a hand-loomed strawberry rug of remarkable size, for it covered nearly the entire floor. A Governor Winthrop desk was accompanied by a square-backed chair with beautifully carved detail. A tall bookcase—containing the books she had lent the Major—was painted with classic decoration that took her breath. She had to touch the upholstered fruitwood chair to be sure she wasn't dreaming of being in a fine Georgian historical landmark home. She smelled beeswax and lemon polish.

Close on the startling discovery came fury. Either she was crazy as a hoot owl, or the Major had rifled a half-dozen classic mansions—perhaps even a museum—and appropriated a fortune in fine pieces.

"Benjamin Blair," she said sharply, "Now you have something *serious* to answer for!"

Naturally, when she wanted to be haunted, early sunlight merely beamed through the south and west corner windows and glinted off the glorious antiques and a number of small accessories any connoisseur of fine eighteenth and early nineteenth century pieces would drool over. The perfectly appointed furnishings made Room 201 unique. She remembered telling him that if her arrangements didn't suit him, he should suit himself. She swallowed convulsively, backed out, and locked the door on the fortune within the room.

Workmen's voices echoed from the first floor. She raced down the broad temporary stairs and hailed the construction super. "I want security installed on every ground-floor window *today.*"

The super and workmen looked at her blankly. In retrospect, she heard her own sharp panic and smoothed it over. "We wouldn't want what's already been stored here in the building to be disturbed in any way. Vandalized, or—or..." The thought of an intruder damaging or removing *anything* from Room 201 before she could make the Major return his ill-acquired collection gave her an instant daytime nightmare.

After deep breathing quieted her panic, she pointed out the unfinished facility's vulnerability. "Stored items here are valuable historically if not monetarily, and some trespasser might start a fire that could burn down the whole complex. Not to mention the damage vandals could do." She calmly ordered special attention to building security. "I'm not so concerned about the third floor because it's on the well-lighted street with its one high window more than three normal stories from the sidewalk. But anyone could come over the garden or alley wall and climb through the first floor windows after Wharton and Badger close at night to visitors." *And they have!* She shuddered, remembering the awful creature who had accosted her in the garden.

"We'll put electronic security on all the windows today, if we can," the foreman promised. "If you like, I can put a security guard on duty between shifts."

Fervently she agreed. "I should have suggested that earlier. Please have him report to me the moment he arrives."

She didn't care to hint at the value of what was in Room 201. She was experienced enough to have a good ball-park idea. With a security man on the job, perhaps a call to the Association's insurance company wouldn't be necessary before she ordered the Major to put everything back where he'd gotten it, and just as quickly.

With the crew working during the day and Mr. Thorpe's eagle eye on everything within sight of Badger House, there was little chance of anything happening within the current daylight hours. Nevertheless, she added cautions. "From now on, report immediately if anyone goes near Underwood who isn't part of your crew."

"Right," the foreman said, but her knees were weak with the shock of what she had seen in Room 201.

***

The furnishings Janis had seen came eerily close to her own unrealistic dream of ideal surroundings for the Major. She was less than attentive to Ryan Aherne who picked her up at one o'clock to go to the United Way-CHAD meeting. She couldn't in all conscience fail to attend, or she would have.

"Do you have another appointment?" he asked. "You've checked your watch every thirty seconds."

With every glance at her Rolex she hoped a great deal more time was passing than her watch revealed. The very moment the sun went down, she certainly did have another appointment. With a major ghost headache.

Automatically she murmured polite responses to Ryan while devising the dressing down she meant to deliver to Benjamin Blair.

Dimly she became aware of Ryan's words. "...I'm glad you like the idea of looking in on the Chili Cook-off at the Convention Center."

She realized her non-committal murmurs had almost committed her to going on from the United Way-CHAD meeting to eating chili for supper. "Sorry, Ryan. I have a crucial appointment at five." Silently she amended: *And it could last all night—if I have to help move furniture.*

"I hope that being over-scheduled doesn't mean you've changed your mind about the Civic Theater tomorrow night?"

She oriented herself to the Salvation Army affair with some confusion. He was speaking of the benefit performance of *Scrooge* and her knee-jerk reaction was to make some excuse for that too. "...Of course not."

He brightened. "As planned, then."

She managed to return to Wharton House by four-thirty. Nancy Rogers had the usual stack of phone messages, including one from Keith.

"I told him I wasn't sure when you'd be back, but I didn't expect you until after three. He has a project in North County today and a construction company meeting tonight. He needs an Okay on showing *Rincon* on Saturday at ten in the morning and called it a 'hot prospect.'"

Janis suppressed a sigh. Keith was still pushing for that

quick sale. "Leave a message on his machine, would you? Saturday morning will be fine."

"The workmen left at four, but a security guard reported for duty. I've wondered about keeping all that old furniture over there with everything so open."

Nancy was already concerned about the relatively expendable items in Underwood. If she knew what was locked in Room 201, she would go ballistic.

With a breezy, dismissive wave that belied her anxiety about insurance liability, Janis said there was no need for concern and went to check on the security man's itinerary.

The beefy guard seemed to know his duties. She said, "I'll be working back and forth among the three buildings for several hours into this evening, and I expect an—er—visitor to show up eventually. I may bring him over to Underwood. Keep everyone else off the premises."

"Your foreman had the electrician string outside lights so everything will be brighter than The Qualcomm on a playoff night. I have good visibility of the garden from the kitchen of Badger House, too. Trust me, everything in these three buildings'll be safe as Fort Knox."

Little did he know Room 201 contained treasures not a lot less valuable than Fort Knox! But she breathed a little easier with him on duty. "All rooms containing antiques or important records are padlocked and the windows barred. I don't anticipate particular problems. Help yourself to coffee and doughnuts in the staff kitchen."

At five o'clock, darkness fell like a black drape with a weighted hem. She fairly danced with impatience until Millard Thorpe had checked out of Badger and escorted Nancy to her car in the staff parking space. Alone at last, except for the burly guard somewhere on the grounds, she concentrated. "Major Benjamin Blair!"

"You roared?"

Every time she heard that richly resonant voice, astral mice ran up and down her spine. If ever a voice could make a woman's knees wobble, Blair had one. He looked entirely too pleased with himself, but made it difficult for her to remember how angry he made her.

He was wearing a new sweater, one that Sigourney's Boutique half a block west had just received for the Christmas trade and Janis had admired. A knitted green silhouette of a pine forest marched across his pecs, and stylized reindeer cavorted in perfect coordination on the snowy band above the green border. No ghost should look so gloriously ready for, or fresh from, a skiing weekend.

"I thought you might like this one with a varmint knitted in," he said and handed her one of Sigourney Boutique's imaginatively printed paper carrying-sacks.

She unfolded a sweater decorated with a knit design of a prowling panther. "So this is a varmint?" A great wild cat stalked the sweater with faux-jeweled, opalescent eyes that reminded her of the Major's own and cleverly appeared to fix on her own gaze. She hardly knew how to say thank you and then pounce on him for the antiques in room 201.

She resisted asking what he might have purchased for the blonde at the Westgate or any other jacuzzi partners, admired her sweater and his and segued into business. "We have to talk about what you did to Room 201," she said firmly. "I went up there today and got the shock of my life."

"I *knew* you could appreciate it. Last night I was as busy on the project as one Comanche attacking three cavalry units coming at him from three directions at once."

"Benjamin, where and how you came by those priceless items I don't know, but what may seem a harmless collecting expedition to you could put us all in jail for grand theft and create terrible publicity for the city of San Diego."

He looked hurt. "You think I got them by questionable means? I paid good hard cash for each of those pieces—a great deal of cash—and you'll find the receipts and certifications in the safe in your office. I had a hunch you would want to see receipts and all that."

Not that she didn't believe him, but she couldn't grasp how he had managed it all—granted, whenever he disappeared he accomplished miracles in the space of a few seconds' absence.

"How in the world did you do it all in one night? And why? I require an explanation which, if I choose to accept it, must be certified absolutely legal."

"To your first question, do not presume to ask. I am not sure how I seem to get things done, but the less I worry about it, the more efficient I am. To your second question, some things never change. Enough money buys anything."

"But, why—when by your own conditions, you're here only temporarily?"

He shrugged. "I can't take the cash with me, nor that treasure I dug up. Even though I shall not be hereabouts much longer, you can say I reacted to being a bit homesick after more than a hundred and thirty years away from anything that reminds me of home. I wished to surround myself with what I remember of my family that still exists...not reminders of a catch-as-catch-can life from the time I ran away from my aunt."

"Ben—everything in Room 201 is a treasure. Along with my interest in local historical homes, I long ago developed an interest in antique furniture and accessories, the kinds that meant gracious living in early America and are seen now only in our great estate homes, private and public. You said, *your family's things,* but the name `Blair' isn't one that comes to mind when I have the distinct impression I've seen pictures of some of those pieces upstairs before today."

"No doubt," he cheerfully agreed. "They were pointed out to strangers even in my day as important heirlooms. I can answer all your questions. Most were once in the home of William Henry Harrison, signer of the Declaration of Independence and his family home at Berkeley in Virginia. Some were in the home of Martha Washington's sister."

"Ben, they have to go back! Right away."

"Why? I bought them without any tricks or sleight of hand. Elizabeth Bassett Harrison brought these three pieces to Berkeley when she married my grandfather, William Henry Harrison. Martha Washington's sister was married to my grandmother Elizabeth Bassett Harrison's brother."

"You're related to William Henry Harrison?"

"He was my paternal grandfather, and Martha

Washington's sister was married to my grandfather's brother-in-law. I found in your *Time Lines* book that twenty years after I was murdered, another grandson of William Henry's—who played with me when I was a tad—was elected the twenty-third President."

Janis's head reeled. "How did the name Blair become connected with the Harrison family?"

"Grandfather William's daughter Elizabeth married Mr. Joseph Blair, who begat my older brother Joe Blair and me. Bottom line, if I may use a phrase from one of your books—I wanted to surround myself for a few moments in time with some of the relics of my childhood, so I bought them."

"You *couldn't* have!" she exclaimed, still dazed.

"Why not? My money is good. The purchase is not only legal, it was in your Association's name."

"Don't start confusing this problem with the Association's interests."

"Janis, you've mentioned your hopes for Underwood's future. What I put in Room 201 can go a long way toward making those plans come true when I am finally out of your way. You will have legitimate papers bequeathing to you the Harrison antiques *and* the story of a ghost supposed to haunt Room 201. The ghost of one Major Benjamin Blair whom you can further relate to `The Blair Suite,' with all its bloody memories, if you so wish."

"It seems so—" she protested.

"So practical? Blair's bloody death in the Underwood, his relationship to two Presidents of the United States and a family related to Martha Washington. Presto! Underwood House becomes one step closer to being a mighty tourist attraction in the State of California."

"That isn't the point! The—"

"Visitors will line up to see the reproduction of a place where an admittedly minor but morbidly interesting person was said to have been murdered. They can shiver at the rumor—well embroidered—of a ghost and his family."

"When you leave," she said, the prospect depressing her when it should by all rights be a joyful thought as he pictured it, "you won't *be* a ghost any more. You'll be at rest."

"A mere detail. Work up a story that the Major's ghost rocks the chair by the book case when he reads. Or that it's rumored a lady glimpsed the blood-stained ghost of the murdered man entangled in the bed sheets. Now, you *know* perfectly well that rumor would create a certain tingle in vulnerable old ladies, if no one else."

He put an arm around her shoulder, which accomplished wonders to distract her from her initial concerns. He tickled her under her chin. "*You* will know there really was a ghost for a brief time, Janis. You can honestly begin the legend for the gormless. Think of all the aged houses your Association can save with the admission tickets."

"You would think of being discovered naked in bed?"

"Have you not heard any other word I said? Would you not enjoy finding me naked in bed? No? How sad! You disappoint me." He bent close over her. His breath ruffled her eyelashes and heated her cheeks. "Trust me, darling girl with charming noses, I would never appear to a lady genuinely offended by the sight." He placed his hand over his heart region and lifted the other in dramatic promise of sincerity and discretion.

Persuasively he suggested, "Hire an artist to do a painting of the legend. I particularly arranged the room, incidentally, to exactly resemble the guest bedroom at Berkeley I remember well from my visits as a tad."

"You may not wish to seduce me as a woman, but you are terribly tempting me with this." She pressed fingers to her temples and attempted to come to the right decision.

"Think over the status potential to your Association, the sincere memorial to me and my family, the pleasure it will give me while I am briefly here."

She succumbed to temptation. "You're not a ghost, you're a devil! And I'm no saint. What did you do with the furniture I put in there?"

"Part of it I put next door in 203. The rest is in room 204. In both rooms I set for you the proper tone for Old San Diego's first hotel. You will see why I would wish to choose more pleasant accommodations."

"Do you imply my setting was incorrect for the era?"

"It was dirty out here, my dear. Water had to be carried up from the river. Only very important hotel patrons received fresh sheets on their first night, and not again for a month of Sundays unless someone like me bled all over them. Hot baths cost a dollar if you got first water, and a dollar was big money then. In the dry season, dirt was removed from cooking and eating utensils with sand. There you have a firsthand report on the realities of life in the Old West."

No wonder he was so easily addicted to jacuzzis. "In other words, if I'm to present an authentic picture, the hotel room should be dingy and dusty?"

"And faded, not pretty. The grand homes of the South were as far removed from conditions in the West as chalk from cheese. Make the contrast part of your historical ambience."

The picture he drew infected her imagination. "The big room with all the lovely Georgian furnishings, if contrasted with a small room showing how it really was in the early days...is a novel idea..."

"There you go! About the time I met my end, I had become tired of being a wanderer—wanted to settle down, build my own house, live decently again. I had a prospective bride, though matters had not progressed far. Before I declared myself, I meant to have something to offer her. House and well, furnishings. I never had a chance to get started, and my intended bride married my assassin much too closely after my funeral to have grieved even in passing."

Touched, she said, "Perhaps your thoughts of revenge are understandable, but they can't help you find what you lost—like a positive project could." She made up her mind. "I'm going to accept your gift, Benjamin, in the spirit I trust it was intended. Let me offer a small but sincere token in return. My favorite stepmother always said the best revenge is to live well and be happy. I would much rather steward your touching bit of hedonism than think about your taking revenge."

"When your murderer is about to be successful, I will need to be doing something more drastic than living well and being smug about it."

"I certainly hope so."

He sighed. "So don't be careless when I'm not around during the day."

"I...won't. Thank you for the beautiful sweater and the beautiful gift to the Association when you're through enjoying it yourself. I'll be on pins and needles until insurance is in place."

"I, er, need you to convert another gem or two. My pockets are ready to be rented again."

She groaned. "You spent it *all?* At this rate you can only afford to exist about another ten days!"

"We'll just have to conclude our primary project successfully before then." He held the back hall door open, and they walked down the brick path to Underwood.

The security guard came out of Badger House and through the circular garden path. She nudged the Major. "He was hired this morning because I couldn't breathe from worrying about what was in Room 201."

"You should have simply asked me to do the job temporarily."

"*If* you could keep your mind and presence here instead of in some blonde's jacuzzi."

He halted on the brick walk, put his arm around her and tilted her chin. When he looked deep into her eyes, she felt she was as transparent as a blush, and probably very silly. He deliberately side-tracked her automatic inclination toward him by holding her off until she straightened. "You know, you have quite a fixation on my enjoyment of jacuzzis and hot tubs. You ought to share one with that serious colleague of yours from the other agency. It might mellow you."

"You can indulge. I can't."

"All work and no play makes Janis dull. And crotchety."

"I have my moments."

"When?"

"Tomorrow night, for one. If you were to be haunting the Westgate Hotel before the performance at the Civic Theater—or more likely haunting the supper dance at the U.S. Grant

Hotel after the performance—you would see me enjoying myself. It's the opening of the season's first production of *Scrooge* which is a dramatic adaptation of *A Christmas Carol,* by your own favorite author, Mr. Dickens. Groups all over the county will put on the production before the season's over, but this one is a road show with a famous actor. Opening night is a charity affair. You might be familiar with the story of Mr. Scrooge, but it would not have been produced as theater entertainment in your day, and this is to be an elegant affair."

"I can see you in deep emerald green with a skirt like a water-fall over your elegant bones, inaugurating the holiday season. Say you are wearing green?"

"I'm wearing my serviceable black silk-velvet collector's prize, a Vionnet, as timeless today as it was in 1920."

"You can't have a good time in a dress that is a piece of history. Neither can you dress like a crow and expect to enjoy high spirits."

"Nonsense to both arguments. Times change. Black's no longer a dreary color for widows and the elderly."

"I still think you should wear emerald green. But, everyone to her own taste."

"I've worn my Vionnet for the last five years and each year donated the cost of a new designer dress to the Salvation Army." Hastily, she added, "I think *you* should tear yourself away from jacuzzis long enough to see what the modern age has done to Mr. Dickens' story. You might also take a break from thoughts of vengeance."

"I will take your suggestion under advisement. Here are two more rubies to exchange."

The guard walked toward them, flashlight trained on them. He touched his billed uniform cap. "Everything's quiet, Mrs. Carter."

"We're just going into Underwood. I have my set of keys. You don't have to use yours."

The guard nodded at the Major and stepped aside so they could pass him on the brick walk.

"He'll do," the Major said. "He certainly took my measure." He waved away her key ring. Opening the padlock as if it were unlocked, he stood aside and held the door for her.

"The rubies will give the jewelry store owner a heart attack from delight," Janis predicted. "May I mention a matter of the initial insurance premium and our limited budget? I don't suppose that you would care to—"

"Stop!" he said and pushed her rudely aside.

"What—?"

"The murderer has been here." His eyes glowed in the gloom of Underwood's interior.

"Benjamin, I was so worried about the antiques upstairs that I made a big thing out of security. No one—and I mean *no one*—has been in this building all day except the workmen."

He seized her arm and pulled her to his side. "He *has* been here. You are in grave danger, Janis."

His touch didn't freeze her blood, but his words did. "I'll call the guard—"

"The villain is not here now, but I want you out of here until I find what mischief he was up to."

"I'll go into my office and wait."

"Only after I check it out."

She automatically reached for the padlock on the office door, but he snatched her aside. "The aura is strong in this lobby. He may be inside the office."

"He couldn't be," Janis said. "I padlocked the door myself. After the workmen put security bars on the window."

She reached again for the padlock, and the world exploded.

NINE

Janis lay on the floor seeing stars, right arm numb.

Benjamin Blair bent over her. "Janis, love, speak to me! I couldn't have failed to keep you from being harmed. I couldn't!"

So pleasant was the sound of concern and the idea he was really upset anything had happened to her that it took another moment or two before she realized he had physically struck her away from the door and *knocked her out.* She struggled to a sitting position. "You *hit* me!"

The twisted distress on his face ironed away, and he left off his self-accusations to begin massaging his own right hand and wrist. "I never hit a woman before. But you were nearly killed by a bolt of lightning from the padlock."

She attempted to get to her feet, difficult though it was when buzzing all over, or perhaps frizzling like a piece of bacon on a hot frying pan. She mumbled, "Only s-static electricity."

"A weapon," he insisted. "Designed to kill you—if you had received the full force of it."

He still massaged his own arm. Thin curls of smoke rose from his hand and smelled like burning bacon grease. Since he had struck her hand from the padlock just at the second it touched, he had received most of the jolt himself.

His hand was cooking, from the smell of it.

"You're the one hurt!" She grasped his wrist and turned it to see the palm. Even in the less than adequate light from Underwood's lobby, she could see the ugly, black burn charring his flesh. The sight gagged her, as did the odor.

He gently forced her to release his wrist and flexed the

injured hand while the last shreds of smoke dissipated. "I will be all right in a moment. Thank your stars it was my hand not yours, dearest girl."

"You can't be all right in a minute. You're terribly burned!"

"You would have been unable to let go of the padlock." He flexed his fingers. The horrid signs of the accident faded before her eyes until his palm looked quite normal again, with no sign of injury and no lingering odor of burn. "I doubt your flesh would regenerate as quickly as mine."

His injury brought only too clearly to her the horrible probability she would indeed have been electrocuted.

He took her right hand in both of his and examined it. The fingertips were definitely blistered where she had grazed the deadly knob.

"Alas, I have no cure for these blisters of yours." He touched his tongue to each and blew gently on them. "My own fingertips ache that you should suffer pain. I hate feeling your pain more than I hate this diabolical plan of your would-be assassin."

He may have thought his kisses no cure, but their caress on her fingertips caused her first to become more buzzy-headed than ever. The sharp pain which had supplanted the numbness faded because she was so focussed on him.

"You've saved my life *again.*"

She began to tremble violently, and Benjamin gathered her against his warm chest. His heart beat as rapidly as hers, and both sets slowed together to normal. A ghost he was, she had to admit, but so real—so solid—that she could draw into her lungs the essence of new clothes, of a session in a jacuzzi, of coffee on his breath, and even of some herb crushed under his feet as they had walked through the garden.

"He's real, this murderer who's stalking me. Why does he want to kill me?"

"We'll have to discover that when we know who he is, Janis. I've asked myself over and over why I have arrived here without the piece of information that would make the picture clear."

"We have to come up with the name. Tell me more about

your partner."

"I can see him clear, a big man for his day, though lean. His wife bore him one child, a female the only heir. And so the line continued. It meant no rest for me for another generation. I don't usually make war on women, so I didn't bother her. I just waited for nature to take its course and provide a male heir."

"She must have married, and that was how the name was lost to you. You said your partner was interested in marrying the same girl you had your eye on. Who was she? That might help us find descendants."

"She was one of the Bandinis. Arcadia."

Janis bolted upright, shocked again. "But I know who married Arcadia Bandini! Dexter's great-great grandfather. They're high-nosed proud of their Bandini connection. Just as much as we are of ours with the Figueroa family."

He frowned. "Then that's a dead end. I assure you that butcher's no descendant of my assassin, in spite of his delight in carving you up like an ice sculpture. At least Doug didn't benefit with Arcadia or the strongbox. A portion of my annoyance while sitting on the bricks has been relieved.

"And I did have time to be concerned about the effect my death would have on innocents. One year, the river rampaged. My assassin's fine home went bobbing to sea with other houses, cattle and horses. In point of fact, I thought I might spend the rest of eternity at the bottom of False Bay with the bricks."

Janis murmured. "Our first family home was carried down the river in a flood. So was Dexter's."

She flashed a thought of the Major's womanizing and said briskly, "You were right about being no saint. But you have made points somewhere. Don't go messing up, whatever happens. Promise?"

"It depends," he said morosely. "I'm contracted to that oath, you realize."

Janis rubbed her cheek against his sweater. "I'll begin to go through all the names from your time who have descendants still around. At the moment I'm grateful to be alive myself, thanks to you."

His opalescent eyes glowed down at her in the moonlit dark. "You know I cannot be about to guard you during the daytime, so take care, Janis. Life is precious." His long fingers stroked her cheek. They trailed sparks like Fourth of July fireworks in the wake of his fingers.

His personal essence mixed with the sandalwood soap she had left in his room with water in the pitcher for washing and shaving. She smelled a crisp, electric, smokey aura on the hand that came under her chin to push her head up enough to look him in the eyes. His mouth came down to meet hers in a long sweet kiss that nibbled at her and deepened, parting her lips until he could slide his tongue into her mouth.

His sweet tongue questioned, teased and melted her.

Her arms circled his neck so she could return the kiss with the conviction of her feelings, whether he could love her or not, or whether he could save her life or not, whether they had a future or not.

This moment was all. Reality did not exist beyond Benjamin's lips. The pressure of his hand against the small of her back, the way she fitted against him and his body, told her that ghost or not he was all aroused male. This moment was their world.

The world ended abruptly when he raised his head, put her firmly away from him, and retreated. He turned his back to her. "I must be mad."

"Don't say anything mean or callous, Benjamin. Please, don't."

"I cannot make love to you."

"I wouldn't bet on that. You would have my enthusiastic cooperation."

"*Belissima,* I won't let it happen even though you could tempt the devil himself. My conscience won't allow it. No angels promise me heaven, no hell frightens me. I am only here to find my murderer and prevent your murder—though to date I have not made the most professional job of it. I don't want to cause you more regrets and disappointments than you have already experienced."

"You would never disappoint me, Benjamin. I'd have no regrets."

"Ah, but I would. You deserve a flesh and blood man, dear girl. Someone to cherish you the rest of your life. Someone with whom to share your life. You must connect with him as soon as possible and leave off any idea of a fantasy love life with this old haunter."

She laid her cheek against his back. "Benjamin, you're more real to me than anyone else I've known in my whole life."

He turned and put his hand over her mouth as though to push the words back. "You never have taken spirits seriously before. Do not begin at this late date." He began to fade.

Desperately she cried, "Come back! I won't take you seriously. I promise! Not...that way. If you leave, the murderer might try again. He might be anywhere. He might be anyone! Come back, Benjamin Blair! Come back here!"

A faint, mocking voice came from high above her, near the door to 201. "The security guard will see you safely off the premises. Convince yourself again that I am a hallucination."

She shrank back into the shadows, appallingly alone when she had almost been in heaven. Obviously she had no charm for even a ghost!

***

She was on her way back to *Rincon* when elusive information returned to nip at her, then to become solidly chilling. A name he'd said...*Doug?*

"...at least Doug didn't benefit with Arcadia or the strongbox." Or had he said *Doc?* Even *Duff?*

Her paternal San Diego great-great-grandfather was Robert *Douglass.*

But nothing in the family records mentioned a nickname of "Doug."

Benjamin had never turned a hair when she said the family name was Logan. She had not thought to mention Great-Great-Grandfather Douglass, *had she?*

Surely she was wrong because she was upset. Benjamin

would already know she was *not* one of his hereditary enemies—since he knew her potential murderer was a descendant of his own assassin—and he had never identified *her* with his assassin. On the other hand, there were all those details one would think he would surely know, that he didn't.

TEN

Great-great grandfather Douglass, formal and forbidding by every account, had been sternly conscious of his status as one of the city's founding fathers. He would never have tolerated a nickname derived from the shortening of his last name to "Doug." All the old newspapers back to the time Robert Douglass had arrived in Southern California referred to him as *Mr.* Douglass, with no nuance of familiarity or disrespect. He was local royalty.

But Ocho had said on occasion when describing the earliest arrival of San Diego's premier Yankee family that Robert Douglass—who never encouraged friendships and was a ruthless man in an era of dog eat dog—also always thought everyone was out to get him.

Her own father, also a ruthless man and known for being a womanizer and serial monogamist, had been ineradicably saddled with a nickname linking him to raunchy old King Henry the Eighth. Once Ocho threatened a local newspaper with a suit for putting that nickname in print. Everyone laughed at him, and all the papers picked up any excuse to use the nickname and report the results. Ocho finally accepted it as if he had invented the name for himself. Robert Douglass' far more friendly nickname of "Doug" was probably never used in records because his times were more formal, and even the use of first names was limited to intimates. Her father's lacking sense of humor about his nickname had not eradicated it, but the opposite. Though he left newspaper articles out of his own preserved records which referred to him in a derogatory manner, *Ocho* cropped up in his obituary because no one really knew him by any other name.

Perhaps Robert Douglass had had more control over the media in his day, but there were missing newspapers in the oldest portion of the collection.

Family history had it that Great-great-grandmother Cirenia's marriage to Robert Douglass was an unhappy one, and she was emotionally unstable. Ben said his partner had married Arcadia Bandini, Cirenia's sister. Janis's head swam. Nothing in the puzzle fit. She found no relief in thinking that if Robert Douglass had been partnered before Malcolm Logan by a Benjamin Blair, her situation could be more than depressing. Terrifying perhaps. She steadfastly refused to consider the ramifications...yet. Her great-great-grandfather's possible role in the scary mystery had to be examined. If he was related to it, she couldn't escape knowing she, too, must be an object of Benjamin's eventual wrath, even though he *had* said he didn't extend his vengeance to Douglass's surviving daughter.

Considering three attacks had been directed at her in as many days, she should eliminate the probability of random incidents. One other dark thought tried to insinuate and spotlight itself. She just had to believe neither awful possibility could be true.

Keith could be in a quicksand of addiction to high flyer gambling again and had pulled down on himself the wrath of a syndicate. That did not make him a killer. Syndicate's hit men were a different matter.

She needed to face Keith with the Major's warnings. If Keith still could not bring himself to reveal to her the extent of his gambling debts so she could help him off the hook, Benjamin might have to save her and let Keith take the consequences of his weakness. Of one thing she was sure. Keith was not the would-be murderer.

Keith's answering machine took the message that she had to speak to him as soon as possible. Then she rushed home.

Millard Thorpe's car sat at the curb outside her gate. In the library, Maggie Wythy sat atop the book ladder leafing through one of Ocho's books. At the copy machine, Millard Thorpe talked animatedly—*laughing*—and copying from a stack of records.

He looked around with a guilty expression on his Woodrow Wilsonesque features. “I know it’s late to find me here, Janis. I hope you don’t mind my helping your house guest with her research material?”

Distractedly, Janis encouraged him. “I’m glad Maggie has an able assistant. Don’t let me interrupt you. I have a bit of my own homework to do.”

She lugged the oldest family scrapbook, nearly the size of a steamer trunk, into the dining room, leaving Thorpe and Maggie to their own discoveries.

The scrapbook, outlining the family’s history from newspaper articles, was augmented by old daguerreotypes and snapshots, and carefully handwritten notations. A tintype of Robert Douglass scowled out at her, sandwiched between the two first sheets, framed by articles from old local papers about Robert Douglass, *one of the Old West’s royalty,* an article called him two generations later, extolling the lasting quality of Douglass-Logan city buildings still in use or long razed.

The scrapbook included material about many other local families and how they braided with the Yankee migration westward—Douglass and Logan men punctuating many of them.

She had never noticed a certain pattern before, but the scrapbook brought it to her attention. Every one of the men in the family had inglorious incidents in their record. Robert had driven Indians from property and claimed it for his own. Malcolm Logan’s oldest son died of a gunshot wound in a dispute over property with his younger brother. Her grandfather Logan had twice been sued by the city, and twice exonerated, for use of substandard materials in city construction. Ocho had been accused of draft dodging. Keith...Keith had been out of one scrape into another all his life excepting during the previous year, though none of the scandals were written into the records. The information had been handed down one way and another, generally played down except as in-family stories to snicker over.

Never a word of Benjamin Blair. Was that because he never

existed, was not part of the family's dark secrets, or had been excised from public records, just as some of the other family secrets had been?

If the Major had been murdered in the Underwood, there should be a record *somewhere* attesting to it even if only because he was a known murder victim. Part of old vital statistics. She would have to start by going through Ocho's collection of newspapers from that period.

Once a psychiatrist had called Keith a borderline psychopathic personality. If she were tainted with a borderline disordered mind, perhaps she could fantasize a murderer. Or a ghost with a family vendetta soon to target her.

The records showed Janis Logan Carter and Keith Logan were the last direct, and as far as any records, the only descendants of the family branch that led from old Robert Douglass. She shivered as though someone were stomping over her grave. Benjamin's memory would click in if she asked him about Robert Douglass. Wouldn't it?

But Keith would never...would he? Her nape prickled unbearably. If Robert Douglass wasn't the key, she *must* be the target of syndicate killers after Keith. The alternate possibility was too hideous.

Keith could easily have come into Underwood House as project supervisor, and just as easily have done the lethal electrical work. No one would have questioned him. He was part of SunSol's structure on a roving basis.

All of which made no sense to her. Keith's half of the estate would keep him in comfort for more than a lifetime.

Even as she argued with herself, she remembered Keith had no control of his own inheritance. Was it enough justification in his mind to murder her and inherit, as principal legatee, most of her half without the same restrictions? If that were true, it made her the loneliest person in the world. If he could not inherit without restrictions, he could be planning a murder with no benefit to himself. Not her own brother....

Unfortunately, Keith's multitude of serious childhood, adolescent, and adult problems offered no positive character references. His major emotional breakdown at seventeen had long been the rhinoceros in the *Rincon* living room. Everyone stepped over it, pretending it wasn't there. Keith's psychiatrist had warned them all before releasing him that there was nothing he could do to help him. *"You can't help a sociopath,"* the psychiatrist had said.

She even learned in graduate school that sociopaths lied, stole, and killed as easily as normal people said *"Hello"* or shook hands. And she had never thought about Keith in relation to such behavior until this very moment.

Something else she remembered from graduate school. Lawyers and psychiatrists wouldn't touch sociopaths with a twenty-foot pole unless they were forced to. Lawyers wouldn't bring the aberrance into court because it was so difficult to prove. And after an acquittal, the sociopath often went after the lawyer for the prosecution, or even his own lawyer—for not having represented him to his complete satisfaction.

Ocho never believed his son was a sociopath, not for a moment. And she never had and still didn't want to. But Keith *could* be the descendant of Benjamin's assassin.

He would have been more likely to have tried to kill Ocho after Ocho fired him from SunSol when he had told Keith he was going to disinherit him.

Ocho had told Keith then, *"By God, I won't turn over good money to be tossed away like confetti by someone with as little common sense of responsibility as you have. Only a fool would have tried to pull what you did, boy. I won't leave what four generations worked their tails off to build to a weakling who chews his own tail. That's what stealing from your family is, boy. Chewing your own tail."*

If Keith were a sociopath, he would have tried to murder Ocho before Ocho sold SunSol lock, stock and barrel. He didn't. That was proof enough for Janis that whatever Keith's weaknesses, being a sociopath wasn't one of them.

But Ocho had welcomed Keith back into the family after he sold the company.

Ocho believed in hard work, even if he was a sharp-dealing business competitor. He only meant to put respect for hard work into Keith by one means or another. That was why the trust income had the complicated incentive increments. Ocho explained his rationale to Janis before his death. *"By the time the boy's sixty, the administrators I chose for their wizardry with investments will have his half on so firm a foundation that he could spend pretty nearly until he was blue in the face and never end his days in poverty. That's why I advise you to let them handle your investments. I know you'll do the right thing for the family. You've always been responsible. If Keith wants to prove himself and have unlimited gambling money before he's a senior citizen, he'll have to put some muscle into it. That would probably be the making of him."*

Keith was already proving himself. *But her instincts told her Keith needed money...*a great deal of money. She had no proof he needed so much money, except for two unrelated details.

He had said, *"When you marry again, Sis, you'll make other arrangements, but if we don't keep finances under our control, the State of California will take it by default if one of us kicks the bucket unexpectedly. It happens. So, why let them pound it down a rat hole?"*

That was when he had given her a copy of his will. A simple one, leaving everything except a few personal mementos to his half-sister, Janis Logan Carter. Naturally, it followed, she gave him a copy of her own will. Except for the bequests to charities, the bulk of her half of Ocho's fortune was to go to Keith with no conditions.

She had also solemnly promised him half the proceeds from the sale *Rincon,* a promise he knew she meant to keep, and one that would put a considerable small fortune into his hands right then. His anxiety that she sell no matter how poor the offer compared to the value of the estate pointed to his urgent need for money he otherwise wouldn't have available.

Janis pushed down growing terror of the truth, but could not eliminate it once raised. One lesson she had certainly learned in the preceding few days: Don't dismiss anything out of hand, no matter how far-fetched.

Sick at heart she held up her right hand to study the blisters from the padlock. They glared at her like angry Argus eyes.

No illusion. Someone had been quite ready to fry her to death. *The monster might be Keith.*

She put her palms over her eyes. If she could bring herself to believe her brother might be trying to kill her for her inheritance, then she must believe Benjamin's curse was directed also at her. It would explain his unwillingness to make love to her when he drew the line at no one else.

No one disputed their great-great grandfather ended his life renowned as a mean old robber baron. One family story held that on his deathbed he had called for his wife's priest—a man he had hitherto only tolerated. Supposedly he remained sequestered with the priest for a significantly long period, which greatly comforted his Spanish wife, Cirenia.

Cirenia, rumored to be mental, was the one Ocho always brought up when he was most disgusted with Keith. *"You're like your crazy great-great grandmother!"*

Benjamin had said of his assassin, *"He drove his wife mad."*

Dear God! She could not stand the possibility that she was truly alone, the target of not one but two enemies—each for his own reasons, and neither of her own making. She adored her brother. She had fallen in love with Benjamin Blair, but he would soon learn that she might be one of *his* enemies.

If Benjamin proved the existence of an afterlife—heaven, hell, and in-between—Robert Douglass, on his death bed, having finally confessed to being the assassin and truly penitent, had been admitted to heaven. If he hadn't confessed, or hadn't been penitent, he was writhing somewhere in hell. Surely that ought to satisfy Benjamin.

Except that Benjamin was, by his own claim, no saint geared to forgiving enemies. He was more human than any ghost had a right to be.

She desperately needed to look for another answer that did not make her brother a would-be murderer like his great-great-grandfather and possibly others in the line if Robert Douglass had tainted the family. If Robert Douglass had made her one of Benjamin Blair's hereditary enemies, he had one more monstrous sin charged to him, and he would be forcing her help him carry it unless there was...the ghost of an alternative.

She did not want to be responsible for Benjamin having to spend eternity in limbo. He was doing no harm spending it in a jacuzzi.

Heavy with her burden of misery as well as the scrapbook, Janis went back to the library. Her hand on the library door, she heard Maggie say her name. Mother Anne used to say that eavesdroppers never hear any good of themselves, but she listened anyway.

"...Janis was one of the sweetest girls on campus in her time, and always a nice-looking girl. Her lovely complexion was a blessing not granted to many under twenty-one."

Millard Thorpe, who had known her at least peripherally since she was in grammar school, agreed.

Maggie chattered on. "She has always had such lovely eyes, too. Of course now she's what they call a raving beauty, but I was never so surprised in my life as when she returned to campus after her divorce looking so *different* from her undergraduate days. Still, I never could understand why she felt the need for the surgery. She wasn't a vain girl at all."

They were talking discreetly enough, and if Janis had properly closed the library door when she left with the scrapbook, she wouldn't have had to overhear Maggie and Millard's idle conversation.

"We feel fortunate she sought the position of Association Director," Millard Thorpe said. "I can tell you she takes after her father. Ocho could sell iceboxes to Eskimos. She stood firm on the matter of top salary. Said we must pay a comparable salary to other agencies. She donates it back to the building fund, which leaves the item in the operations budget. She's already hit us up for a raise this coming year. And they'll vote for it because they know she's giving it back. As long as she's director, fine. If another agency ever steals her from us, we'll be able to afford the salaried director and nothing else."

Janis stopped eavesdropping before she really did hear something to lower her spirits even more than they already were depressed. Enough that Millard Thorpe was discussing a matter intended to be kept quiet.

She bumped the library door with the huge book, and noisily pushed it open. Millard and Maggie stood silent at the copy machine, looking uncomfortable at her abrupt entry.

"You're still here?" Janis asked.

"We thought you had gone up for the evening," Maggie said. "Millard was just saying that on top of the time you've already given to your job today, you probably were putting in another day's work upstairs in your home office."

Millard Thorpe said, "We were actually discussing efficiency. Maggie agrees with me that all work and no play reduces efficiency. I had just suggested to Dr. Wythy here, that she might enjoy a recess from her research and attend a baroque concert with me on Thursday and you might be persuaded to join us."

Maggie looked more likely to find Janis a fifth wheel. Janis smiled brightly. "What a nice idea! But my week's booked solid with pre-holiday-season meetings. I can't possibly join you. However, you both might like to share my box at the opening night of *A Christmas Carol* at the Civic Theater, Friday evening. Four tickets go with the box and include the reception and supper dance following the performance. I'd really like to make use of all four tickets included in my position of sponsorship."

Millard said cautiously, with a hopeful eye to Maggie, "I have no other plans for Friday."

Maggie gushed, "How gracious of you to include us, Jan.We'd be delighted to join you, wouldn't we, Millard?"

Thorpe was looking less horsey than Janis had ever seen him. Almost handsome. By the look Maggie gave him, he was as sexy as Sean Connery. If Janis weren't mistaken, there was a smell of springtime and the merry month of May in the room even though it was the first week of December outside the house.

Certainly Janis didn't know *anyone* else who ever called Mr. Thorpe by his first name. "Then it's settled. Incidentally, dress at the event runs the gamut from casual to white tie. I'm going to wear an old black, floor-length dress. An old black dress everyone in town has seen a dozen times or more."

Maggie preened. "I happened to have brought a holiday dress with me, in case of an appropriate opportunity to wear it."

Millard Thorpe looked as close to eager as Janis had ever seen him look. "I could brush off my dinner jacket."

The prospect of the benefit performance and all its perks roused little enthusiasm in Janis. Nevertheless, she pasted a smile on her face and pretended for their benefit that it would be great fun.

ELEVEN

Friday morning, Nordstrom's delivered a large box to Janis Carter at Wharton House.

"I didn't order this," she said.

"Paid for, ma'am." The delivery man whipped out the receipt and directions plainly showing it was for Janis Logan Carter, care of Wharton House, to be delivered no later than Friday noon.

"Let me check the contents. I haven't been near Nordstrom's in months." She dug through a generous amount of tissue until she came to iridescent blue-green taffeta and lifted out an Oscar de la Renta very bare of shoulder and back. In her size.

"It's you, all right," the delivery man said.

The gown was a far cry from the ancient Vionnet respected as a collector's item and for its timeless elegance and history. The de la Renta iridescent green, slit to high on the thigh and lavishly ruffled, was utterly fantastic, to the minute drop-dead gorgeous. With it was an enormous triangular ruffled wrap, lined in matching velvet. She simply had to throw the sensual wrap around her shoulders, just to test its silky, sensual embrace. The effort of removing it simply to place it back in the tissue instead of wearing it for the rest of the day was considerable. She couldn't possibly send the ensemble back unless she had to.

"No buyer's name?"

"You have the receipt right there, lady."

She made a weak compromise. "I'll call the department and tell them if anyone asks about it before this evening, I'll see it gets where it was meant to go."

***

Ryan crooked his arm. Millard Thorpe, every passing minute looking less like Woodrow Wilson and more like Sean Connery, echoed the gesture with Maggie.

Maggie was smashing in what was for her a subdued dinner dress of crepe in garnet color, with a matching evening coat embroidered in gold, silver, and bronze. Ryan could turn a few heads himself.

He wore a dinner jacket well. His auburn hair *sans* freckles and with the even tan of someone who pays attention to the acquiring of it also made him stand out in a crowd.

She said as tactfully as possible, "Ryan, we'll need to take my rental car, because there are so many of us, and your little Porsche won't hold us."

Ryan puffed a bit. "Didn't bring the Porsche. We go in style." He ushered them onto the portico of *Rincon.* In the circular driveway, a silver-gray stretch limousine idled, chauffeur standing ready.

Janis's eyes popped. "Ryan Aherne, you have no business spending such money on a limo!"

"Didn't," he whispered into her ear.

She drew back, her eyebrows making a question mark.

"This afternoon the A-Triple-A Limousine Service contacted me and told me one was mine for the evening."

"Curiouser and curiouser," as Alice in Wonderland would say. If the committee for the charity had seen fit to get a limo company to *donate* the service because she had written a ten-thousand-dollar check to the Salvation Army benefit for the homeless, she could see it. But Nordstrom's had not donated the dress. And if the committee had for some inexplicable reason taken the limo out of expenses, she intended to blow whistles so loudly at the organizers that they would never again waste what was meant to go to charity. She knew from being on the Salvation Army Board that her ten thousand dollar donation entitled her to the box, the reception, the supper, and nothing else.

Not that she believed in the easy discharge of her charities by writing checks. On every holiday the last three years she had washed dishes in the kitchen of the Salvation Army Shelter while some of the most important people in the city served turkey and gravy in the dining room. Christmas she would no doubt be doing the same, as well as whenever she could during the rainy season. At least one Sunday a month she helped out at the Community Services Shelter, and she wrote other charity checks.

She avoided distressing Ryan and her other two guests with her feelings about stewardship of charity funds. They were impressed with the luxury transportation. When push came to crunch, she would pay the bill gladly out of pocket and never miss it.

Millard Thorpe advised Maggie as they sipped sherry from the limousine bar, "The patrons pulled a coup this year, getting an actor of the status they did for a weekend of performances. You're in for a treat."

"I've had to sit through so many productions of this," Ryan said, "that my attitude is `Bah Humbug.' I saw him in it a year or two ago at the La Jolla Playhouse."

Janis glanced at him from the corner of her eye, wishing he would not put on a jaded act.

When their group entered the lobby of the Westgate, flashbulbs popped, and the lights from the TV crews blinded. Janis smiled brightly at Ryan for the benefit of the cameras, gave Maggie's titles and the spelling of her name to the Channel Ten TV people, and moved toward the stairs leading to the reception area. She couldn't help overhearing one of the TV crew say, "Wish every couple we shot was that photogenic. They'll make the tape."

Ryan squeezed her arm. He'd heard the cameraman, too. "Surefire publicity for the ConVis Bureau *and* the Historical Association!"

The four moved on up the stairs with the crowd. Janis uneasily scanned everyone hoping Keith hadn't decided to attend the opening night. Until her grave suspicions about his gambling activities were allayed, she really didn't want to deal with him. He was unlikely to make even small donations, and the evening's version of culture, whether connected to charity or not, was not Keith's idea of entertainment. His idea of charity, Janis had heard him say more than once, was to put all the homeless to work at stoop labor and get them off welfare. His idea of entertainment was a high stakes gambling casino.

The concerned and wealthy of San Diego crowded the glittering reception area. Janis didn't object to the five foot silver champagne fountain. That was annually donated for the occasion along with the champagne.

Maggie gave an odd little gasp. "...Oh, my dear, back by the door—they just came in—the man with the two blondes, one almost in a red dress, or slip or whatever it is, and the other girl in outrageous purple sequins...?"

Through a temporary aisle, Janis focused on the group of three and received a direct wink from the man escorting the blondes.

Benjamin Blair!

He strolled toward them, a blonde on each arm. His midnight blue dinner jacket came from Versace and fit to the millimeter. Heads turned, because, regardless of the one blonde's minimum dress—a Nolan Miller; and the other blonde's blinding sequins; a Bob Mackie—San Diego rarely displayed such a gorgeous man. The two girls would eclipse everyone but the star of the charity show. Benjamin Blair would succeed in eclipsing the star.

Benjamin, giving Janis a happy little high sign as he steamrolled across the floor toward her with the girls, annoyed her beyond reason. How dare he!

"He's smiling and waving at you, dear. Good heavens, what an attractive man!"

"I know," Janis acknowledged through gritted teeth.

Careful! her instincts warned. She could say the wrong thing and never be able to get her feet out of her mouth. "His name is Benjamin Blair. He hasn't been in San Diego long, but I met him recently."

On consideration, she ran glibly through his genealogy as he had given it to her. She might as well lay a foundation of explanation for his donating the Harrison and Washington family antiques—information sure to be necessary sooner or later.

Millard Thorpe peered over his tri-focals. "Really? I never heard of him, and I have made an avocation of studying our country's first families. As far as I know, the Harrison line died out."

Dr. Maggie came to the rescue from left field. "Wrong, Millard. When I was a student at UCLA, I knew an architect who was descended from the Harrisons. And very proud of it. That was years ago, I admit, but his name wasn't Harrison, and as I remember his family tree was fairly extensive. There's no reason to doubt Mr. Blair's family tree just because his branch moved out of the limelight. He might even be related to the man I knew."

Janis improvised. "He stopped by Wharton House, and we had a brief visit earlier this week—I don't think any of you were there at the time. Maj—Mr. Blair's something of a genius at making money—er—through commodities. And very interested in our Historical Association."

Before Benjamin came up to them, Rudy Rodriguez from the County Board of Supervisors intercepted the trio. He welcomed Benjamin like a long-lost brother, was introduced to the blondes, and after a moment of conversation during which Janis nearly popped her eardrums in an unsuccessful attempt to hear what was being said, drew Benjamin the last few yards to where the four from the Historical Association stood.

"One of our new patrons," Supervisor Rodriguez said. "A very *generous* patron, too, you'll be glad to know, Mrs. Carter. I know you already are aware of his strong interest in the work of the Historical Association."

"I know Maj—Mr. Blair," she said, and introduced her companions.

Rudy Rodriguez harrumphed at Maggie. "Ah, yes! A friend told me of the—ahem, interesting—experiments you've been doing at the Horton Grand. Have you turned up any new and improved spirits in our fair city?"

Maggie said calmly, "One or two, Mr. Rodriguez. You must read my report in the quarterly *Journal of Psychic*

Research and Parapsychology."

"I'll do that, Doctor." Rudy Rodriguez was wearing his most distinctly patronizing tone of voice. He turned his attention to Benjamin's dazzling female companions.

Janis was possessed of a sudden desire to see Benjamin Blair de-materialize slowly, taking his blondes with him, leaving nothing but the after-image of opalescent blue eyes. He remained maddeningly corporeal.

Ryan asked, "How long have you been in San Diego, Mr. Blair? I pride myself on being the first to welcome visitors and newcomers, but I hadn't heard of your arrival until this evening."

"I think I may have met you before, Mr. Blair," Millard Thorpe said. "I do seem to have a strong sense of it—you'll forgive an old man's bad memory?"

"I visited Wharton House earlier this week. But our paths evidently did not cross." Benjamin gave them all his easy smile. "I generally keep a low profile. Did Mrs. Carter tell you I may be interested in parting with some of my family's things for your projected museum in Underwood House?"

Millard Thorpe looked questioningly at Janis. "We will see if we can help her to be far-sighted regarding some matters she and I aren't in agreement with as yet."

Maggie, strangely subdued, thrust forth a hand, which Benjamin took in both of his. "I knew who you were from the moment I came in the door," he said. "I have read many of your reports and have wanted to meet you for some time. Your research affects me deeply. I say that sincerely."

Maggie stared down at the hands clasping hers. Janis didn't dare guess what might be running through Maggie's mind. The parapsychologist must be confused by something about the handclasp, for her face wore a totally bemused expression. Janis held her breath.

When Benjamin released Maggie's hand, she looked dazed and turned towards Millard Thorpe, shaking her head as if to clear cobwebs. Benjamin meanwhile turned his prismatic gaze on Janis.

She had received the dress and had worn it. The girl was

so beautiful he wanted to burst into an Italian love song on the spot, but he refrained. "You look wonderful, Ms. Carter. Mr. Aherne is a lucky man."

Ryan moved closer and claimed her arm. "I'll say." His chin moved forward pugnaciously, and Benjamin Blair worked hard to keep himself from literally turning green with jealousy, from thundering, from producing lightning that would strike the pup down.

Hastily Janis asked Ryan to bring her a glass of champagne. He released her arm with obvious reluctance to brave the crowd around the champagne fountain.

Tongue-tied at the moment, she was unable to blurt out her suspicions regarding her family. "I—er—have you seen the paintings on exhibit here? All by local artists, and all donated to the cause." She drew him away from the others to the far side of the room where the paintings had been hung.

She wondered if she should tell him before she did more digging into the records. If she told him prematurely, she could endanger Keith. And she simply could not bear to think of him towering over her and the others in all his vengeful anger when she was an innocent bystander. But of course he would know if her suspicions were true or misplaced, and what must be would be. She gathered her courage.

"Surprised to see me?" he asked.

The question distracted her from her intentions. "Why did you decide to come?"

He lifted an eyebrow. "You expressly advised me to do so. I even joined you in becoming a patron."

Temporarily forgetting her resolve to speak to him about her great-great-grandfather, she glanced back at the two blondes being entertained by Rudy Rodriguez and the Deputy Mayor of San Diego. "I presume those are proud possessors of jacuzzis?"

He grinned but lowered his expressive left eyebrow at her. "You have no right to complain. You're flaunting your agency friend. We are both free to flirt with whom we like."

"I am *not* flirting with Ryan! My association with him is a simple working one, quite different from your—!"

"How different?" he teased.

"Different!" she said petulantly. "My ex-husband is also going to be here—probably escorting one or another of my bridesmaids. I must admit the man has no shame, but I long ago scratched the whole perfidious bridal party off my Christmas card list." She looked about at the exponentially increasing crowd. "I wonder why I don't see him yet. He never misses a social situation, and he's never late."

Benjamin cleared his throat. "He is unavoidably detained. He had a minor accident coming up the stairs."

"Benjamin—What do you mean?"

He lifted his hands in a gesture of innocence. "I *swear* I didn't touch him. My friends and I were already at the top of the stairs and stood for a second looking back. There he was, halfway up. He saw me and stumbled. There were dozens of people between us. Every one of them are my witnesses, if you must quiz them."

Janis wasn't convinced. "Exactly how serious an accident was it?"

"The management handled it with a minimum of fuss and distraction. I understand he hit his nose on the bannister as he went down." Benjamin pushed his own aristocratic nose to the right until it lay obligingly against his cheek. The moment he removed his finger, his nose snapped back into alignment. She doubted Dexter's had.

Benjamin regarded her righteously. "Unfortunately, he will now need to undergo corrective surgery by one of his colleagues and, for odd genetic reasons, his nose will henceforth be as obliging to him as mine is to me, but perhaps a bit trickier to manage. It does sound a note of retribution, does it not? I cannot blame you for your initial suspicion."

"You know entirely too much about the accident to convince me you had *nothing* to do with it."

He maintained his air of injured innocence. "You harbor too many suspicions, but I admit I have no appreciation for what he did and is planning to do to you. Have I mentioned that?"

"You refer to his sleight of hand in real estate dealings,

infidelities, or performing his own brand of magic, plastic surgery on wealthy women?"

"All of them," he said promptly.

She whispered fiercely, "You just can't—"

"Now, now! If we are to get along as friends, you must believe I would never lay a hand on him."

She had to say what she had dragged him to this isolated corner to say. "I don't know if we can continue to be friends, Benjamin. There's something I need to discuss with you *very* seriously."

"Such a serious face, ma'am! I declare a moratorium for tonight on serious. We will talk tomorrow night when I meet you in your office after dark."

"But—"

He put a firm forefinger on her lips. "Hush, if you do not wish everyone to hear thunder and see lightning. Here comes your dashing escort."

He was forcing twenty-four hours on her to confirm or discard her suspicions. "All right, but I warn you, I mean *very* serious."

He grinned. "I wouldn't have Mr. Dickens' play spoiled for the world by my ill humor at receiving `serious.' Speaking of serious matters, you will admit my choice of green is superior to your choice of black?"

She stared. "It was *you!"*

"Bought it last night just before the store closed its doors."

"And the limo!"

"I wanted your evening to be memorable."

"Don't worry. It's rapidly totaling up all sorts of points to make it memorable!"

"Good. I shall therefore admit to having pricked your ex-husband's conscience. And that conscience made him stumble, not I. By the way—one of the young ladies I am escorting tonight—has *three* noses. It seems she wasn't fond of the second one, done by your ex-husband. However, though she had the job done again, she still isn't entirely happy. I advised her to let well enough alone. This era of yours is vastly odd in its demand for bland good looks. There are so many other more interesting aspects than bland."

"For those of us who can't see the whole truth and nothing but the truth, there are some justifications for reconstructive surgeons."

"Not in my estimation so far. Which brings me to this fellow, Aherne. Pleasant. I perceive he is well-liked by the hierarchy and his co-workers. Has a future, is ethical, proud as punch to be seen with you. Half in love already."

Stiffly she warned him, "I told you—he's only a working colleague."

"I wish only to let you know he has a good heart and would treat you like a queen. You could go further and do worse than fall in love with him. He would be faithful once brought up to the mark."

"All I need is you to play matchmaker. Don't you *dare!*"

"I simply wanted to bring him to your attention."

She turned and looked for Ryan. If Benjamin spoke intimately into her ear for one more minute, she would do something absolutely...outrageous. She supposed it was his total non-availability which allowed her to give free rein to her romantic fantasies' need for an outlet. That made her certifiable. Nevertheless, he reduced her to a breathless inability to concentrate on why she should be terribly annoyed with him, inability to keep her mind on her work or on logic or....

"You can go a long way down the road of life and not find a better man than the red-headed one," Benjamin said insidiously into her ear.

She turned to tell him he was far off the track, collided with him, and made no move to step back. Into the corner of his mouth she said, "Sometimes I wish you had even as much intuition as Maggie has. Yours is awful, or you'd know I feel no attraction to Ryan except that he's one of the best public relations executives I've ever met. Don't you know I'm attracted to you so much I'm in danger of creating a scandal right here in this crowd!"

Now *that* was the state to which he had reduced her. Totally vulnerable and open to total rejection.

"I should be flattered," he said, and he did not step back either. "Here comes Ryan. You will not wish to embarrass yourself, my girl."

He was immune to her cow-eyed obsession with him.

Ryan pushed by Benjamin to present her with a glass of champagne and a plate of chilled shrimp, crab, and lobster shishkebab. "Whew, this is some crowd! People might wonder how well you and whatsisname know each other if they weren't all in the same predicament. Just slither over toward the window wall, where there's room to lift your elbow. That's it. Careful now."

Once Ryan had her separated from the Major to a reasonable extent, he said cheerfully, "The actor was a star in that pop series that went on for years, and he's now in a movie derived from the series. Good in the role of Scrooge, of course, but after one has seen a story about ghosts a dozen times, spirits lose their charm, don't you think?"

"Certain spirits can be nothing but charming," Benjamin said blandly. "It happens this will be the first time I've seen the play, and I look forward with all the excitement of a tad."

Janis surreptitiously pinched Ryan to keep him from saying one more stupid word.

Benjamin went right on as though she couldn't tell he had noticed the pinch. "I am in Janis's debt for telling me about tonight. I would not wish to have missed any part of such a pleasant evening."

She suspected the bloodthirsty, randy Major considered part of his pleasant experience had been dealing with Dexter, however indirectly. And then there were the two blondes. She wanted to hate him for the blondes, and for being unattainable where she was concerned, but she couldn't even begin to hate him.

"Libbi and Rhonda would rather have gone to something they called a `rap concert' at the Sports Arena. I promised I would attend with them tomorrow night."

Ryan winked. "Not my idea of culture, though you do have attractive company to take your mind off the noise."

"You cannot recommend the performance?" Benjamin

asked.

"Wouldn't be caught dead. Neither would Jan, would you, Jan?"

She wished he would speak only for himself.

"It happens I have no objection to being caught dead." Benjamin snagged a passing waiter with an hors d'oeuvres tray.

"There goes the ten-minute bell," Ryan said. "We'd best be getting across to the Civic Theater, Janis."

The peripatetic Major went to collect his ladies.

Later, seated comfortably in the upholstered box seats, she delivered to Maggie her spare pair of opera glasses.

"Mysterious Mr. Blair has the box opposite us," Maggie observed via the glasses.

Janis scanned discreetly, and there he sat on the other side of the proscenium. He looked right at her, winked and put his arm around both the blondes. Janis scowled through her opera glasses.

"I know that Benjamin Blair—from somewhere," Maggie said. "I can't think from where, but I do."

Janis glowered at him. He needn't be having such a good time over there in his box. The girls appeared to be having much too good a time, too. He was an absolutely unspeakable flirt if not a downright tomcat!

She stiffened when Ryan slid his arm around her shoulders, only too aware in the minute or two before the play began, that Benjamin was visibly endorsing Ryan's familiarity, and she was not.

"The thing I like most about you, Jan," Ryan said, "is that we like the same things in life. For example, neither of us would be caught dead at a rap concert."

In truth she longed to be a mouse at the rap concert. No one had ever suggested she go to one, but who knew but she might like it. She wished she could share in Benjamin's introduction to Rap. She looked across at the other box. Benjamin still appeared to be having a wonderful time. The blondes still looked as if they were having an even more wonderful time helping him have a wonderful time, whether any of them were spell-bound by the spirit of Christmas according to Dickens or not.

Beside Janis, Maggie whispered, "You look more relaxed than I have seen you since I came."

Janis glanced at her, controlling her desire to scream. Maggie's ability to tune on the paranormal was amazing, but in zeroing in on what was going on in front of her nose, she wasn't infallible.

The infuriating man in the box on the other side of the auditorium continued to allow the blondes to whisper into his ears, if indeed that was all they were doing. Janis wished the blondes in limbo, and from across the way, Benjamin admonished her with a wagging forefinger.

Janis lowered her opera glasses and with the utmost dignity concentrated on the stage.

After the final curtain, Maggie discovered she had left her scarf in the ladies' lounge and went to retrieve it.

Millard Thorpe took the opportunity to thank Janis effusively. "A most enjoyable evening. Most enjoyable." He cleared his throat and regarded her through his tri-focals. "Although Dr. Wythy has obviously outrageous pursuits, I can't understand why she never married."

"The story on campus was that she loved a man with whom she quarreled. He enlisted in the army, was precipitately sent to Viet Nam, and was reported as missing and presumed dead. She tried to contact him through psychics and seances to let him know she deeply regretted their misunderstanding. Though she was unable to reach him, she found what to her were definite evidences of other paranormal activities. By the time she could go ahead with her life because she was over her loss, she had fallen in love with parapsychology. A number of years later, she found her lover was still very much alive, but he had decided not to return to *her.*"

Mr. Thorpe looked deeply distressed at the story.

"Maggie is quite philosophical about it," Janis stated. "She even uses the story in her lectures to point out that many veterans came home much changed by the experience, and he was one of those. She took his being alive as a proof of her hypothesis and believes to this day that if he had been killed in action, she would somehow have contacted him on the other side."

"Misdirected passions," he said sadly. "No wonder she's a bit about in the head. Poor woman. We all have our odd side. There are some who consider me a bit around the bend in my perhaps over-weaning obsession with nineteenth century military history in this area. "

"Not at all, Mr. Thorpe," Janis assured him. "People like you keep history alive. Have you ever run across any mention of one of Mr. Blair's antecedents, a Major Blair, supposedly here in the San Diego area 1869 and before?"

"Stationed with a local military unit?"

"A Civil War veteran in local trade, but still known by his military title, I believe."

He considered. "I can't say I have."

She hadn't expected Mr. Thorpe to have heard of the Major, but that eliminated possibility was disappointing. Mr. Thorpe mentioned several men of San Diego's early era who had been involved in the Civil War, including her own great-great grandfather. She listened, semi-distracted. Benjamin, arm and arm with his two blondes, was descending the opposite stair. She smiled down frostily at them.

I'm so jealous! She had discovered she did have murderous impulses. Inherited? She wanted to strangle Benjamin Blair. Lucky for him, he was already dead.

***

Maggie accepted a nightcap cup of hot cocoa. "What a lovely evening! I don't know when I've enjoyed *A Christmas Carol* as much. He's quite a wonderful actor."

"I think Mr. Thorpe enjoyed himself, too," Janis said.

"He doesn't say a great deal, except about historical military figures in the San Diego area."

"It's a serious hobby with him, Maggie. He's rather lonely, having been a widower these last two years."

"Really?" Maggie asked casually.

"They were married forty years. Mrs. Thorpe was an inspiration to everyone locally who cared about the area's original community. Almost single-handedly she started the movement to preserve historical landmark homes. He joined her efforts and, since her death and his retirement, he has been one hundred percent active in the work of the Association. He also is noted for his knowledge of American military uniforms and customs from Colonial days and was a military man himself at one time."

"In the Engineering Corps, no doubt. He has the personality of an engineer," Maggie mused. "And if he was truly happy with his wife, I'm sure she was a very nice lady." After a considering silence she said, "Probably very conservative, probably a D.A.R., certainly a lady who never made a spontaneous move in her life."

Janis wondered if Maggie was a little jealous of a different sort of ghost herself. But Maggie's problems were nothing to her own.

Maggie came over and firmly placed her blue-veined hand on Janis's arm. "My dear, I found some extremely interesting material in your Underwood House attic archives this morning, and this is the first I've had an opportunity to speak of it to you."

Janis jumped up, almost breathless at the possibilities. "You found material on Major Benjamin Blair?"

"What? No, dear, if you had mentioned you were researching Mr. Blair's background I should have been pleased to do so. Perhaps on Monday? No, what I found is rather more of a negative nature. I thought you might like the papers in your own keeping, not in a public place."

"Then...what in the world—?"

"I'll go fetch it. Forgive me for having smuggled it back here and put it in my room. If you would rather it be put back where I found it, I'll do so."

She ran upstairs and immediately returned with a dog-eared manila folder marked *Tax records prior to 1980.* She placed it firmly in Janis's hands.

Janis raised a questioning eyebrow.

"Not what you think, dear. It must have been misplaced at some time prior to your father's death."

Janis opened the envelope. There were a few tax records from her grandfather's time—of the kind probably saved as interesting historical bits and pieces. But there was principally another folder within the folder. An envelope folder, the kind that comes with a flap and is tied closed. Someone had bordered that secondary file folder front and back with a black marking pen as some kind of special designation. Obviously it was no ordinary file folder

Flushing slightly, Maggie said, "Whoever tied that tape wanted it to stay tied. I broke a fingernail working it open because I was determined to see what it contained. Even old tax records can be most informative and hide bits of information that lead to all sorts of things. But I didn't expect to find what I did."

Janis opened the second folder, well-filled with every variety of material. None were tax records.

The first sheet was a letter from the head psychiatrist at the private hospital where Keith had been a patient in his adolescence. The letter advised Ocho that release of his patient was necessary because state law mandated it under new laws regarding holding patients against their will when said patients were nondelusional and showed no tendencies to be of danger to self or others. In his considered opinion, such a release was a serious mistake. Therapy had simply taught Keith how to protect his sociopathic tendencies.

Other papers included police reports, school reports and therapist reports dating back to Keith's early childhood. To before she was born. To before his mother had run away with the accountant.

Her brother had led far more than a high-spirited childhood and adolescence. More than a rebellious childhood and adolescence. More than the one psychiatrist's diagnosis of *sociopathic personality* seemed born out by evidence seen previously. Keith's quixotic or violent impulses were often followed by a targeted path to whatever goal he fancied might suit his purpose, however illogical it would seem to anyone else.

And in most cases his action was blind to any sign he

could not possibly get away with it undetected.

Janis could not look at the material without understanding why Keith's mother might have chosen to leave *everything* behind her. The material gave adequate insight into why Ocho had run out of patience, yet finally relented enough to provide for him.

"I feel sure your father didn't intend this to be in the other file," Maggie said. "It must have been misplaced."

Janis felt sure Maggie was right. "I'll put this in the house safe for the time being," she said. Especially since that folder needed to be considered in light of the threats to Janis' life. And why.

She considered the postponed discussion with Benjamin. Before she discussed with him her concerns about the Logan-Douglass ties to him, she wanted to know for sure they had irrefutably existed. She was determined not to precipitate an unnecessary tragedy involving her own relationship with Keith.

The suspicions, the circumstantial evidence, all were unfounded. They had to be.

TWELVE

All night Janis tossed and fretted, trying to think of a way she would not be forced by her own sense of ethics to tell Benjamin what she had uncovered. If she didn't, would he think she had attempted to deceive him? Yes, all things being equal, he would.

She was sure his powers of intuition, though fallible, would be well up to seeing the truth. He would *know.* And Keith would not be the one Benjamin was looking for....

Conversely, she thought about her misery if they were the descendants Benjamin was sworn to see die. She would rather he simply showed up in the worst of his thunder and lightning storms and delivered retribution without her having to wait for it, dread it.

As for Keith, there was a perfectly logical, though none too comforting conclusion. Regardless of Keith's place in the horror she faced, the demon that pursued him most fiercely was his proved gambling addiction, and the possibility he was again being threatened for gambling debt.

She sat bolt upright in bed at one point, *knowing* in that way one has when everything comes together, that Keith was in trouble with a gambling syndicate again, knowing they were using her to get to him.

She had no appetite for breakfast, but put on a cheery face. Maggie consumed enough for both of them, and having no idea what was eating at her hostess, drove off to Villa Montezuma intent on yet another paranormal investigation. Janis listlessly dragged off to work—late, but it was Saturday and she wasn't scheduled, so it didn't make any difference what time she arrived.

Nancy Rogers interrupted a training session with new docents to say workmen had been on duty since before she had come in and she had received a call from the Central Downtown Library.

"The young man said they're doing a display on early San Diego newspapers and asked if we might make copies of any newspapers they don't have that we do, from the earliest in the 1840s through 1870. They gave me their list. He didn't give his name. He said your brother said you knew more about this sort of thing than he did, and you probably could find the papers in the third floor loft. The library needs them soonest. The librarian said if they have any you don't have, they'll be happy to make copies of theirs for your collection."

"I'll take care of it this morning. I want to browse the old files anyway."

"It's a madhouse over at Underwood even though it's Saturday. A double crew's on the job."

"We need double crews if we're going to open by our target date, the week before Christmas. That's another reason I'm here today—to work on details of the opening event."

The paint crew crawled about the exterior scaffolding finishing the exterior painting. Janis's head spun and her stomach bounced alarmingly even to glance at them. Inside, the free-standing staircase had been set firmly in place and spiraled up into the dark woods of the high interior. She was able to appreciate it from across the lobby, at a distance.

"Ain't it a handsome piece?" the foreman asked her. "You wouldn't think a rough old frontier hotel would put on that kinda dog."

She laughed. "The Gold Rush era builder of the Sacramento hotel that was similar to Underwood commissioned this for his hotel and considered money no object where his rough and ready miner patrons were concerned." As she passed on the way to her office, she touched the yellow warning ribbon threaded across the bottom layer. "What's the danger?" Her stomach jumped just identifying a possible problem. "Surely, not of...collapsing?"

"Heck no, Ms. Logan Carter. The thing's up there to stay.

I don't want my men roughing it up, that's all. They're to use the temporary work stairs."

She cautiously admired the considerable achievement it had been to install the antique. It swept from first floor to third, but the effort to look at it from so close nauseated her even with her feet on the solid local stone of the first floor lobby.

"You can get an impressive look at the symmetry of it from right here by leaning back as far as you can and looking straight up," the foreman invited.

She became dizzy just listening to his well-meant suggestion. Merely looking at just the bottom step with her two feet planted on the marble lobby floor was quite enough to trigger her fear of heights and disorient her sense of balance. She swallowed down phantom vertigo and smiled weakly at the foreman. "I'll be using the back stairs or that nice little closed Otis."

"The Otis ain't in operation this weekend. The man has to come back Monday and work on the cable system. If you need to go up to the third floor, use the workmen's stairs to the second floor, then the back stairs to the third floor."

She left her things in the office, and he left her at the back stairs. She closed her eyes, even though the staircase was well-railed, graded, and enclosed. All the newspaper collection was by this time stored in the third floor shell. Up to the third floor she meant to go and would have braved the circular stairs if need be.

Inside the cavernous unfinished third floor, the light from the heavy-duty extension cord over a rough beam was sufficient to illuminate the area packed with stored equipment and furnishings miscellany. Another bare bulb lit the area where Ocho's newspaper files and old Association files were stored in file cabinets lined against the back wall amidst cartons of books and records no one but she had looked at in years.

She had sat through the last three Association meetings while a vocal battle raged over the merits of establishing offices on the third floor versus leasing more central offices off Fifth or Sixth Avenue, near the Park in downtown San Diego. She still hoped to persuade them to use Underwood's third floor and keep the Association in the area where most of the Heritage Homes were grouped. Utilize a building they owned. Her voice, backed by the Logan money, was important.

She threaded past the remaining furniture from Adams Avenue Antiques, and pulled on the second extension light before delving into Ocho's newspaper files. Issues of the city's first newspapers were surprisingly numerous in the first years, and equally surprising gaps occurred which she had never particularly marked earlier—such as the last two weeks of January, 1869; all but one issue of February the same year, and two in March—crucial issues that would likely cover any information about the murder of one Major Benjamin Blair if such murder had occurred.

She removed the library's requested materials, which she found in one of the fireproof-waterproof boxes, and took them over to Wharton House for Nancy. She could work after that, undisturbed, on the opening program arrangements. The job helped her avoid thinking about meeting with Benjamin after sunset. How could she find words to tell him about Robert Douglass?

The sun slid across the early December sky; the workers left; the security guard began making rounds. Every passing minute increased her anxiety, but she had no choice. If Benjamin was bent on revenge, and that revenge included herself, she wanted to know it without any accusation that she had lied or tried to hide it from him. She wanted to get the worst over with. She comforted herself with knowing that aside from his one little hang-up he had a wonderfully kind nature. Surely he knew she had no malice in her.

The sky darkened. Resolutely, she said into the empty lobby, "Major Blair? Benjamin?" *Dear Benjamin? Sweet Benjamin?*

No answer.

She climbed the workmen's set of stairs and politely knocked on the door to Room 201.

With her hand raised for another knock, a flash of revelation struck. She had been entirely too confident that

Ocho's files contained every newspaper copy extant. She had not searched the *Association* files for any but dates of issues the library wanted, and they had not included that era.

Could it be those issues were really missing from Ocho's files by other than coincidence?

The gap question began to nag at her. Why should those *particular* issues be missing?

The Association Files, admittedly inferior to Ocho's, could conceivably have one or more missing copies from the winter of 1869 that would prove once and for all that the original Major Benjamin Blair had existed and had been murdered in the original Underwood Hotel, and what his connection might or might not be to her family.

Her oversight stemmed from Ocho's own smug assurance that his father's, grandfather's and great-grandfather's collection was the most complete that could be found. Perhaps it was incomplete for a reason her great-great-grandfather could have explained had he wished.

As surely as if drawn by a magnet, she was again drawn to the third floor and this time to delving into the Association's newspaper editions.

To her dismay, since her morning trek upstairs, the back stairs to the third floor from the second floor had a one-by-four nailed across the safety rail posts. Though she hated to have to use the spiral, she stepped from the main gallery onto it and climbed resolutely toward the third floor level. She kept her eyes on the risers and steps and concentrated on her mission, not her height from the lobby floor.

Near the top she succumbed to the temptation to look up, and vertigo instantly overwhelmed her. *Don't be a baby!* she commanded herself and gripped the banister for dear life—only to realize the final section was loose. Incompletely installed, the banister broke away from the rest of the staircase. Before she could simply collapse and hang onto the treads for dear life, she toppled.

As her mother had done, as she had always subconsciously feared, she was falling from the sky. *And she knew who the murderer was.* She knew the only one it could be.

Also, instead of her entire life flashing before her eyes, she heard herself scold, *Now you know why you've had this phobia, and you've done this to yourself, you stupid, bird-brained girl—!*

For one horrible moment in free fall, she could see the marbled lobby rise from two floors below. Then she was no longer falling, but jerked up short.

Benjamin leaned over the side of the stairs, clasping her around her waist, supporting her entire weight with one arm, although her feet dangled over the abyss.

"Whoa!" he said. "Couldn't you have had sense enough to use the back stairs?"

There she was, hanging over the edge of the spiral staircase with her stomach heaving up and down as though she had bungee-jumped—as if she ever would deliberately—and there Benjamin was, telling her she should have had better sense.

"Don't wiggle," he said. "I'm not Superman. Easy does it. Want to float down with me? Or join me here on the steps?"

Janis closed her eyes. Best to get the worst over with. "...Before we go anywhere," she said, talking as fast as a speeded-up recording, "you might as well know I may be one of the murderer's descendants you're looking for."

She half-expected him to drop her right then.

After an eternity of being crunched by her own weight and his iron grip, she opened her eyes and looked up at him. "Our family goes back in a straight line here in San Diego County to before the time you were assassinated. My great-great-grandfather's name was Robert Douglass. Is he the `Doug' you mentioned? If he is...oh, Benjamin—that makes me your enemy, too." In misery, she squeezed her eyelids closed again.

He hauled her onto the stair beside him.

She opened her eyes and peeked at him. No reassurance there, but no lightning flashing or thunderous noises, either. Just his sober expression and expressively mournful blue eyes. "It's true, isn't it?"

He nodded.

"You could have dropped me. Then you would have only

one other descendant to catch up with. We haven't been a prolific family for one reason or another—wars, accidents, failure of some of the females to marry, and others marrying late in life."

Benjamin looked horrified. "Why would I want to drop you?"

"I'm one of your murderer's descendants. I can't begin to tell you how sorry I am, but that's the way it is."

"If you think I should let you splatter on the lobby floor when I showed up expressly to save you, you must think very badly of me, Janis Logan Carter. But I forgive you. You have been under understandable pressures."

"Aren't you upset? About me being one of the descendants? It means my own brother wants to...he's the only one who knows I'm deathly afraid of climbing stairs or ladders or...anything high. He could have predicted practically to the inch exactly where I'd cling to the bannister for all I'm worth. I have to face knowing he wants my death badly enough to cause it in the way it could happen in my worst nightmare. Oh, Benjamin, I'm still terrified, just *sitting* here."

"Put your head into my shoulder and keep your eyes shut. I'll get us downstairs."

Obediently, she shut her eyes again. He picked her up, cradled her securely, and before she knew it, he was lowering her onto a comfortable surface and had a pillow under her head.

"You can open your eyes now."

She was on the bed in Room 201.

He poured her a glass of the wine from her cellar. "If you had to go up to your storage area, why didn't you use the back stairs?"

"A board's nailed across the back stair access to the third floor, and the elevator isn't operating. The foreman told me the reason the circular stair was roped off was to keep the workmen off it—that it was perfectly okay!"

"It amazes me how your brother is able to persuade you to be exactly where he wants you at the time he wants you to be there."

"I'm the only one with the key to the third floor, and I've been up and down today already. There's no reason for anyone else to go up there." She burst into noisy, gulping tears. And though her nose always reddened when she cried, and her eyelids always swelled, she couldn't seem to stop.

"The screws to one end of each section on the highest level were deliberately removed. Just waiting for you to grab for balance. No one would have known it was anything but a simple accident happening to someone using the wrong access, against warnings."

"If only Keith had confided in me that gamblers are after him!" she wailed.

"I don't presume to know why the Powers that Be made me so blind, except that I was distracted by your not so pleasant ex-husband."

"Last night and today I've worried about having to tell you I'm the last descendant of your m-m-murderer. I know you must hate me, no matter how nice you're being, and I can't blame you. Oh, Benjamin, I'm so *sorry* you have to hate me!"

His arms around her did not confirm her discovery. "I think you are as brave as they come, but with an unfortunate blind spot in regards your brother. Did you run away when you knew you must tell me, after you finally figured out the answer? Not for a minute."

"Oh, I flinched. But going over the bannister wasn't as bad as having to face you, now I think about it."

"I should have showed up when you called me. I have my own moments of cowardice. I had no wish to hear what you had to say. There— you see? Your bravery exceeds mine. I have been studying one of those books of yours—an amalgam of various psychoanalytic disciplines, so perhaps I should label myself more into denial than cowardice on this matter. *You,*" he digressed in a petty manner, "are more into denial than I am, so I will not put too much guilt on myself. I knew what you were going to tell me, and I didn't like to face having my own curse thrown back at me."

She went on crying. There were a lot of tears bottled up

that had very little to do with him except that he had drawn the cork from the bottle.

Finally he had had enough. "You're going to be all right. Now you know, and I know, who we are dealing with. That is half of any battle."

"It has something to do with his obsession with racing. He's in trouble with a syndicate again. I'm sure of it. That's why he wanted me to sell the house, even at a loss. He must need a great deal of money very quickly."

"You think that excuses him?"

"Of course not, but you have to understand, he's not like other—"

"Right. He most certainly is not. I should very much like to know how he thought he could get away with it. He has empty rooms in his second story, your brother. If you will allow me to make the observation."

She began sobbing again, adding hiccups.

He sat on the Harrison tester bed holding her fiercely in his arms, and after a time she began to feel safe, absolutely calm—in spite of the horrible situation.

He sighed and regarded her with resignation. "You are no shining star of intelligence," he said, "where your brother is concerned."

Her tears drenched his silk shirt. "I'm s-sorry. I can't seem to help myself. I was so f-frightened...and now I'm so c-c-cold..."

He produced a clean cotton handkerchief and wiped her face. "This will never do, you know. You'll make yourself ill." He kissed her wet eyes, said firmly, but as if to himself, "I want you to know I'm only trying to calm you down and comfort you. This is not to be confused with any other kind of kissing."

"Poor Benjamin, it must be awful to find out all a tiger like you can find to kill is a stupid mouse like me!" She really sympathized with him.

If he meant the kiss to be comforting, it was the most comfort she had ever known. He was baked custard with a dusting of cinnamon, a crackling great fire in the library fireplace on a rainy night—he was the definition of comfort. She didn't want such comfort ever to stop. His kissing warmed her from a bright center that spread until she sizzled from the edges to her center and back again. From custard and cozy fireplace it became champagne and Napoleon brandy and Fourth of July, and comfort left off and became excitement.

She stopped crying in order to appreciate the extraordinary excitement of Benjamin Blair's brand of comfort.

Clothes suffocated and constricted. They assisted each other with doing away with the clothes in order to be able to comfort each other properly.

His arms became lover's arms. The cold bright night reeled around their heat. The only thing existing for Janis was being introduced to what passion was all about. She had only vaguely known what was missing in her marriage. She would never again be ignorant of passion. And she wanted to give as good as he gave.

After a time, she was aware of the perfume drifting through the window from the savor garden and the orange tree at the end of the garden nearest Underwood. It was technically winter, but the night smelled like spring. She had never been so intoxicated by aromas. Or by silver moonlight illuminating the room with magic. Benjamin knew where every sensitive nerve of her body was, though she had never known them herself. She was sure he was memorizing her by touch, and she followed his lead.

She memorized him with her own searching lips and caresses.

Oh, his hands were so sure! His body so sure! She could not learn fast enough all the lessons he was teaching her. They were together in a way that was so perfect it was far beyond tears or laughter or excitement.

The passion that couldn't possibly be more wonderful grew increasingly more so. She centered in a vortex of music and color and just plain healthy lust.

Passion temporarily spent, he cradled her. "Devil take me, Janis, what have I done?"

"Don't you dare tell me you don't know!" she kissed the

hollow of his throat.

"The whole business of our making love is a terrible mistake for both of us." He rolled over on his back and looked up at the ceiling.

"If it's a mistake, I hope no one ever comes up with a way to erase it," she said dreamily. "Let's stay right here in this room forever, making mistakes one after the other." She was almost ready to bless her greedy sibling for having inadvertently brought this marvelously impossible situation about.

Benjamin gently disengaged her arms, rose and began to dress.

"Where are you going?" she asked from the depths of the tester bed.

"I can't stay. I'm complicating your life in a tragically unproductive way."

"Don't you *dare* make perfect love to me and then just—disappear!"

"I am not `just disappearing,' Janis, my darling, but I have to put a stop to this before your life is irreparably muddled."

"If you leave me now, that's the irreparable muddle. I'd have preferred you to let me finish the fall. I can't bear not being with you after this. Now I know what loving you can really be like, I'll be more unhappy than if you'd never made love to me at all. I'll wish I were never born. I'll wish I were dead like you wanted me to be when you didn't even know who you wanted to take revenge on! Is that what you want? I don't believe it."

He scowled. "Stow talk about being dead. The last thing that is needed around here is another earthbound spirit. Get it through your head—I wouldn't revenge myself on you if you stuck pins in me. Heaven knows you have turned into a terrible millstone on my conscience, but you are meant to live until you are well up in your eighties. Remember, you have this monstrosity of a tourist attraction to complete and a number of other projects even bigger in your future, as well. But as soon as I see to it that your brother doesn't bother you any more, I'm gone. Not abandoning you. Just...gone." His voice was bleak. "You'll have to make do with your reconstructed monstrosity."

"The reconstructed Underwood is *not* a monstrosity!" She could tell he didn't mean a word he said about leaving.

"Of course it's a monstrosity. Just the ridiculous fact you had the nonsensical idea to install a circular staircase out of that notorious Sacramento hotel where `entertainment' was Mademoiselle De Lourge sliding the length of the banister four times nightly into the arms of the miner who had won the latest lottery makes the place ridiculous."

"Good heavens! Is *that* in its history? I only knew it was similar to the one in the old Underwood, but more ornate. Now I've gone and *ruined* it, when the story is worth thousands of tourist dollars!"

In a dry voice he said, "The broken section is still attached on one end. They can re-attach it."

"What are you going to do about *him?"*

"Your damned brother? And I regret to say, he is. Your brother is not going to kill you. Stay here, be calm and I will settle his hash with a conference that will put the fear of the devil into him." With a regretful expression he began to fade away.

She hated that he was so anxious to leave her when she loved him so.

His voice came faintly, "One day you will come to know I did what was best for you. Stop those tears! They absolutely destroy me."

"I'm thinking of my poor brother." She hiccupped.

Abruptly he faded in. "Not sympathizing with him again, are you? The sooner I put a stop to his nonsense, the less apt you are to go prematurely into the hereafter, which I, for one, can guarantee from experience is not the greatest place in the universe to be."

She opened her mouth and he kissed it shut, which was an absolute wonder because his talented tongue was in no way allowing her to reject it—as if she would ever want to.

"Don't try to tell me he was a dear child. He didn't start thinking along lines of killing his sister for her half of an inheritance in just the last few weeks."

"There has to be a way to reform him. *Scare* him into it the way you scared that awful mugger. Please, Benjamin! He's in enough trouble with the toughs he has on his case. I'll see his gambling debts are paid. That should take care of the problem."

"You can pour every cent you have into that project, and all you'll be doing is pounding sand into a rat hole."

She sat up. "If you put the kind of fear into him that only you can—that can change him. You and I, Benjamin, we could honestly reform him."

"Ye Gods!" he said in resigned disgust. "Well...I shall find a way to face the stupid aging juvenile and convince him it is less healthy to irritate a vengeful spirit than to get on the wrong side of what you call a syndicate and I call thugs."

"He really isn't a bad person, Benjamin."

Benjamin groaned. "You are more naive than a spring lamb being led to slaughter. Your brother has had psychiatrists, military schools, and carrots and disinheritance and open death threats dangled in front of his nose all his life and none of them worked. Whatever I do, it has to wait until this coming night because the sun is about to rise."

"You've lost all track of time. It's not even midnight."

"You are the one with no sense of time. We have made love all night, the more shame to me for my fine resolves!"

He patted her rear. "You will be safe enough, *today,* but after that—he might decide to shoot you in broad daylight. And in broad daylight, I'm nowhere, remember."

"Think of a way to reform him by tonight. Promise?"

He groaned again. "You want him alive so I will have to stay around and look out for you. Don't you realize that if he reforms and fathers any children in the next few years, I'm still chained by my oath to see the last descendent in the grave. Consider yourself. You are not destined to go through life alone. That red-haired colleague of yours, I expect," he predicted morosely. "You'll both likely have children, and eventually instead of you and your brother—a manageable, finite number—I suppose there will be dozens of descendants—breeding like rabbits because I will have softened my attitude toward their personal lives, but be unable to rescind the curse that tinkers with their moods. Result—I will be doomed to stay in limbo forever."

"It won't work out that way! Keith's never been married, dislikes even the idea of being a father, and perhaps doesn't like women very well, either."

She thought bleakly of one or two of the papers in Ocho's file on Keith and knew he was not at all apt to be attracted to any female.

"If he only knew he is missing one of the joys of life," Benjamin said.

"I definitely think he'll never have any children," she said firmly. "And I know I won't—now I know how it would affect you."

"Oh, what a waste!" Benjamin exclaimed. "I will not have you moping about, acting weirdly."

"...While you seem to go everywhere and enjoy doing everything, even if it does have to be between sunset and dawn. Can't you resign yourself to leading a comfortable life for a few years? Then, after we're gone, you can fade away for good. *Just don't take revenge on Keith. Please?"* She clasped her hands behind his head, holding him prisoner while she pleaded.

"You can be most persuasive. Not to mention the most adorable female in this world or the next." He nuzzled her ear. He kissed her again and disengaged her arms. "No more argumentation. I must be off and away before I let you complicate things further."

"Promise me you'll come directly tonight. No blondes in jacuzzis."

"I gave up blondes and jacuzzis."

"Since when?"

He shifted. "Since you made such a fuss about it, if you must know."

She began to cry. She had never been so happy. "Thank you, Benjamin. Don't go yet, Benjamin. The sun isn't up. It's still dark."

"If I have told you once, I have told you a dozen times, it is against my principles to trifle with a woman looking for love. This night proves I was right to hew to the principles and criminal to forget myself. You deserve a man who can be with you day *or* night for the rest of your life."

"I would rather have someone who really cares about *me,* Benjamin. I *know* you care about me, no matter what you say. And I trust you more than anyone else in the world."

"The problem exactly. I am not in the world."

"You are! From dusk to dawn, *you are!"*

He touched her cheek lightly, leaving a sizzling trail of sensations. "Goodbye until tonight, Janis. One way or another, your brother shan't bother you again after tonight, and that is a promise I will not break." He walked straight through the door.

THIRTEEN

Benjamin's head extruded through the door like a mounted trophy. "I will not leave you locked in there unable to explain how and why to your colleagues. Here's the padlock. Use the bar on the inside." He pushed the padlock through as if the door were well-tinted fog. "Have no concerns about tonight, Janis. I will be on the spot, I promise. No matter what happens."

With this enigmatic hint of the difficulties the day might otherwise produce, he removed himself in the disconcerting way he had.

The last sight of him worried her. Something about the way he looked...as if he knew there would be a problem but he could not tell her what to expect. She pondered whether she was more frustrated by him without memory or with it recovered.

She accounted for all her pieces of clothing...no way did she wish to have to explain anything inadvertently left behind. When the counterpane was smooth and the room in perfect order, the sun was illuminating dew diamonds all over the garden, but she was still bemused by how marvelously the night had passed, folded around them.

The world would call her a fool to fall so terribly in love with a ghost. She was even more foolish not to want to believe in her bones that her brother had nothing to do with the attempts to murder her. Her faith in him insisted there had to be another answer. The gambling syndicate was really the villain.

She had a harder time convincing herself Benjamin's plan to confront Keith would establish that neither she nor Keith had a part in his curse except that of innocent bystanders.

Keith was guilty only of an unfortunate coincidental addiction. Her ghost would not abandon her once all was straightened out.

She curled into the carved leather-backed chair and nibbled on one of the packaged peanut butter and cracker sandwiches in the snack supply she had packed in the top bureau drawer. Ocho had often said she and Keith took more after their mothers than after him. He had meant those comments as accusations, even though Keith looked so much like him as he grew older. Once those accusations had hurt. But however much she had yearned for her father's love and approval, she grew also to know he was in his own way as much a pirate as his father and his grandfather before him. For all she knew, all the men of his line had pillaged and burned their way to decadence. The signs pointed to the last male of his line, Keith, being no better. Perhaps worse, if Keith was able to stand by and let miserable hit-men from a gambling syndicate murder his sister before he could be persuaded to pay gambling losses. She could not ignore his character deficits, but he wasn't the one actually pursuing her. He was merely the catalyst for that pursuit.

How could he be so naive as to believe he would not be found an accessory, if not the prime suspect? She reminded herself that if worse became worst—and she still wouldn't believe that could be true—Keith would be all the more dangerous because guilty or innocent he was *unpredictable*. Her denials of danger always came back to one incontrovertible point—one could hardly argue with a ghost.

What difference did Keith make in her world if she loved a ghost who had no intention of seeing her again except to confront her brother about his sins. With a sigh she pushed back the bar that secured the door to Room 201 when occupied, let herself out and padlocked the door behind her.

As soon as she entered her office, she wrote a letter, marked the envelope *To be opened by the police if Janis Logan Carter is found dead under suspicious circumstances,* and locked it in the office safe. She ripped the misleading yellow caution tape away from the back stairs and climbed again to the third floor.

The early morning sun poked only tentatively through the one high, north window of the dark floor. She stubbed her toe on a bag of workman's tools and a large roll of electrical tape spilled out. When she pulled the chain to the light bulb, the bare globe swung back and forth from the extension cord over the beam, blazing erratically into the shadows, causing them to dance throughout the otherwise ill-lighted, cavernous room.

She prepared to delve into the Association's old files in her determined search for issues from the missing period in Ocho's collection. If she found any preserved by the other prime private source of local history—even if they carried no notice of the Major's murder—the overall value of the combined collection was increased and the results not simply to satisfy herself.

In the Association's own file of early newspapers, mostly *The Herald,* rather than the city's earliest newspaper, *The Crier,* she made the stunning discovery of every issue for January, February, and March of 1869, though the overall number of issues owned by the Association was considerably fewer than the Logan collection. She took the first issue printed after the major claimed to have been killed...the issue dated Thursday, January, 25th, 1869, under the still-swaying light bulb to better read the old-fashioned print.

The fragile yellowed paper, enclosed in clear preserving film, was tabbed with a label showing it to be one of several donated in 1992 by heirs of a Mrs. Quentin J. Smith whose daughter had found them lining attic trunks containing clothing stored by Mrs. Smith's own great-grandmother.

Janis's hand trembled. Her heart pounded. The banner headline for the week was what she had looked for.

TRADING COMPANY'S JUNIOR PARTNER MURDERED

Last Saturday noon, the Room Clerk on the request of Mr. Robert Douglass, opened Room 201 of the Underwood Hotel and found the body of Mr. Douglass' junior partner, Major Benjamin Blair.

Douglass had been concerned over his partner's failure to arrive at a dinner engagement the previous evening in the home of the Zunega family.

Major Blair had numerous stab wounds and his room had been ransacked. Mr. Douglass, greatly overcome by the tragedy, advised authorities that the Major, who had returned late the preceding afternoon of the 18th from a business trip to the Presidio of San Francisco, was a man "without an enemy in the world."

There are as yet no suspects, but a number of the hotel staff have been questioned regarding comings and goings during the afternoon and evening of the 19th.

The following week's paper of the era, Thursday, February first, a follow-up story was on the issue's back page.

DEATH OF DOUGLASS PARTNER STILL A MYSTERY

Authorities claim all efforts to apprehend the murderer of Major Benjamin Blair have so far led to nought. The sheriff determined the assassin entered Major Blair's rooms by way of a roof window in the Third Floor and rope to the window to Major Blair's room at the southwest corner of the second floor.

Mr. Douglass, the owner of Douglass Land Office Company and Douglass and Blair Trading Company, offers a REWARD of Five Hundred Dollars for information leading to the Arrest and Conviction of his junior partner's assassin. Still overcome by the tragedy, Mr. Douglass stated, "Major Blair's passing will be sorely felt by our community."

All doubts Janis ever harbored about dealing with a ghost vanished. She was sure the unusual circumstances surrounding the disappearance of all other copies of *The Herald* issued that date could be laid to the determination of her wicked old Great-great grandfather, Robert Douglass having bought them up discreetly and perhaps by illegal means. She shivered. She was equally sure Ocho had not known the copies existed. His obsession with a complete collection would have made him pay anything for the copies and gloat over coming closer to a complete collection than his own progenitors. He would not, of course, have had the slightest inkling *why* they were to all purposes the only copies left in existence. Old Robert Douglass had almost managed to do away with all records of the very existence of Major Benjamin Blair. In her heart, Janis knew Robert Douglass had managed to eliminate or alter all mention of Major Benjamin Blair in the annals of Old Town San Diego.

How he had missed the papers used by Mrs. Smith's thrifty ancestor to line her trunks was only to be guessed. She had forgotten they lined the trunks—and however many handsome payments were discreetly advertised for the issues, the lining papers had survived. The date of acquisition showed the finds surfaced during Ocho's last illness. They had been put in the Association's files at a time when her family's attention was on other matters than adding an item to their collection. Otherwise, she would have seen them much earlier. Ocho would have crowed over discovery that Robert Douglass's first partner was not Malcolm Logan, but a Major Blair, killed by person or persons unknown before the Douglass-Logan star began to rise.

The gift of the Smith newspaper issues also came at a time when the Association itself was in sufficient state of administrative upheaval that no mention of the acquisition was given the media. Whatever had been the course of the early investigation, the major's death never involved suspicion of her great-great-grandfather's connection to it.

Family records had shown Robert Douglass becoming more and more reclusive and suspicious as he aged, while Cirenia Figueroa Douglass was said to have decidedly "turned mental" in her later years. Poor woman—what had she suspected or learned of her husband's secrets that unhinged her!

Janis wanted to look for further information into Major Blair's death, but the extension cord light bulb hanging over the files fizzled and blew, casting the third floor into gloom too dim for reading. Putting the newspapers with the files for the library, she prepared to leave. She was almost to the door when it abruptly opened.

For a moment the intruder looked dear and familiar. Then she remembered this man had probably already tried four times—that she knew of—to kill her.

His eyes were dead coals in their sockets. He stood between her and the door, six inches taller than she, lean and fit through his construction work. With sunlight filtering through the window on the north wall, she realized she could hope for no help from Benjamin until dark.

Keith moved toward her. "You were supposed to go over the bannister, you know."

Frozen in place, she found her voice could be as casual as his. "Why, Keith? *Why?* I have always been your support, your friend, your loving sister. In every sort of sad circumstance, I always stood up for you. Always."

"True, but they're after me. Time's run out, and I have to pay them. You have to understand, there's no other way."

"If this is why you were so anxious for me to sell the house, I'll sell it to Dexter. You can have all the profit from it."

"You should have grabbed when the grabbing was possible, Beaky. The problem's gone way beyond that estate sale. They pushed the interest on the debt to twenty-five percent *a week.* Before long, there wouldn't be anything left for either of us. Damn, I hate to do it this way, I really do, but the indirect way didn't work. They'll wait for probate but not for anything else."

"I'd have given the money to you if you were short and threatened."

"Oh, sure, Lady Bountiful doling out the dollars and holding the reason over my head. Like Ocho. This is the better way. I'll have it all. Debt paid. No money worries even if

Simonson manages my half until I'm a doddering senior cit and it all goes to nursing home care."

"Keith, I'll still stand behind you. We'll work things out."

"Well, Sis, the whole story is that I put the syndicate off with funds from SunSol. So I have to put those funds back, too."

She choked on the new bit."Not again!"

"See how easy it is for me to come to you for money? Already you're scolding me."

"You won't have any trouble with the syndicate! I have a friend who can take care of—"

He sneered.

"I've been making *peanuts* with the stupid, mucking job *and* the trust income, compared to what you get in income from your half of the principal. And all you do is throw it away on your precious causes. So I'm working things out to my advantage. I intend to live the way Ocho kept me from living."

He glanced at the workman's industrial size roll of electrical tape on the floor by the door. "I'm not about to let my knees get nailed to floor boards, which is what will happen if I don't get the money back in the SunSol accounts by the 31st of December."

"Even if I'm *dead* and you get away with murder, you could never get the money earlier than *next* December!"

"There's that one nasty little fly in the soup, them raking in that much more interest while your estate's settled. But they'll wait for probate. They'll even fix the SunSol problem for a price. I'll be able to afford the interest as soon as the estate's all mine."

"You'll never get a dime out of it if they've got *their* hooks in. Unless you let my friend help you, believe me, you won't."

He ignored her words. Desperately, she sought a crack in his confidence. "If I die, my friend already knows who's responsible. We guessed the accidents stemmed from you."

"You mean with the crackpot from Claremont? I should have taken care of both of you the night I came over to turn on all the gas cocks in the house, and you two were still up. If you'd been asleep, you never would have heard the explosion. I'd be collecting the insurance, and it would all be over. I suppose I'll have to tie up that little loose thread." He sighed.

Janis struggled to stay calm. She couldn't let Maggie be dragged into the picture. She forced a surprised little laugh. "If you mean Maggie, she doesn't know anything at all about you that you didn't tell her. I'm talking about my friend Benjamin Blair. You haven't met him. I was supposed to call you this very morning and set up a time for you to meet with us."

"That's convenient," he said. "When did he suggest I accommodate him?"

"Tonight. Just after dark. At Wharton House. Benjamin's been—investigating the accidents with me. He said you needed help with your problem, and he has that help for you."

"A do-gooder type? Okay, I'll see him, but you won't be with me. I have other plans for you that will work out just great with this chance encounter of ours being right here."

Keith had never been normal, and she saw he had gone over the edge to total sociopath or psychopath. "Nothing can be so bad you have to kill me."

He widened his eyes at her. "Why, Jan, baby, you're my sister. I'm not going to kill you."

He lied of course. The car, the mugger, the wired light switch in the office, the staircase—even the plan to open the gas cocks.

"Was I *there* any of those times? Would I have actually done the deed? No. The mugger would. The car would. The light switch didn't work right." He smirked. "The staircase would have been a pure case of your stupidity—failure to observe warnings, plus, everyone knows you're dingy about heights."

She took advantage of the moment to dart around a credenza and outflank him, but he snaked out faster than she could move and captured her arm in a painful grip.

She inhaled to scream, but had no time before he struck her on the edge of her jaw with his fist. Red stars exploded and she descended into black.

***

She came to her senses to find he had taped her wrists together and wound more tape over her mouth. Numbly she looked up at him. In spite of her determination not to cry, tears welled.

"I'm just going to leave you up here—behind the bank of metal files."

She moaned, beat her heels against the floor and writhed, but was helpless.

He looked down at her with a considering frown, picked up a one-by- eight board and balanced it at a slant on the credenza. The other end of the board he braced against the floor where it met the wall. Maneuvering her, tape bound as she was, onto the board, he was able to whip electrical tape around her in a spiral from ankles to ribs and up over her shoulders, immobilizing her on the board. One last strip over her forehead, and she could move not a fraction of an inch. Satisfied, he said, "That ought to keep you from making any fuss that draws attention."

Keith's psychiatrist had said sociopaths weren't insane, but thought the world was there to march to their tune. If anyone was in their way by whatever accident, they would not be apt to ask if he might pass, but to swat the obstruction with the nearest and most effective blunt instrument that would remove the obstacle permanently. They could walk over the body without looking back.

Benjamin? You said I would be safe here today.

"I'll do a bit of creative ransacking," Keith said pleasantly. "Take a couple of things to make it look good when you are found, hmm? Mother's ring for a start." He pulled the ring from her finger. "I see you brought Ocho's local gem and mineral collection up here. Bits and pieces from that will send investigators in conflicting directions." He broke open the case with the workman's hammer and removed specimens. "Wouldn't be surprised if the men I owe won't take them on account, hmm? It'll look like you interrupted a burglar when they find you...in a few weeks."

He selected an antique railroad watch and the rare

lighthouse clock that had always fascinated him as a boy. He smiled her. "Don't worry, I won't turn these over to the Mob. I'll keep them as souvenirs of my happy childhood."

He looked around. "Let's see—where are your keys?" He snapped his fingers. "You can't answer, but I remember now. You left the key ring in the padlock. I'll lock the door up here, put the keys in your purse and toss the purse somewhere it can be found in a few days. They'll think you left here...until they find you."

Her face ached where he had hit her. Best not to struggle, just wait for the day to pass, for Benjamin to find her. She heard a truck pull up, and the voices of workmen. Perhaps she would not have to wait the whole day, if they found Keith up here.

Keith heard the workmen too because he cocked his head. "Damn."

He grasped her, taped as she was to the board like a package, and lowered the board to the floor. "I'd best make myself scarce, hadn't I? Let's see—the crew today are painters. They won't have any reason to come up to this level, and they're through up here for good, anyway. They'll leave by three. I'll be back when the coast's clear and settle you in behind the files."

He snapped off his flash. She heard the padlock snick into place over the hasp on the other side of the door.

She lay like a chicken trussed for the oven, unable to make a sound. She hadn't seen the security man when she came up, and even if he had seen her, he was unlikely to go farther than the padlocked door. If he had seen Keith, one of SunSol's men, he wouldn't have thought about it twice.

Even the workman who had left his tools would not show up until Monday and by then, if she were still there, she would be bundled away in the back and as unable to communicate as she was right at the moment. She could only wait, trusting in Benjamin.

FOURTEEN

The crew's scheduled job that Sunday was painting the library and rest-rooms on the first floor. Janis tried calling, shouting, but though the effort nearly caused her to black out, and the noise seemed deafening to her own ears, she knew it was merely a muffled mumble through the tape, probably impossible to hear even if someone were standing right outside the door. The two advantages she had were that she was breathing and Benjamin would come.

Unfortunately, and in spite of its closeness to the shortest day of the year, her faith did not make her day short. It was the longest day of her life.

She could see only the unfinished rafters above. Time stood still. She imagined at one point that she was like an insect captured in amber, or even something like Benjamin during his long days and years of immobilization.

When it was three o'clock someone called "Quitting time!" so loudly she heard the words even where she was. *Don't leave!* she screamed silently.

After a brief flurry of noise and rattling of equipment, she heard only silence except for the faint noise of traffic from the street two floors below and behind her. The sparse light allowed into the room by the meager windows faded.

Benjamin Blair, I desperately need you! There's no way I can let anyone else know where I am, if you don't come!"

He wouldn't be cruel enough to take a turn skating along the Boardwalk at Pacific Beach. Nor would he take the time to try raw baby squid at a Japanese sushi bar. Nor would he dally to splash a blonde in a steamy jacuzzi. *If you leave me here another minute, Benjamin Harrison Blair, I'll haunt* you *through all eternity!*

"Here I am," he said. "The sun just set, and I came as fast as I could." He climbed atop a chair to screw a new light bulb into the socket with the burned out bulb.

He had been carrying a tennis racket and a can of balls and wore pristine white shorts, the blue Izod shirt she had bought him, athletic shoes and socks.

Rescue, revenge, then a spot of tennis? She might have wept, but for some insane reason, she felt like laughing.

He hunkered down beside her. "That tape across your mouth and over your hair isn't going to be easy to get off without a few `ouches'. I'll be as careful as I can."

Janis closed her eyes and attempted to relax, resigned to the problem which at worst would leave a red mark and break a few strands of hair.

He worked the tape loose with infinitely gentle fingers. It wasn't as bad as she had steeled herself to endure, except where the tape painfully adhered to the top layer of her hair. Never again, she vowed, would she wince when a beautician ran a comb through a mere snarl.

Her head was free. "That's the worst of it," he said.

"Is anything bleeding?" She touched her stinging lips with her tongue. "I knew you would come...Oh, please hurry and free my arms and legs!"

He smoothed her hair. "Janis, I can't."

"Of course you can! Don't tease. I'm in such cramped torture."

"I know." He bent to kiss her, and his touch was a perfect balm. "I promise you, in just a little while you'll understand. I'm sorry I couldn't prevent this. Believe me, there's no other way to be sure you're *safe.*"

"But you can free me *now!* Before Keith comes back! He's truly a monster. Oh, why did I think his demons were all in the past...What are you waiting for, Benjamin? Get rid of the rest of the tape and take me away from here."

He regarded her with sad blue eyes. "You're going to be all right. Patience, my poor darling."

"Benjamin, pl—"

Whatever she had been about to say broke off at the sound of the key turning in the door's padlock. Benjamin stood and watched the door open.

Keith stood on the threshold staring from Janis to Benjamin, his dark brows drawing together over the bridge of his nose. From the pocket of his black leather jacket he took a snub-nosed pistol and pointed it at Benjamin.

"Isn't this nice? I didn't have a chance to get up here, and have been waiting before I needed to slip into Wharton where you were supposed to meet me. You saved me the trouble of getting you up here to join Jan. So I'll have no problem killing *you,* and you'll take any suspicion from *me.* Prepare to meet your maker, after which I'll put Jan back behind the files. It wouldn't do for someone to come in in the next few days and find her here by the door."

His angelic smile never wavered. She heard a soft *pop!*

Benjamin dropped with a thud to the board floor. She would have cried out with the shock of seeing him fall, except that as quickly as Keith aimed and shot, he muffled her with a hard hand before dropping the pistol back into his pocket.

With his free hand he reached for the roll of electrical tape. "Can't risk anyone hearing you, can I? I'd have been here sooner, except that I had to wait for the looky-loos to leave, and the staff, and wait for the security guard to go around Wharton House on a round."

Behind Keith, Benjamin rose and stared down with a frown at the hole in his Izod shirt. He said in an aggrieved voice, "You've just ruined a gift from a lady, a gift I prized. It was my first gift in over a hundred and thirty years, and I take exception to your mean-spirited behavior."

Keith whirled and stared, eyes bulging first at Benjamin, appearing anything but wounded—though definitely annoyed—then at the scorched hole in the blue Izod shirt which was neatly positioned over Benjamin's heart area. Even a small caliber bullet would have done enormous damage in the unlikely event the one who was shot hadn't been killed outright. In spite of the blackened hole in the shirt and the nasty smell of what Janis assumed was cordite, she knew vast relief that the impact had only knocked Benjamin off his feet and his invulnerability was naturally intact.

Keith looked puzzled. "You can't—?" and pulled the little pistol out of his pocket. He fired twice more at short range. Two other little black holes appeared in Benjamin's shirt.

"Surprised me first time, shame on you. Surprised me twice, no way," Benjamin said gently. "It's my turn, now, my lad."

Moving faster than Janis's eyes could follow, he grasped Keith in a headlock and began the crunch. Keith dropped the pistol, which skittered across the floor to the threshold of the door.

"Benjamin, no!" she wailed.

He halted, though he did not release Keith. "None of that 'take pity on him' nonsense, Janis. It would be a blasted nuisance trying to keep you alive with him loose. I prefer more amusing pursuits."

Her frantic struggle to free herself was limited to futile twistings of her head. After a moment she gasped, "I don't care about him! It's *you* I care about, Benjamin—I know you don't want anything to do with me, but I don't want his blood on your hands!"

Patiently, he reminded her, "For eons, we ghosts have been wreaking revenge on our enemies. Revenge, reprisal, and villains receiving their just desserts goes with the territory. Ghosts are already in a limbo and what more can happen to them, as I've more than once reminded you?"

"Oh, Benjamin, please listen! You already have so many more privileges than any other ghost I ever heard of! You've been having the time of your life or existence! Plays, rap concerts, mud wrestling, television, shopping, restaurants...the—the jacuzzis—everything. You have all the convenience of being alive and none of the inconveniences."

"You don't call disappearing into nothing at sunrise, and this sort of thing, an inconvenience?"

"Your daylight time out isn't boring or monotonous or frustrating. You don't have to fight traffic to and from the job. You don't have to deal tactfully with the public or put up with a boss or customers or clients like hundreds of thousands of the people you see on the street endure at least some of the time on their jobs."

"It's a point, but, since I don't, then all the more reason to get rid of this rodent and make sure you don't have to be worrying about him all the time while you cope with the daily disadvantages of living."

"Don't you realize how truly blessed you are? None of the reality of life, just the enjoyment of it about half of every twenty-four hours. And all because you were a wonderfully kind and decent person in your lifetime."

"Now *that* is piling it on a bit thick, Janis," he protested.

"I don't think so. But, if you take revenge on Keith, no matter how much he deserves it, your *Karma* will be changed. I just know it."

"Karma belongs to a different set of spirits. If I have a Karma, it demands I see no more descendants of Robert Douglass inherit his tendencies and then, not only is my job on Earth complete, the world is better off by half."

"Don't risk it, Benjamin! Please don't risk losing your unique status. Don't risk what lies somewhere ahead for you."

"I know not if there is a future for me, after all is said and done. But there is a future for you only without this abomination—" he twisted Keith's head, and Keith howled.

"*Please* don't do something that will change everything for you. I promise I'll never be a nuisance to you again. Don't worry. I won't marry. I won't have children. I won't extend your curse if that's what you call it. You can enjoy every minute of the time I'm on Earth without the slightest interference from me, I promise. Don't endanger your sentient time between now and the time Keith and I die our natural deaths. *Think about after all your assassin's descendants finally are dead and gone.* Think about *that,* Benjamin. Please?"

"What if he takes it into his head to do something on this order to you again?" Benjamin scowled at her.

"Oh, he *won't!* Will you, Keith?"

Keith's eyes rolled wildly. His face had turned an interesting shade of puce.

"Of course he will, you dear, silly woman. So far, he only knows he can bully and cheat and try to murder a hopelessly sentimental sister. He hasn't quite grasped he's dealing with someone from the spirit world. Have you, Logan?" Benjamin tightened the headlock slightly, assuring Keith's full attention.

Keith found his voice. "Sure, Ben. Sir. Sure. I know you've got me where you want me."

"Do you? I am not at all convinced," Benjamin said in his light, pleasant way. "But your sister has an oddly persuasive way with me. So you *are* going to reform, are you not? You *are* going to be a the most valuable man in the construction company or wherever you choose to put your efforts. Be a loving and solicitous brother. Be a good, loyal friend to your acquaintances? In short, you will be a good boy, or else. Will you not?"

"You're right—I am. I will!"

"In exchange, I will persuade your friends to cancel your gambling debt."

Keith said, "Anything you say. Just let me go, man." His glance flicked toward the gun on the floor.

Benjamin sighed. "Time to convince you that any further attempts to shorten the life, damage the health, or diminish your sister's enjoyment of life will bring you more trouble than you ever thought you could be in, young man. You also will give up gambling. Completely. Understand me? Ready for the demonstration of why?"

"Sure," Keith said. "Take it easy, man! You're breaking my neck."

"I could, if I wished, break every bone in your miserable body and leave you like a slug on the floor, unable to move a muscle for the rest of a long, really miserable life."

"You have me convinced," Keith moaned.

Janis fervently hoped he was convinced, but having persuaded Benjamin to be merciful, even she was holding her breath, suspiciously alert for Keith to take it into his head to say whatever he thought he needed to say to get away from Benjamin's stranglehold.

"Now the demonstration that I mean business," Benjamin

said.

He released Keith, who collapsed, and his eyes narrowed at the gun even as Keith groaned in obvious relief.

"Take a look at what you will deal with when I'm really angry."

Instead, Keith dove for the gun.

With a roar that shook the rafters, the ghost changed from Benjamin Blair, mild-mannered tennis player in ruined blue Izod shirt to giant warrior in Civil War uniform. He raised his arms and writhed, slashing the air with his saber as he swelled to twice—three times—his normal size.

A hell's fire flashed and smoked behind him and from within the blazing opal of his eyes. From his hands smoke issued, and a heat Janis felt so strongly she feared her beautiful Underwood House would burst into flames.

Though thick black clouds blocked most of the light from the bulb at the end of the extension cord, the scene was clear in the flashes of lightning, and Benjamin's words could be heard through the shattering thunder that accompanied the lightning. He swelled to the rooftree and larger still, so that he had to bend almost double. He curled above the cowering man on the floor, and roared down at Keith, "If you thought you were dealing with a gullible idiot, you deluded fool, think again!"

With that, he gave a magnified version of a Rebel yell and burst into laughter that bounced and echoed hideously from rafter to rafter.

Keith's scream left no doubt he understood he was not dealing with some ordinary friend of his sister. He scrambled up from where he had cowered as the apparition towered over him. Whimpering, he backed out of the door, his eyes bulging in undiluted terror.

He backed as far as the bannister around the gallery and wailed again at the chilling sight of a boiling monster seemingly about to burst the walls of the third floor.

The bannister against which he pressed gave way. He flailed, yelling anew as he toppled. His shriek dwindled then stopped abruptly.

Paralyzed by shock as well as the tape bonds, Janis could not believe what had happened. It simply didn't register for a moment. When it did register, she took a long breath preliminary to a scream that once begun might never end.

Benjamin dwindled quickly to his normal, unintimidating height and enfolded her, board and all, with arms as solid and comforting as they had always been to her. "I meant to put the fear of backsliding into him," he said penitently. "Believe me, Janis. He backed into another section of safety rail which he had booby-trapped for you."

She could turn her head enough to hide her eyes against his shoulder and shudder. "Is he—is he—?"

Benjamin left her momentarily to saunter out and look down at the lobby floor. "Hoist by his own petard," he murmured.

He returned. "He will never bother you again. He never gave a thought to whether his plan could kill others not involved in his life. He would have kept on devising other outrageous schemes to kill you and probably others if he had been unable to find you here when he did this morning."

After a moment, she whispered, "I know it wasn't your fault, Benjamin. You tried to warn him. I know you did. Even after he saw you at your most terrible, he still meant to shoot you, not to be sensible and change his ways."

She began to weep for Keith, whom she had never known at all. No one had ever known him, not even the psychiatrist who had told Ocho he was a sociopath.

"I am not going to remove the rest of the tape, Janis. Even if no one heard your brother's scream, and I am sure the Security Guard did and will be here in a minute or two, someone will shortly be investigating the gunshots. As soon as they see what has happened, they will be up here. The door is wide open, the light is on. Your brother's gun is over by the door. The watch, your ring, the gem specimens are in his pockets. Only his prints are on the roll of tape and the gun. And here you are, taped up, probably hysterical when you start to think about it. You could never have had anything to do with the accident."

"I—I'll have to answer questions. They'll say I'm insane."

"Tell them what your brother did to you, what he was about to do. Say he talked wildly to someone or something he thought he could see. Describe how terrified he was. There are doctors who will back up any suggestion he was out of his mind. You'll be all right now, Janis. You won't need me. Have a good life..." He rose and regarded her sadly, "or I shall be forced to haunt you."

"Don't go!" she begged, then remembered she had promised not to stop him if he would only refrain from killing her brother. He hadn't touched Keith. He had kept his promise. "I'm sorry, Benjamin. I release you."

He kissed her forehead with a touch as light as a moth's. "Cry, scream, yell—get it out of your system. It will do you good and bring rescue that much faster." He faded to the opal-blue eye glow, and it, too, faded, leaving her alone, strapped to the board, and in tears which became the commanded torrent.

FIFTEEN

Maggie looked anxiously at Janis. "You're sure you'll be all right here at *Rincon?"*

"I'll be fine. Mrs. Cadigan has taken care of me beautifully for years. There's nothing she likes better than clucking over me like a mother hen and complaining about my poor eating habits. But my goodness, Maggie—after your first meeting, I would never have expected your relationship with Millard Thorpe to take the turn it has."

"Dear Jan! If it hadn't been for you, he and I might never have met. We definitely would never have had the opportunity to get to know each other and fall in love. We would be married later, if there weren't compelling reasons to have the ceremony while Millard's sister and her family are here over the holidays. I would have asked you to be my attendant, even under the circumstances, but it seemed important to ask Millard's sister."

"Absolutely. I'm glad you aren't wasting valuable time, Maggie. It's so precious."

"At our age, we can't afford to, but I feel a need to see you happy, too, dear." Maggie's anxious expression did not clear.

Janis hugged her and lied, "I'll bounce back. Don't worry about me. When is the wedding?"

"New Year's Eve. The side chapel of St. Luke's will look lovely, filled with holiday poinsettias."

"That chapel at old St. Luke's is always lovely, Maggie, and I want you to let me give the catered reception, please, as my wedding present?"

"I shouldn't let you spend so much." Maggie hugged her. "But I accept. And, dear, I took the liberty of sending an invitational note to your friend Ryan Aherne at the Convention and Visitors' Bureau. I'd also like to send one to Benjamin Blair, but I don't have his address."

"I—don't have an address for him, Maggie."

Maggie Wythy regarded her with raised eyebrows. "I could have sworn, even from the little I saw of him, that he would be in touch. I really liked him. A lot. There was something about him...his aura, you know."

"What kind of aura, exactly?" Janis cautiously inquired. "Exactly, now, Maggie!"

"I can't be exact. That has puzzled me. Some white flashes. Higher consciousness, you know. Energy build-up. Spirituality. But dark red, too. Rage and anger, malice, wrath. And light red. Sexuality, passion. Sensitivity. Oh, yes, and *orange.* Joy of life. Joy of expression."

She raised both hands and fluttered them while frowning in concentration. "Every time I saw him, a different aura, but I think the violet fluctuating to lavender impressed me most. Supernatural abilities and incorporeality. Yes, very strong at times. Mysterious factors. Mysticism, magic. Obsession," she murmured. "And intolerance, alternating with tolerance. One could never be certain what such a person was thinking or going to do. I'm not surprised he vanished without notice. But the light yelow moments...open, clear intellectual facilities, freshness...I wish I could study him at length."

"He would drive you crazy," Janis said.

Maggie chortled. "Not at all. I felt a kinship to him! I think we could have had such discussions."

"I'm sure."

Janis remembered how Maggie had skirted any discussion of Keith. "What was Keith's aura like, Maggie. No dissembling, now!"

"Brown," Maggie said promptly. "Very brown. Egotistical, unloving, addictive. Also diseased, and destructive. I was horrified, but I couldn't very well tell my hostess her brother seemed so evil! When I learned about his childhood, though, I put it down to a constitutional emotional weakness and hoped for the best."

"I wouldn't have believed you if you had told me," Janis said sadly.

"I know. But I did so hope you and Benjamin Blair..."

Janis managed what she hoped looked like a casual shrug. "Yes. He had nothing if not charisma, but it was one of those `Don't call me, I'll call you' kind of endings."

Maggie leaned forward and took Janis's hands in hers. "There's something you're not saying. Can't you talk about it?"

Janis shook her head. The media feeding orgy over the bizarre death of Keith Logan, only son of old Ocho Logan, had left her drained, even while it served a purpose. She had been spared dwelling exclusively on the fate of never seeing Benjamin Blair again. As far as she was concerned, that was punishment enough for being Robert Douglass' last living descendant.

With the scandal turned to old news thoroughly milked by the media, she could not refrain from facing up to Benjamin's having taken himself to—where, she didn't know. She hoped he was not spending his time on a pile of old bricks, though she doubted he was reduced to such an existence. His cache of gems and gold would hold out as long as she, Janis, lived. He was undoubtedly having a good time in some blonde's jacuzzi.

Wherever he might be, she was painfully aware of his murderer's last descendant keeping him tied to an existence from which he should have been long free.

As far as she knew he wasn't haunting anyone or anyplace. Except her heart. If she needed to live another sixty or so years in the hope he would return, she intended to keep going. And not in the nature of a revenge on him from a woman scorned, either.

He had chosen to live by his vow. She could soldier on. She mourned that the two could not be mutually supportive.

He knew where to contact her again if he ever changed his mind. She intended to carry a piece of Underwood brick with her everywhere, as long as she lived, to assure herself he could find her any time after dusk, any day of any year.

"Perhaps something will come of your friendship with Ryan Aherne," Dr. Maggie ventured. "He's quite obviously smitten."

Janis turned away. She had made two mistakes. Dexter and Benjamin. Three, if she counted unshakable faith in Keith. She had no intention of making another. Any relationship for as long as she could project into her future would be nothing but a substitute for the real thing. She sidestepped Maggie's implied questions. "I'm back at work, going full blast on Underwood's delayed grand opening, and at night when I can't sleep I work on getting ready to move as soon as possible, and of course, dance at your wedding, Maggie."

***

Volunteers came out of the woodwork to prepare for the gala Underwood opening. Even in a season of more activities than many could handle, the invitational champagne reception had drawn positive responses from a large portion of the mailing list. The Mayor cut the ribbon. Guests streamed in.

Association Board members shook Janis's hand with more than normal warmth. "Your stamina is remarkable, Janis. None of us thought the opening could be pulled off this soon even under the best circumstances. In light of your dreadful personal tragedy, it's unbelievable. You're truly an admirable woman to carry on no matter what."

Aware the board member was examining her closely for signs of only heaven could guess what emotional undercurrents, due no doubt to headline news about her psychotic brother, she said simply, "I needed something to pull me through the worst period, and work has been a life-saver."

None of them could know that her pain in knowing she would never see Benjamin again far overpowered the ambivalence she felt for Keith.

"We anticipate your next triumph will be solving the necessity for professional office space," the board member said. "We have every confidence in you."

"I do hope so." Janis smiled politely at the woman—and her husband. From the man's long acquaintance with Ocho,

Janis was aware he could make those offices possible with a wave of his hand at one of his own executive suite rentals along Sixth Avenue. He had made no such gesture, though he had mentioned that if the Association ever decided to go that route he would give them a "deal they'd be happy to accept." A deal, she presumed, equal to the kind of deal Dexter had contemplated making for *Rincon.* That deal for *Rincon* had been firmly rejected. He then had lucked out with a distress sale in La Jolla which he had happily boasted of to her in a phone call that, between the lines, let her know she could remain sitting on her white elephant and her pride until the house collapsed, because he had made a real deal for a "better place." Hardly. She was sure that come spring, *Rincon* would find a new owner.

Two other Association members arrived to congratulate her on the wonderful Harrison room, which had of course become the Association's instant pride and joy.

"Yes," she answered their question about Benjamin Harrison Blair's absence, "it's too bad Mr. Blair couldn't be here to see the excitement over his unique donation."

She stood smiling and nodding like one of those Chinese dolls with their heads on springs. The volunteers burbled inanities. She wondered if she had turned into a smiling plastic mannequin in a black Vionnet.

Her countless hours of overtime were about to catch up with her. She wanted desperately to go home and fall into a coma until the wedding. "Excuse me," she said to the group. "I must catch the caterer before she leaves..."

Returning from the kitchen, she encountered another crush that temporarily barred her return to the reception line, but the Association President could handle that without her help. Behind her was a grouping of rented Australian ferns and palms in huge pots hiding the identities of two men whose voices she didn't recognize.

"...Aherne, you dog, where's this gal of yours you've been bragging about? We want to check out if she's as gorgeous as you say."

"...Yeah, Ryan. The heck with gorgeous, it's the rich that

piques my interest. Not hard to take, rich and gorgeous."

Ryan's voice came in response. "No, rich doesn't hurt, and neither do her great community contacts."

"Better tie her up quick before someone beats you to the gate," the second voice advised.

"I know a smart move when I see it." Ryan's voice was smug with pride.

The other two laughed.

It might be unfair to be so struck with the conviction that she was strictly a trophy to Ryan Aherne, but if anyone knew what it was like to be a trophy, she was that person. Their comments, coupled with Ryan's attitude, came across like a slap in the face with a wet dishcloth.

She waited a moment and followed a couple of the other guests around the palm grouping. Keeping her smile, she spoke loudly enough to someone who came up to her that Ryan turned and beckoned.

The trophy was about to be displayed.

She was not a trophy, even if she didn't matter to the one person in or out of the world who really mattered to her.

She missed Benjamin so much she was one big, dull ache. She wouldn't even mind that lazy voice accusing her of being a nag. But she would never be able to nag him again. Well, she had overcome pain before, and work was the way to do it.

Her small smile, which had been carefully polished and in place before the first guests arrived, was still unchanged when she made polite conversation with the two volunteers looking expectantly at her.

Ryan threaded his way through the crowd toward her, flanked by his two buddies. Janis braced herself.

He took possession of her arm. "Got a minute? I want you to meet a couple of friends."

She excused herself to the volunteers, and cordially acknowledged Ryan's introductions. "Do you work with Ryan? He's been incredibly sharing of his time and expertise during this tremendously difficult period. I'm sure he must be relieved my burden on his time is over with this opening of yet another tourist attraction."

"Jan, I never think of our time together as a burden," Ryan protested.

"You wouldn't, because you're so supportive. I've absorbed an education in community organization skills from you these last few months. I only hope I can offer return assistance to the ConVis Bureau in the future."

"I say, Janis, I hope we—"

"You were thoughtful to ask me to your sister's open house, but I won't be going about socially for some time. I know you will understand."

"Naturally..."

She patted his arm as an older relative might. "I understand Dr. Wythy invited you to her wedding. I'll probably see you there."

She in no way cut him, but her words and her demeanor were those of someone who could only be a colleague. With a rueful glance at her Rolex, she said, "Nine forty-five! The crowd's thinned out enough I can actually believe it will be over in a quarter of an hour. How do you think it went, Ryan? I do so rely on your professional opinion."

A little hollowly, he assured her it had been an unqualified success.

"And no little bit due to your good advice! I suppose you're all about to call it a day, too? Let me wish you and your friends best wishes for the coming year—you'll have to excuse me. I see Millard Thorpe, my veep, giving me a high sign."

She kissed air at his cheek, kissed air at the cheeks of his two friends, and removed herself as quickly as she could. She might crawl into a corner to lick her wounds and heal in private, but she wasn't going to lose her professional demeanor in public.

***

The evening of the wedding, she stood in the second pew on the bride's side of the pretty chapel, watching Maggie join Millard at the altar. The two old darlings looked blissful and incandescent, with a new, youthful lease on their lives. For the thousandth time since she had last seen Benjamin on the third floor of Underwood House that terrible evening in early

December, Janis thought wistfully of Benjamin and herself and how sad it was to know that if only they hadn't been born separated by time, they might have...

Breath warmed her neck, and a whisper sounded in her ear like an organ chord. "They can look forward to at least twenty years together. I guarantee it."

She didn't dare turn even a fraction to look up into the opal blue eyes. She looked instead at his warm hand clasping hers at her side.

"What are you doing here?" she whispered.

"I was invited."

She looked up at him then, startled. "How did she find you?"

"Slipped the invitation under the door of Room 201 at Underwood House."

"How did she know where—?"

"Very astute lady," he whispered. "She knows I made a mistake, running away from the best thing for me in all of eternity. She told me so in no uncertain words. I'll let you see the note later."

Janis's heart leaped.

"I told you I was ready to settle down more than a century ago. Glad it wasn't an irrevocable decision at the time. In the infinity since I last saw you, I've thought of no one but you. My brief enjoyment of being alive in the night is empty, Janis. I need you to enjoy it with me. The idea of you settling for that fellow from the Convention and Visitors' Bureau has haunted me until I'm half crazy. He's wrong for you."

"I know that," she whispered. "Hush!"

His eyes gleamed. "Come with me into the courtyard. I have a proposition to discuss with you."

"Afterwards," Janis whispered, because Maggie had turned from the altar and was looking at them, smiling. She winked and turned back. Janis put a forefinger to her lips and shook her head at Benjamin in silent warning.

"To have me around—or unable to be around—will be dashed inconvenient for you many, many times in the next fifty or sixty years," he whispered.

If he meant what she thought he meant, her heart was going to expand like a soap bubble and enclose the universe. "I'll manage to tough it out as long as there are sunsets."

The minister said to Millard Thorpe, "Wilt thou have this woman to thy wedded wife?"

Benjamin's hand tightened on Janis's. His lips formed the words, *I will.*

She was sure her now gigantic soap bubble heart was going to burst.

The minister turned to Maggie with the same question. Janis formed the same response silently.

She had been to as many or more weddings than most young women her age, but never to one where the church was more beautiful, the essence of commitment so strong. Her very own ghost held her hand so tightly she knew he would never leave her again except every dawn, and then with the unbreakable promise of return at sunset. Maggie and Millard kissed, and the minister said to those present, "I present to you, Mr. and Mrs. Millard Thorpe."

Maggie and Millard drifted in a world of their own out to the parish hall that had been turned into as elegant a reception area as could be produced in any place its size. Janis murmured to Benjamin, who looked splendid in a midnight blue Versace suit and school tie, "I must tip the caterer generously. I don't know how she did this on such short notice."

Everyone from Claremont had made the trip, but eventually, Janis and Benjamin arrived in front of the bridal couple in the receiving line. Maggie hugged Janis. "I didn't see Ryan Aherne here, but I do see the man I'd most hoped to see—other than Millard, of course." Diminutive Maggie's eyes positively sparkled as she craned to look up into Benjamin's blue eyes. "You don't know how glad I am my note reached you!"

Gravely, he kissed her cheek. "You don't know how glad I am you were clever enough to deliver it, lecture and all. Thanks. From both of us."

"Go along with you both. Don't waste time with two old crocks like us," Maggie said.

"Many years of happiness to you. A precious gift I know you appreciate," Benjamin said.

He and Janis slipped out into the late December night air of the enclosed church courtyard. "If she doesn't know outright, she knows by instinct," Janis said.

"So, why wasn't the Convention man here?"

"He knew it was all business between us. He never had a chance. Ever."

"Didn't he? When I first came along, I would have sworn there was something brewing there."

"Benjamin, in a way he's like Dexter—anxious to have a beautiful trophy wife. He also liked knowing I'm rich. Finally, I know everyone who's anyone in the county, and that's a great asset to a career-minded man. He never saw *me,* the real me. The way you do. Nobody else ever has, or ever will. It's so wonderful being *just me* with you."

"I don't know about the trophy part, but I see nothing wrong with a beautiful rich wife who's an asset in other ways as well."

"I know you don't, Benjamin. What's special to me is that it's me you want, not a rich girl. Not a beauty. Not my connections. Me." She laughed. "But I have to be rich and know how to steward money, the way you spend as if there's no tomorrow!"

"Until now, I thought there was no tomorrow. But you aren't perfect, you know. All work and no play. I aim to work on adjusting your priorities." He smiled down at her. "I'll aim to get your work hours to eight and your time with me sunset to sunrise."

"Is any left over for sleeping and eating?"

"Do that on your own time. Ah, *mi bella nazo Italiano,* I wonder how after over so long in limbo I've become so lucky."

Still pondering his criticism of thinking too much about work, Janis asked, "How can I pay less attention to work if I am to partner a man who doesn't work for his living and spends money the way you do?"

He drew back with an exaggeratedly wounded look and gesture. "I have every intention of being gainfully, responsibly—even over-remuneratively employed! To begin with, whenever you must reasonably be separated from me after sunset and before midnight because of official evening activities from which I am necessarily removed, I shall be writing my memoirs. I know the Orient, Africa, and South America in a way that should present a fascinating light on the life of the nineteenth century man in a most sensational fashion."

"What, no jacuzzi blondes?"

"First, my green-eyed lady, I have been doing nothing but enjoying the jacuzzis, not the blondes."

"Oh, it's not true that ghosts can't lie. You just told a whopper!"

"Let me rephrase my statement. From the time I received the message that you disapproved, I restrained myself from indulging in anything *but* the jacuzzis, aside from providing the blondes with a genuinely entertaining escort. I am not at all averse to being a trophy escort."

"I will accept that, Benjamin. However, I plan to provide you with the jacuzzi to end all jacuzzis, and you can keep your escorting duties to me."

"Platonic?"

"Absolutely *not.*"

"Where will the jacuzzi be?" he asked with great interest. "I don't see it fitting into Room 201. But I can, if necessary, put everything I own in my pockets, so I see no problem with wherever we live."

"I want us to have a real home, Benjamin. And I have an idea..."

"The third floor of Underwood?"

"The third floor of...Benjamin!"

He lifted his hands. "I didn't read your mind. Our minds are simply in tune."

"Just think, Benjamin. The third floor of Underwood can be turned into an elegant apartment. I'll personally finance it, then lease it from the Association. A *lifetime* lease. I'm sure my very satisfactory monetary arrangement for them will allow them to secure their prestige suite of offices right where they wanted one all the time—on Sixth Avenue."

And, she reflected briefly, she would see the Sixth Avenue lease agreement was also a definite bargain for the Association.

"I'll use my money to furnish our little love nest," Benjamin said compacently. "You will agree I am a connoisseur of jacuzzis, first priority? Then to find the second priority. Our own bed, no sharing with the Association's visitors. And then my third priority."

She dreamily echoed his vision. "Jacuzzi on the roof, perhaps? Along with a pleasant private garden...What third priority. Benjamin?"

"I fancy a particular small piano that is rumored to have been played by Mozart at one time. I do like to listen to you play 'The Ash Grove.'"

She glowed with pleasure in the sincerity of his compliment to her long under-valued musical skills. "I might, with a bit of practice—not when you are present for it to bother you, of course—manage a fair repertoire, with Mozart's inspiration as an incentive."

"My dear, it would be my great pleasure to hear you practice and inspire me while I write at my memoirs, and you know I would not say I appreciated that talent of yours were it not the veriest truth."

Janis heaved a great sigh of satisfaction and tucked her head under his chin, where it fit to perfection. "There is plenty of room for a piano on the third floor, along with anything else we fancy."

"Our own little nest, convenient to both our roots in the world."

"Theoretically you could write your memoirs anywhere, Benjamin, so long as you keep the crumb of Underwood brick with you. Do you think we might travel during my vacation times?"

"If I can jaunt all around San Diego, I see no problem with anywhere else you fancy visiting. I'd like to show you many places I've been, though no doubt there have been changes since my time."

"I shall hire a bright young graduate in Private Sector Non-

Profit Agency Administration to be the Association's Assistant Director. When the time seems appropriate, she can segue into my job, and I'll serve on the Board."

"Already I have turned your mind from work to a more relaxed attitude."

"Perhaps you will turn out to be the breadwinner with your memoirs and have a far more shining career than I. I'd be so proud of you, Benjamin!"

"I consider writing my avocation," he said modestly. "My *work* will be to set up a certain attractive aura for Underwood's visitors. I shall apply immediately to the Director of the Association for position of Spirit in Charge of Haunting Underwood House and Environs."

"We don't want to display anything blatant, Benjamin—"

"No, indeed. But I see myself appearing solely by your direction, perhaps at full moon or winter solstice or whatever, transparent on the spiral staircase, wearing my uniform. Or perhaps on rare occasions, freezing the arms of visitors to Room 201 where they have been told the Civil War major was murdered."

She dimpled at him. "I do believe your haunting presence might be a valuable asset to the Association."

"Perhaps certain suggestible elderly ladies should glimpse the murdered major in the Harrison bed."

"I think you are an unreformed exhibitionist, Benjamin, and there will be no lewd materializations. Promise me?"

"I shall be lewd only with you, *mia piccolo naso Italiana.* However, consider an increasingly enlarging middle-aged and elderly female population beating a path to the Wharton Heritage Complex in the hope of seeing the ghost, dear girl. Consider the revenue they would engender for all your ambitious projects I dare not project at this time."

"I think you would much more usefully and companionably be employed as my official escort to community fund-raising projects. That will add a certain cachet when they say, *'What do you know of that fascinating younger man devoted to aging Mrs. Logan-Carter?'*"

He frowned at her. "I shall manage to age with grace at

the same rate as you, but they will never consider age when they are in the presence of the fascinating Mrs. Logan-Carter."

Janis rubbed her cheek against his silk suit and inhaled his essence and that of the roses blooming in dead of winter in the church courtyard. "I rather like to think of you arriving home every night as though you've come from a prestigious downtown high-rise executive position. You can materialize discreetly in the shrubbery, walk briskly through the savory garden. I'll come running to meet you, and we can take the elevator to our apartment or decide where we are going for our early evening entertainment."

"The prime entertainment will be found in our own apartment, ma'am. Before supper a passionate session in the jacuzzi. After supper a tender session on a fur rug before the fireplace. Later, a rowdy bit of exercise chasing each other through the apartment before an outing...and after the outing...another passionate session in our very own bed. Or wherever."

"Your plans are going to make me a very late riser, Benjamin, waking late afternoon, I should think, after leading the most important part of my life from sundown to sunrise and—"

Firmly he stopped her with a kiss. "We needn't plan it all right now. But I am going to teach you to appreciate all kinds of adventures in the night. When we are not making love in our own little hideaway, you must allow me to show you all the wonderful places I have discovered in this very city that you have never found. That is, if I can ever persuade you to enjoy flying with me. We could take many fantastic trips all in a night. And you can show me all the adventures you know of that I have yet to learn. I've read enough the last few nights to know I'll enjoy catching up completely with the twentieth century and looking with you to more than half of the twenty-first."

"Fifty or sixty years of being together as lovers and dearest friends, you said?"

"Together we'll find out afterwards what lies beyond." He wrapped her in his arms. "No one cares if we stay any longer at the reception. Care to waft with me back to Room 201, our temporary hideaway?"

She was surprised to realize the prospect of flying wherever he chose to take her did not make her dizzy at all—not, at least, in the sense of being acrophobic.

"I'm ready if you are," she said, and stood on tip-toe in anticipation.

ABOUT THE AUTHOR

Marian Jones was first published with a poem in a national children's magazine when she was seven, and she was rewarded with pen pals from all over the world—some of whom she still corresponds with faithfully. She has written no more poems, but is an eclectic writer, having been published by Harlequin Romance and other romance houses, by Random Century House and Picasso Publications with historicals, and in numerous national publications in fiction and non fiction. She has served with distinction on the National Board of Romance Writers.

She lives with her retired U.S. Navy Motion Picture specialist husband, whom she met while she was the director of a U.S.O. facility. He is now Media tech at a local college while she teaches writing. They have one daughter and a toddler granddaughter. Two office cats keep her devoted company while she writes. She keeps them separated from the koi pond, a backyard full of orchids and bromeliads, and a host of hummingbirds.

Visit her web site at http://www.marianjones.com.